"I want you to go to the celebration with me."

Ryan drew in a deep breath and let it out slowly. She didn't want to have this conversation. "Keir, I can't do that."

"Why not?"

"What do you mean, 'why not?' I thought we agreed to keep our relationship away from the gossipmongers. I can't jeopardize my career."

"Nobody said you had to."

Annoyed, Ryan shut her eyes, reaching for a way to describe her fears. Facing him, she said, "Keir, I really like being with you. But my career is very important to me. Just like yours is to you. When we started seeing each other, you agreed to stay low-key. Now you want to change the rules."

"You are right," Keir said, taking her hand. "I did agree. But, I also said we'd revisit this subject if things changed. That's happened and we're revisiting."

"Don't!" Panicked, Ryan shook off his hand and placed hers in her lap.

Frustration was etched into his normally pleasant features. He grabbed her hand and held it tightly. "The situation has changed. Our situation is different. I'm not going to pretend anymore. Why should we act like teenagers worried about how our friends and parents will react? This isn't Romeo and Juliet. We're too damn old to play games, and I don't live that way. And I'm not going to."

Now Until Forever

Karen White-Owens

Dafina
Books

Kensington Publishing Corp.

http://www.kensingtonbooks.com

I would like to dedicate *Now Until Forever* to my family and reading audience. Without both groups' unwavering encouragement and support, I'd probably give in to my lazy side and sit in the center of my bed watching soap operas and eating popcorn instead of writing. Thank you.

DAFINA BOOKS are published by

Kensington Publishing Corp.
850 Third Avenue
New York, NY 10022

All Kensington Titles, Imprints, and Distributed Lines are available at special quantity discounts for bulk purchases for sales promotions, premiums, fund-raising, and educational or institutional use. Special book excerpts or customized printings can also be created to fit specific needs. For details, write or phone the office of the Kensington special sales manager: Kensington Publishing Corp., 850 Third Avenue, New York, NY 10022, attn: Special Sales Department, Phone: 1-800-221-2647.

Dafina and the Dafina logo Reg. U.S. Pat. & TM Off.

First Dafina mass market printing: December 2006
10 9 8 7 6 5 4 3 2 1

Printed in the United States of America

Chapter 1

Keir Southhall kicked the black leather executive chair away from the desk at his Los Angeles production company, One Leaf Studios. He rose, stretched, and strolled to the coffeemaker, with his mug in hand. As he passed the floor-to-ceiling windows, he took a minute to examine the set, zeroing in on a petite female figure buzzing in and out of the construction area.

Who is she? Unable to resist, he trailed her movements across the studio. Eager for a better glimpse of the woman with skin the color of warm mocha, Keir leaned closer.

Slightly built, with jet-black hair that framed her face with short wisps, she looked gorgeous, striking. One of the workers called her, and the woman turned and smiled. Her entire face lit up.

Jesus! Keir felt as if he'd been sucker punched. With a shaky hand, he placed the mug on the desk. The desire to vacate his office and head down to the set warred with his common sense.

He wondered how it would feel to hold that ray of sunshine in his arms, be inside and a part of her. Keir allowed that fantasy to emerge, conjuring images of himself and that woman intertwined in the heat of passion. "Damn," he muttered, feeling his flesh grow hard as stone.

Man, get a grip, he admonished silently, shaking his head and laughing out loud. *She's only a woman, and you were just released from thirteen years of turmoil and hell that lesser men refer to as marriage. You don't need any new complications, especially not with a chick that works for you.*

Yet, Keir remained glued to the window. From this distance, he barely made out her straight nose and full, lush lips. "What color are her eyes?" he mumbled, lingering over her heart-shaped face and the smoothness of her skin.

A rap on the door reluctantly pulled him away as the pungent odor of tobacco crept into the office, making his nose twitch. With one final glance at the woman, he strolled reluctantly to his desk, opened a drawer, and removed an ashtray. After he gave the black plastic dish a shove, it slid across the highly polished mahogany surface and teetered on the opposite edge of the desk.

"Phil, come on in," Keir called, returning to his vigil at the window.

A tall, lanky man with thinning red hair entered, with a clipboard in one hand and a pen in the other. An inch of ash hung from the cigar glued to the right side of his mouth. "Hey, my man. How'd you know it was me?"

"Cigar. No one in their right mind has the guts to come to my office with that stench doggin' them."

"Hey!" Phil protested, chewing on his cigar. "I'll have you know, this is the best one-dollar cigar you can buy."

Keir chuckled, searching the set below for the tiny figure. "I believe you. But, it might be advantageous to our cast and crew if you'd upgrade your cigars to a two-dollar brand." He pointed at the desk. "There's an ashtray with your name on it over there."

"Right." Phil moved to the desk and stamped out his cigar, leaving the butt in the ashtray. "How's life in the Eiffel Tower?"

Laughing softly, Keir perched on the edge of his desk

and folded his arms across his chest. "Eiffel Tower? Who came up with that?"

"A few people on the construction crew." Phil glanced around the office and nodded. "It fits."

Keir's office sat above the sets and was surrounded by windows. The place resembled a lighthouse more than a tower. It offered him a perfect view of all the activities that went on the sets below. Often, he watched the hustle and bustle of the daily shoots from this vantage point and found it useful.

"Here you are, up here watching your subjects do your dirty work," said Phil.

"Hey," Keir admonished good-naturedly, "you better check yourself."

Phil waved a dismissing hand at his boss. "I'm not worried about you. We go way back."

"That may be true. But I'm still your boss. Don't forget it." Standing, Keir dropped his hands to his sides. "What brings you my way? Everything okay on the set?"

"We're fine." Phil scraped his thumb across his tongue and then flipped a page on his clipboard. "I want to go over the shooting schedule for episode six and talk about the guest stars."

Keir's eyebrow flew up, and a giant grin of approval curved his lips. "Six? We're ahead of schedule."

"That we are."

Pleased, Keir pursed his lips, considering the situation. "Good! Once five is in the can, we'll have a celebration lunch. I want the crew to know how much I appreciate their hard work."

"Won't be long. Maybe another day or two." Phil moved across the office and stood next to his boss, studying the view. "My man, what are you looking at?"

"Her." Keir nodded toward the woman. "I've never seen her. Is she an extra?"

Phil shook his head.

"Who is she?"

"Ryan Mitchell. Costume and set designer. We were lucky to get her."

Keir seldom heard that note of admiration in Phil's voice, and it stirred his curiosity. "Why?"

"She just finished out her contract on an action/adventure series with your buddy Joel. You know the one, *SWAT Command.* Won her an Emmy, too. She's excellent. Comes to work on time, does her job, then goes home. No hassles. No headaches. No drama."

Keir's lips pursed. "It sounds as if we hit the jackpot."

"That we did. Why so interested?"

"No reason," Keir answered, running a hand through his wavy hair. "She caught my eye, that's all."

Phil examined Keir with the practiced eye of a longtime friend, someone who knew him well. "Yeah . . . and?"

"And nothing." Keir turned away from the window.

"You just got out of a funky situation with Shannon. Don't tell me you plan to check her out?"

"I haven't said a word," Keir replied. "You're the one making all the assumptions."

"Yeah, but it's time. I mean, you haven't had a regular bed partner since the divorce. Is that why you're interested? Want me to make the introductions?"

"I'm old enough to handle my dick. Maybe you should worry about your own." Keir returned to his desk, sank into his chair, and waved a hand at the visitor's chair. He leaned back, methodically squeezing a red rubber exercise ball. "I've got two kids, who need my reassurance. Just because their mother and I found it unbearable to live together doesn't mean that I'll forget them. Let me add the fact that I'm the creator/director/writer/producer for *Renewed Case Files,* slated for an October premiere. It's already June, and we need to stay on schedule or exceed it. The last thing I need is an on-the-job romantic situation, which could turn into my worse nightmare if things get out of hand."

Phil raised his hands in an act of surrender. "Hey, my man. I'm sorry. I saw you studying her form, and I thought you might have an interest. Nothing more."

"There's no vibes here. Ms. Mitchell caught my eye because I'd never seen her before. That's all. Got it?"

"Got it. By the way, it's Mrs. Mitchell."

"Mrs.?" A jab of regret stabbed the armor around Keir's heart as a volley of what-ifs raced through his head. Shaking off those feelings, Keir refused to analyze the disquieting sense of disappointment he incurred.

"Widow. Husband's been dead two or three years."

Relief flowed into Keir. For the second time in five minutes, he refused to examine the reasons behind his feelings. He cleared his throat. "That's too bad. Let's get back to work."

"It's your world, boss."

"As long as we understand each other." Keir opened his desk drawer and pulled out a script. He flipped through the pages before tossing it to Phil. "We need some major revisions to this crap. Call a meeting with the writing team so that we can do some brainstorming. This won't fly without rewrites."

Phil reached for the script. "Will do."

Ryan Mitchell sat near the platform of a new set that was being constructed, sketching the new room as she envisioned it. As her fingers flew across the page, she added furniture, window treatments, and accent pieces to give it that lived-in, realistic appearance, while the construction team's boom box spilled the country-western lyrics of the Dixie Chicks. Once she completed her designs, she planned to search the warehouse for the items she needed to bring the set to life.

She studied her drawing as memories from her first interview for this job came back. In preparation, Ryan had boned up on Keir Southhall, studying all the information she'd found on the Internet, in the library, and through her limited circle of friends in the business. From his bio, she learned that he was forty-two years old and the father of two. Born and raised in California, Keir Southhall had capped off his film school years by receiving an Oscar after producing his documentary depicting the plight of children growing up in brothels.

Known for his innovative style of filmmaking, he represented one of the new breeds in Hollywood, a true visionary. He made movies that he wanted to see, rather than what the big brass dictated. No longer satisfied with his movie career, he'd turned to the small screen to write, produce, and direct a weekly television series.

The day of her interview, Ryan had arrived early, expecting to meet Keir Southhall and dazzle him with her knowledge of his background and achievements. No such luck. Instead, she'd met with the set director, Gloria "Glo" Kramer, and the production executive, Phil Berger.

Disappointed, Ryan had walked away from the interview with the distinct impression that she hadn't measured up. Surprise! Not only did she get a call back for a second interview, Glo Kramer offered her the job.

Ryan loved it here. After the restrictive nature of the directors on *SWAT Command,* she enjoyed the encouragement and praise she'd received since joining Southhall's team.

A set of French-manicured fingers curled around Ryan's shoulder and squeezed in a friendly gesture. "Hey, lady. How are things coming?"

She found Glo at her side. The fifty-something blonde oozed excited energy. Her enthusiasm and ideas were legendary in Hollywood.

"Hi. I'm working on the living-room scene for episode six." Ryan shifted the sketch pad in Glo's direction. "The crew promised they'd be finished with the set this afternoon. What's up with you?"

"Things are heating up." Glo laid a hand on a pile of scripts nestled securely in the crook of her arm. "Keir and I are going to meet and go over this stuff." She drew closer, whispering, "Here's a word of advice, don't do too much work on this set. Things may change."

"I hear you. Should I expect this?"

"No. Not at all. Keir's pretty decisive." Glo shifted the pile from the crook of her left arm to her right arm. "The scripts we're looking at are ones that he didn't see until now."

"Why not? I thought he always gives final input before we go hot."

"He does, but his son's been sick. So, he didn't get to read them. While I'm thinking about it, we need to schedule a meeting with you and Keir. You are one of the few new employees that he hasn't met yet."

Finally, I'm going to meet the big man himself, Ryan thought, recalling some of the details she'd learned for her interview. That info might find its way into her meeting. "Whatever you decide is fine with me. By the way, where's his office? Is he in this building or the studio's administrative office?"

"Keir's here." Glo pointed to the tower overlooking the studio. "That's his office. You've probably seen him but didn't know it."

Ryan shrugged. "Possibly."

"If you had, you'd remember. Keir is quite handsome. A real hottie. I have a son close to Keir's age." Glo nudged Ryan playfully, giggling like a teenager on her first date.

Ryan smiled, waiting for the proper moment to steer

the conversation back to work. She didn't need or want this extra info about a man that she'd probably see two or three times while she worked at One Leaf.

"He's about five feet eleven, with the greenest eyes I've ever seen. You could lose yourself in his eyes." Glo used a finger to draw an invisible circle around her face and added, "Round face, toffee-colored skin, dark brown curly hair, and dimples. He's cute."

Sounds like a Cabbage Patch doll to me. "I don't recall seeing him."

"Between his son's illness and drumming up advertising dollars and investors for the show, he's been away from the studio lately."

Nodding, Ryan let Glo ramble on.

"But, that's about to change. Earlier, I noticed the lights were on in the Eiffel Tower, so I took a little trip up there to talk with him. And believe me, he's ready for business."

Ryan's gaze drifted to the office above the set. Lights blazed, and she barely made out the images of two people. One of them must have been Keir Southhall.

"To tell you the truth . . ." Glo began.

Sighing softly, Ryan retracted the lead from her mechanical pencil and braced herself for the inevitable studio gossip headed her way.

"There've been a lot of ladies who would like to become the next Mrs. Keir Southhall."

"Oh?" Ryan muttered appropriately, shifting on her seat. She felt uncomfortable with the direction Glo's conversation had taken.

"Keir got divorced late last year. Back in, oh, 2000, we worked together on a project, and one of the hairstylists fancied herself in love with him. That girl caused all nature of havoc on the set. Eventually, we had to fire her. I hated doing that. But, it had to be done."

A sudden realization hit Ryan as she studied her boss. *Glo's probing to see if I'm going to become a problem.*

"That's too bad. I like to keep my work relationships separate from my home life. This is my job. Period."

"Good." Glo patted Ryan on the shoulder. "I'm glad I won't have that problem with you."

Consider yourself warned, Ryan thought, feeling the sharp edge of loneliness as she offered Glo an understanding smile. *You don't have to worry about me; no man could love me as dearly or deeply as Galen.*

"This is too good an opportunity to screw up. Besides, I don't believe in work romances. They cause entirely too much drama," said Ryan. She waved a dismissing hand in the other woman's direction. *I hope that settles your mind.* The last thing Ryan wanted was an entanglement with the boss.

Although, a bit of physical frolicking wouldn't hurt. Someone to curl up next to for a few encounters would keep her body from screaming with suppressed frustration in the middle of the night. She was widowed, not dead.

Where had that come from? My life doesn't work that way. Enough. Time to get back on track, Ryan decided. "Tell me. Have you worked for Mr. Southhall long?"

"Honey, call him Keir. He's not a real formal kind of a guy. He always says that Mr. Southhall is his father."

"How many films have you done with him?"

"Four," Glo boasted. "This is my first television series. That's why you were a front-runner for this job. You had the background, expertise, plus that Emmy."

"Thank you. I'm hoping to learn a lot from you guys."

"This job should be mutually beneficial."

Glo placed her pile of scripts on the chair next to Ryan and plucked the sketch pad from her hands, admiring the design. "This is good."

With a sigh of relief, Ryan bowed her head in a show of acknowledgment. Good. They were back on track, reviewing the work and getting away from personal stuff. "Glad you like it."

"I knew you were perfect for this job," Glo praised. "Just keep creating work like this, and you'll do well here."

Chapter 2

Ryan selected a carrot to nibble on from a small tray of vegetables provided by the production company. She snapped her fingers to Stevie Wonder's "My Eyes Don't Cry," blasting through the hollow walls of the studio. Giggling, she watched Glo attempt the Hustle with a few production workers clad in steel-toe work boots.

A figure detached itself from the shadows, silently moved forward, and asked in a whiskey-honeyed voice, "How come you're not out there with the rest of the crew?"

Startled, Ryan jumped, spilling vegetables on the floor. As she scooped the carrots and broccoli spears from the tile, she searched the man's olive sweater for a badge but found nothing. Whoever he was, he had clout. No one walked around the set without the express permission of the producer, and everyone wore a badge.

"I beg your pardon?" Ryan choked out, mesmerized by the cool, collected way he approached her.

The man lifted his chin in the direction of the commotion. "They're a lively bunch. Why are you sitting on the sidelines?"

She turned to the boisterous group as Glo tripped over her feet. "Better a spectator than a spectacle."

Keir chuckled. "You've got a point there. But, I've always been told participating can be more fun."

"It depends on the sport," she responded suggestively.

"Are you a person who prefers more private pursuits? More intimate?"

Her tongue did a slow drag across her lips. "Sometimes. But it also depends on with whom and what game we're playing." *Lord help me,* Ryan thought. *I'm openly flirting with this man.* She couldn't help it. It was fun, wicked, and the longest conversation she'd had with a man outside of work in years. Something about him made her drop the personal shield that protected her against new relationships, possible pain, and disappointment.

Smiling, he moved a little closer, and the fresh, clean 'cent of him wafted under her nose. "True."

Ryan's gaze swept over his frame. He was quite perfect to look at. Ryan's brows creased over her chestnut eyes. *Who is he? He's handsome. No doubt about it.* Could he be one of the guest stars or the director for next week's show? Green eyes were unusual. She couldn't think of a single actor that fit this description.

She offered her hand. "Ryan Mitchell."

He took and held her hand a moment longer than necessary, stroking his thumb across her soft skin. The gesture sent her heart galloping. "Keir Southhall."

Ryan's eyes grew large, and her heart pumped faster. *Keir Southhall!*

Oval rather than round described the shape of his face, and the dark brown hair, which Glo had called curly, actually was fairly straight, except for the stubborn wave it had to it. One wayward lock fell across his forehead, adding to his attractive aura. Dimples so deep you were in danger of falling into them added to his overall striking appearance.

Glo had described a Cabbage Patch doll, but Ryan

didn't see one. "Oh," she muttered, instantly replaying her conversation with this man in her head. Had she said anything outrageous or offensive? No. She didn't think so. Although she had to admit, their dialogue had bordered on titillating.

"Good to meet you at last," Keir said.

"At last?" she repeated.

Keir shrugged. "I've heard good things about you. Plus, I've noticed you buzzing around the sets."

"Have you now?"

He nodded, pointing at the Eiffel Tower.

Smiling stiffly, she said, "I'll have to remember that you're always close."

"That I am."

"Keir," Glo yelped, running up to him. She wrapped an arm around his waist and hugged him close. "I didn't think you'd grace us with your presence today."

He gently detached himself from her embrace but kept an arm around her shoulders. "Why wouldn't I be here? This is my party."

"You're the boss. I assumed there were more important things to hold your attention," Glo explained, with a giggle.

"You guys did a great job. I wanted everyone to know how much I appreciate their efforts," Keir said. His gaze strayed in Ryan's direction.

Glo followed the direction of her boss's gaze. "Oh, Keir." She waved a hand at the younger woman. "This is our new set designer, Ryan Mitchell. Keir, Ryan. Ryan, Keir. I don't think you two have met."

The pair shook hands a second time as Glo made introductions. "We were getting acquainted," Keir explained, again holding Ryan's hand a second longer than necessary.

"It's nice to meet you, Mr. Southhall." Ryan tugged at her hand, which was still grasped firmly in Keir's.

Reluctantly, he released her. "My name is Keir. Mr. Southhall is my dad."

Glo laughed out loud, then pointed a long, manicured finger in Ryan's direction. "Told you."

Ryan's hand felt warm and tingly. She rubbed her fingers over the spot where he'd caressed her skin. "Yes, you did."

Frowning, Keir's gaze focused on the older woman, then shifted to the younger. "What's so funny?"

"Oh, nothing," Ryan replied. "Glo predicted you would say that about your father. And you did."

"Mmm," he mumbled softly, stroking his earlobe. "I'll have to work on my lines. I hate to be predictable."

Ryan returned her attention to the antics of the staff, avoiding Keir's penetrating gaze. *You're far from predictable, Mr. Southhall,* she thought, taking a final peek at this handsome man.

Alive with activity, the farmers' market was stuffed with shoppers. The weather was gorgeous on this particular Saturday morning, simply magnificent for outdoor activities. Delighted to be out and about, Ryan strolled along the rows of vendors, checking the prices and quality of the produce.

After weeks of nonstop production, One Leaf Studio had shut down and given the staff a complete weekend off. Ryan loved her job and looked forward to each day, but it felt great to be free of the pressure of daily shoots.

Ryan stopped at a stand and picked up a yellow squash, testing its firmness. Her sister, Helen, and brother, Tony, did Sunday dinner with their baby sister two or three times a year, and Ryan wanted to prepare a great meal. Grilled rainbow trout, green beans, sautéed yellow squash and onions, plus red velvet cake for dessert, should keep them fed, content, and out of her personal affairs for the duration of the evening.

At the next stand, Ryan was fingering the fresh green beans when the eerie sensation of being watched crept down her spine. She lifted her head and scanned the crowded pavilion until her gaze landed on a familiar figure.

Keir Southhall. Of all the people she might meet in a place like this, Keir wasn't on her list. What was he doing here? People like him didn't shop for their own food. Staff and housekeepers did the mundane stuff for them.

He looked extremely handsome dressed in worn denims and a black cable-knit sweater with a deep V-neck. A white crewneck T-shirt winked from under the sweater, while dark sneakers covered his feet.

With a hint of a smile on his full, sensual lips, Keir dipped his head in silent acknowledgment. He returned a melon to the stand and started across the crowded area, heading directly for her.

Ryan's heart danced in her breast and her palms felt clammy as she watched the stunning man move toward her. Something about him spoke to her on a fundamental level, which made it almost impossible for her to resist his strong personality.

Keir stopped in front of her. His eyes swept over her petite frame. "Hi."

She responded to the familiar note in his voice. "Hi, yourself. What are you doing here?"

He lifted a red and green woven bag. "Saturday shopping. And you?"

"The same," she answered, lifting her own bag.

A soft chuckle followed her explanation. "How about a cup of coffee?"

Okay, Ryan, think logically. This is your boss; you want to stay on his good side. "I don't want to bother you."

Keir relieved her of the shopping bag, cupping her elbow. "First of all, it's no bother. It's good to have company while enjoying the sights." He focused on a spot beyond the market. "What about over there? We can have bagels and lattes."

A spark of excitement filled her at the thought of spending time with this interesting man. *Calm down,* Ryan warned herself silently. *This isn't a dinner date.* She shrugged. "Sure."

He settled his warm palm at the base of her spine and steered her through the morning crowd to Starbucks. The wonderful aroma of freshly brewed coffee greeted them as Keir ushered Ryan inside. He guided her to a table. The chairs were decorated in forest green, burgundy, and black. Ryan slid into the spot opposite Keir.

Keir strolled to the counter to place their orders. Five minutes later, he returned with a round, black plastic tray loaded down with coffee, bagels, cream cheese, and fruit cups. He placed everything on the table and sat opposite her, then gave her a sheepish little smile. "I know you only wanted coffee, but this looked too good to pass up."

Actually, it did. "That's fine," Ryan said and distributed the food and condiments. They started on their breakfast while watching the morning crowd. "Do you do the market often?"

"I haven't done this in quite a while. Generally, my housekeeper does all the shopping. I woke up this morning with plans to work, but everything from the vacuum cleaner to the telephone kept breaking my concentration. So, I decided to get out of the house for a while and explore. Maybe by the time I get home, the place will be quiet and conducive for work. What about you?"

She broke off a piece of her cranberry and orange bagel and popped it into her mouth. "I've got family coming to dinner tomorrow evening."

"Oh, family. More work."

Ryan laughed. "True. But they feel the need to check up on me every so often, and I have to show them that I'm okay."

"Are you?" Keir captured her eyes with his.

"Am I what?" she asked softly, fidgeting with her coffee cup. There was an undercurrent of something electrifying flowing between them.

"Okay?" Keir asked. His eyes probed to her very soul.

Stunned, Ryan realized that Keir was asking about her husband. How did he know about Galen? She scoffed. *Glo.* "Yeah, I am."

"Good." Keir's eyes swept over her approvingly. "Family can be a trial."

Her boss's lightning change of topics was difficult to follow. "That's for sure. My brother and sister are more than fifteen years older than I am. Since our parents passed away, Helen and Tony feel they need to watch over me. I was our parents' change of life baby. Their little unexpected bundle of joy."

Reaching for his cup of coffee, Keir nodded. "That's got to be tough for a kid. You had teenage siblings when you were little. You didn't have anyone to play with."

"Yes, I did. My mother filled the void. We did everything together." Smiling, Ryan waved her hands excitedly in front of her. "Because I didn't have anyone my age, Mom kept me busy and got me involved in different programs. I went to after-school activities, Boys & Girls Club, and glee club. You name it, I did it. Until I entered my teens, the only time we weren't together was when I went to school."

"She sounds great."

"Mom was," Ryan agreed, thinking of the times her mother had offered her gentle support and solid advice.

Silence settled between the pair as they finished their meals.

A family of five took the table across from them. The children were animated, loud, vocal, and full of energy. They grabbed at their pastries and bagels with eager hands. Cuddled close, a baby sat in her mother's lap.

Laughing at the kids' antics, Keir asked, "Do you have any children?"

Ryan shook her head. "You?" She already knew he had children but didn't know more.

"Two. Boy and girl."

"That's nice," Ryan managed, feeling the sharp edge of regret. She and Galen had wanted children. A daughter or son. A little person to combat the loneliness after Galen died would have been wonderful. But they'd waited, voting to build their careers before starting a family.

"It can be."

"Tell me about them. What are their names? How old are they?"

Keir drained his cup before answering. "Adam is twelve. Average boy. Baseball and computer games rule his life."

Ryan smiled, getting a mental image of a dark-haired boy with a baseball bat slung over his shoulder. "What about your daughter?"

"Emily's five. She's shy, soft-spoken. In a word, she's a girl."

Refocusing on Keir, Ryan teased, "That much I figured out for myself."

He chuckled, fidgeting with his coffee cup. "I mean she's very feminine. Emily's a girly girl. She loves dresses, dolls, being pretty. I suspect when she gets older, I'll have a diva on my hands."

"I wish you luck with that one."

"Thanks."

"Really. They sound perfect. I think most women like to feel feminine, pretty." Ryan grinned, thinking how much she loved her scented baths and fragrant candles at the end of a stressful day.

"What's so funny?"

"Nothing. I think it's cute. In my mind, I see this delicate little person all dressed up in lace and frilly stuff, looking like a little girl should."

"That's my baby," Keir agreed.

Ryan glanced at her watch and realized that they had been sitting in the cafe for over an hour. Smiling apologetically, she gathered their disposable items and dropped them on the tray. "Keir, I really enjoyed spending time with you, but I've got to finish my shopping and get home. Thank you for breakfast."

He glanced at the clock on the wall behind her. "Yeah, you're right. We have been here a while."

Scooting off of the chair, Ryan picked up the tray and dumped their trash. She returned and gathered her bag before heading for the door.

Keir followed.

Outside Starbucks, she faced him and tossed out, without thinking, "I really enjoyed talking with you. We'll have to do it again. Next time it's my treat."

Grinning broadly, Keir said, "I'm holding you to that."

Surprised, Ryan frowned. Holding her to what?

"Good luck with dinner tomorrow," Keir added. He linked his fingers with hers and squeezed before walking away.

Tingling started in the pit of her stomach, stoking a gentle fire. It had been a while since anyone had made her feel this way. Laughing, Ryan shook her head and warned herself silently. *This is not a romance novel. Come down to earth.*

Chapter 3

Exhausted from the hectic pace of Monday morning's shooting schedule, Ryan dropped into the chair at her desk and sighed. She ran an exasperated hand through her short hair, sending the soft wisps in every direction.

The reputation of this week's guest director as a perfectionist was well earned, and Ryan had worked frantically to stay one step ahead of him. So far, Eric Steinfell's tirades and brilliant directional skills had been dead-on. It made for an exhilarating but completely draining experience.

The workmen had completed construction of the sets for the next few days of filming, and now Ryan had to prepare them according to the shooting schedule, and she needed everything to be perfect. To do a final check on the sets, Ryan had decided to skip lunch, opting instead to run to the workroom for a few minutes of peace before the afternoon schedule began.

"So this is where you hide out."

Ryan jumped at the sound of Keir's voice. What was he doing here? She swiveled her chair in his direction and found him standing in the doorway to the tiny workroom, which she shared with Glo. "Yes, it is. How are you?" she managed through a mouth that felt as if it had been stuffed with cotton.

Keir entered the confined space, sidestepping racks of clothes and props, filling the room with his presence. The fresh aroma of soap and aftershave wafted under her nostrils as he moved closer. Ryan examined the man from the top of his head to his Italian leather shoes. Keir looked exceptionally attractive in a steel gray suit, white shirt, and striped gray and black tie.

Ryan drew her tongue across her dry lips and asked, "What brings you to this end of the studio?"

"Curiosity," Keir answered, taking a moment to look around him. A hint of laughter packed his voice. "I wanted to see where you work. Plus, spend a little extra time with you." He stopped next to her desk, fingering the purple, velvety leaves of her African violet. "You don't know how refreshing it is to talk with someone who's not afraid to say what they mean and mean what they say. I don't get that often. You don't put on airs to impress me."

"Thank you. I think." With a nervous hand, she smoothed the hair at her nape, adding cautiously, "I was being me."

"I know. And I like it."

His warm regard tugged at her heartstrings. *I like you, too,* Ryan thought, taking a minute to compose herself.

They shared a special element that touched a place deep within her. Unfortunately, Ryan had been witness to how the television and movie business used women. She'd never been, and didn't plan to become, one of those females who achieved their career goals through casual sexual encounters with the industry giants.

Ryan lowered her eyelids to conceal her expression and thoughts. Glo's warning remained fresh in Ryan's thoughts. This job was great, and she didn't plan to do anything that would jeopardize it or focus the limelight too closely on her. "I guess I should say thank you."

"Yeah, you should." Keir grinned, sending her pulse into a gallop. "Plus, I wanted to tell you how much I enjoyed having coffee with you Saturday."

"Me, too," Ryan admitted softly. At odd moments her thoughts had kept returning to Keir and the time they'd spent at Starbucks.

Keir perched on the edge of the desk, facing her. "How did it go?"

"What?" Ryan asked, finding his nearness disturbing, yet exciting.

"Dinner with your family."

"Oh!" Ryan rolled her eyes heavenward, seeing her sister's scrunched-up, dill pickle expression in her head. "I found it less painful than major surgery."

Keir laughed out loud. "Ouch. That bad?"

Ryan nodded, leaning back in her chair. She loved the deep, rich sound of his laugh and wanted to hear it again. "Losing a limb might have been easier."

Chuckling, he muttered sympathetically, "Poor thing."

"Well, they're family, and there's nothing I can do about them. They treat me like a four-year-old. And honestly, it's getting really old. It's beyond stale." She dismissed the incident, with a quick shake of her head. "I don't want to talk about them anymore. Let's discuss more interesting topics. How was your weekend?"

"I had my kids. We enjoyed most of our time together. But, we encountered a few tense moments when I had to play the heavy."

Frowning, Ryan sat up straight in her chair. "What happened?"

"I refused to take them to a PG-13-rated movie." Keir folded his arms across his chest and jutted his chin out stubbornly.

"I don't blame you."

"Really?" His eyes lit up, and a smile spread across his face. "Thanks. It's good to know I have backup if I need it. They wanted to see one of those action-packed blood fests with far too much blood, death, and bullets for me. So I told them no, and they were furious."

"What does their mother let them watch?" Ryan asked.

Keir shook his head morosely. "A lot of stuff that they shouldn't see. But I can only regulate what they see when they're with me. I can't take responsibility for anything else."

"I agree." Ryan picked up a pen and twirled it between her fingers. "Your kids are twelve and five, correct?"

"Correct."

"Neither child is old enough for a movie like that. No matter what their mother does, you have to follow your conscience." She touched his arm, feeling the muscles respond to the light touch of her hand. "You did the right thing."

"That's how I felt. Believe me, things were unpleasant for a while. But, I smoothed their ruffled feathers with dinner at IHOP. They love that place."

"Eww!" She laughed softly at him, enjoying the moment and his story about the trials of being a regular dad.

"I'll tell you, after a weekend of nothing but kiddie movies, television programs, and conversation, I'm anxious for some adult interaction."

"Oh?" Ryan's mind raced. *Where is Keir going with this?*

"Yeah, which is my segue into a dinner invitation," said Keir. "Not IHOP," he hastily reassured her. "Wine, dinner, and good conversation. Do you like Chinese? I was thinking P.F. Chang's. What do you say?"

Surprised by the invitation, Ryan rested her head against the back of her chair and studied the man. She didn't know how to answer his question.

Yes, she found him very attractive. The wild, frivolous side of her personality wanted to jump in with both feet and give this new attraction all the attention it deserved. On the other hand, her cautious side recognized the pitfalls in saying yes, considering their work situation and Glo's warning. "Well . . ." she trailed off, leaving his question unanswered.

His eyebrows drew together in a concerned frown. "Did I get this wrong? I felt something between us, and I thought you did, too."

"Keir, what are you really asking"—she paused— "exactly?"

"Food, a meal." Confusion settled uncomfortably on his handsome features. "What do you think I'm asking for?"

Treading lightly, Ryan tried to explain. "You're a nice man."

"I hear a but."

"Look, I don't know what you've heard about me," Ryan began, placing her hands on her chest. "And I know some people are very casual and comfortable with their sexuality. But I'm not that type of person."

"I didn't ask you for sex."

Embarrassed, Ryan felt her cheeks burn, and she refused to meet his gaze, while her hands fluttered in the air nervously. "I know. I'm just afraid that this will cause a lot of problems. I'm not into casual sex. I don't want you to get the wrong impression."

"Wait." Keir captured her hand and held it in his own. "Look, I like you. You're fun and easy to talk to."

"Thank you."

Annoyance flashed across his face, and his tone turned cool. "I don't want your thanks. I want you to have dinner with me."

"Keir, I like this job, and I want to keep it. I'm not

available or interested in an affair, which could turn into an avalanche of crap."

Keir stood, and his green eyes narrowed and hardened. "I'm not a teenager with raging hormones. I'm a forty-two-year-old divorced father of two. And I want company. *Adult* company. I'd like to share a meal with a person whose opinion I respect. Someone I can talk to, eat with, and spend some quality adult time with. Besides, you owe me one," he reminded.

"What are you talking about?" Her lips pursed, and she stared at him suspiciously.

"When we were at Starbucks, you said we should do this again. I'm calling in your marker."

Exasperated, Ryan opened her mouth to respond. That had been a parting remark, nothing more. And Keir knew it.

He raised a hand, stopping her. "Ryan, you've been in this crazy business for a few years and understand how some directors operate. But it's not the way I work. Am I making myself clear?"

"Yes."

"Good."

She sighed, lacing her fingers together to keep herself focused. "Keir, I like you, too. Now, it's my turn to make a point. I work for your production company. And I want to keep the reputation I have of being an upfront, dependable employee who doesn't cause trouble. No entanglements. I come to work, do my business, and go home."

Keir leaned closer. His earnest expression made her ache to say yes. "I'm not asking you to jeopardize any of that. All I want is for you to share a meal with me."

She gazed back at him, realizing how much she wanted to take him up on his offer. Ryan wanted to explore the feelings that were developing between them.

So much of her time was spent alone, and she missed sharing dinner and conversation with someone who had the same interests as she had. She was tired of eating alone, being alone, and not having any fun in her life.

"I promise. This is about having dinner," Keir assured her, with a persuasive smile on his full, sensual lips. "Dinner, good time, fun. I'll have you home by eleven," he muttered in a piss-poor Chris Rock imitation. "How's that?"

Shaking her head, Ryan laughed, then said hesitatingly, "It sounds great. But, what about Glo? She doesn't approve of on-the-job romances."

Keir pursed his lips. "I don't care. This is my personal life, not Glo's. It's got nothing to do with her or One Leaf Studio."

"That's where you're wrong. It has everything to do with my job," she responded in a sharp tone. "I have to work for and with Glo. I don't want problems."

"It won't happen. We can keep our dinner plans under the wire. Between us. How does that work for you?"

"Well . . ." she hedged, wavering. Would one meal really cause that much trouble? Her blood froze when she thought of Glo and what she might do if she found out that Ryan had gone out with the boss. Dinner with Keir didn't have to become a big deal, Ryan decided, dismissing Glo and her warning. She liked this man. If Ryan could believe what Keir said, she was safe. Slow and easy, that was the way to work this Keir thing. "Okay. What time?"

He grinned like a kid on summer vacation. "Great! How about eight? I'll pick you up at your place."

Ryan shook her head, opened the middle drawer of her desk, and fished through the junk for a pencil and scratch pad, ready for directions to the restaurant. "You don't have to do that. Let's meet at the restaurant."

"No," he vetoed, taking her hand between both of his. Her pulse accelerated as his fingers stroked the top of her hand. "I'm a man that takes his dating responsibilities seriously. I asked you out. I'll pick you up."

She scribbled her address and telephone number on the pad, ripped the page from the spine, and handed it to him. "Yes, sir."

He pocketed the paper. Eyes sparkling, he stood, squeezed her hand, and then headed for the door. "Thank you."

Once Keir disappeared out the door, Ryan sat for a moment, reliving his brief visit. Dinner sounded like a great way to spend an evening. Plus, she really liked Keir. On the other hand, the danger of making a major mistake loomed large. Ryan hoped that she hadn't lifted the lid on Pandora's box and allowed one thousand years of misery to escape.

Chapter 4

Jade-colored walls and polished cherry wood furniture adorned P.F. Chang's. White linen tablecloths and petite oriental lamps added a pinch of elegance to the eatery. The Chinese bistro represented one of the upscale restaurants.

Escorted to their table by a blond hostess in a white pleated shirt and black slacks, Keir and Ryan followed the woman through the near-empty restaurant. With a hand at the base of her spine, Keir led Ryan across the hardwood floor. A mushroom-colored suit with a scarlet scoop-necked silk shell, Ryan's outfit complemented Keir's beige cashmere sweater and cocoa silk trousers.

The trio halted at a secluded corner table. Keir helped Ryan into a chair and seated himself opposite her. For the tenth time, Ryan wondered what she had gotten herself into. Why put her career and reputation on the line? If Glo discovered the truth, there'd be hell to pay.

The other part of her blew it all off. It was only one dinner. Plus, it felt great for her ego to be out with this handsome, powerful man who could have his pick of women. Keir had chosen her.

The server approached their table. "Welcome to

P.F. Chang's. My name is Jim. I'll be your server tonight. Can I start you out with a cocktail or an appetizer?"

"Ryan?" Keir prompted. "Would you like something to drink?"

She spread the white linen napkin over her lap, pondering the question for a moment before answering. "Riesling works for me."

"Any brand in particular?" Keir asked. He copied her gesture, tossing the linen cloth across his lap.

"I tend to lean toward German wines. Is that all right with you?"

Kcir smiled back at her and accepted the wine list from the server, studying the selection. "We can do that. How about Mosel-Saar-Ruwer?"

"Excellent choice, sir," Jim complimented.

Ryan nodded, absently drumming her fingers against the tabletop to the soft Asian-themed music playing in the background, while a hint of ginger and onions filled the air.

Keir reached for her hand, held it in both of his, and stroked it reassuringly. Ryan's skin tingled everywhere his fingers touched her. "Relax. It's just dinner," he said. "We're here for fun, food, and adult conversation. I'm not expecting anything more. Okay?"

His words soothed her. Ryan smiled back at him. "I know."

"Great." Keir released her hand and began to flip through the menu. "How about an appetizer? Have you tried Crab Wontons?"

"No. What is it?"

"Crab meat mixed with cream cheese, garlic, and green onions wrapped in a fried wonton skin." Keir ran his tongue across his lips. "It's delicious!"

Laughing softly, Ryan said, "You sound like a commercial. Are you on P.F. Chang's payroll?"

He shut the menu. "No. I happen to truly love Chinese food. Crab Wontons is one of my favorites. Want to try it?"

"You've convinced me," she answered, picking up her water glass.

After placing the appetizer and wine orders, Keir returned his attention to her. "Now we can relax, enjoy our food, and watch the crowd."

With a skeptical eye, Ryan glanced around the sparsely occupied restaurant. "I don't think we're going to do much people watching on a Monday night." She pointed a finger at the empty nearby tables. "Look at this place. It's practically empty."

"Is that a problem for you?"

"No."

"Good. Enough of my life is spent in the limelight. I crave privacy," Keir said.

"I'm not a woman that needs to be the center of attention."

"I'm not surprised. You seem like a very confident, self-composed woman who doesn't want to be placed center stage."

"My privacy is as important to me as yours is to you."

The server returned with the wine, uncorked the bottle, and poured a small portion into Keir's glass. After a quick sip, Keir nodded. The server filled their glasses and placed the bottle in a clay carafe on the edge of the table before quietly disappearing.

For several minutes they sat, sipping their wine and taking note of the goings-on at the restaurant. As if he'd come to a decision, Keir put down his glass and turned to Ryan. "Here's my suggestion for the evening. Let's skip the awkward, getting to know each other phase and hop right into the personal stuff. Agreed?"

Instantly, his suggestion hit a cord within Ryan and put her at ease. "Sounds good."

Settling farther into his chair, Keir admitted, "I hate all those forced silences while you're trying to figure out something clever to say. Let's just skip that. You can ask me anything. I don't want there to be secrets between us."

Intrigued by Keir's offer, Ryan lifted her wineglass and took a sip, stalling for a moment. "I'm going for it. How did you decide to become a director?"

Grinning at her, he said, "Oh, come on. Couldn't you think of something better than that? Like, what were you trying to say in the scene with Viki and Gary at the end of your last movie?"

"No. I'm really interested in how people end up where they do."

"Fair enough. Did you miss the part where I'm bossy and want everything done my way?"

Giggling, Ryan responded to his quip. "I have noticed. But I didn't want to point out the obvious."

With efficient movements, Jim returned with a plate and deposited it in the center of the table, announcing, "Crab Wontons. They look great." Keir served several star-shaped fried noodles to Ryan before putting a couple on his plate.

"Did you always know you were going to be a director?" Ryan asked while nibbling on the food.

"Yes. But I didn't accept that fact right away."

"What do you mean?"

"I started my undergraduate studies in accounting."

Ryan's voice rose an octave from surprise. "Really! How did that go?"

He scoffed. "My spreadsheets refused to balance. They were always off by a penny or two. That drove me nuts."

"You're a director at heart. What were you thinking?"

"I wanted to make it all work out. I figured the easiest way to reconcile the problem was to toss in a penny and make things balance. Didn't work. My instructors wanted to know where that particular penny went, and I had to find it." Keir's forehead wrinkled into a frown. "I hated that."

"Poor baby."

Nodding, Keir muttered, "I was. Anyway, that's how I started out. I finally owned up to the fact that I wanted to direct and transferred to film school in New York. Best thing I ever did. What about you? Did you always want to do set designing?"

"Nope. I started out with the plan to be the next straight Versace or African American Vera Wang."

"Ambitious. You still have time to make that dream a reality," he said.

"It's crossed my mind. Anywho, I also went to New York for fame and fortune and an education. Instead, I found myself involved in set design for one of the soap operas."

"Wow!" Amusement flickered in the eyes that met hers. "Soaps. 'I just fell in love with my sister's boyfriend's cousin who's my secret half brother that my mother never told me about.'"

"Something like that. It paid the bills while I finished college. The good part was my work caught the eye of Joel Collins, and when he started selecting crew for *SWAT Command*, his people gave me a call."

"Got you an Emmy, too."

Embarrassed, Ryan brushed a hand through her short hair. She always felt uncomfortable talking about the Emmy. "There's that. Believe me, that nomination came as quite a surprise. And that's how my career went from zero to two hundred overnight."

"Yeah. I know exactly what you mean."

"Let's turn the spotlight on you. I'll dim it a bit so you won't feel so pressured. Talk to me. You're the one with the Oscar."

"You thought you were surprised. I can't describe how shocked I was. I hadn't finished film school. *Children in Brothels* launched my career and put me on the map with the industry giants. Also gave me an opportunity to collaborate with a few of my idols."

"Like who?"

"Spielberg, for one. John Singleton was another. My all-time favorite, Robert Altman, was the icing on the cake." Keir's green eyes shimmered with admiration. Ryan was impressed by his passion for his work. "That man can capture the essence of a scene better than anyone I know. I loved working with him because I learned so much."

The aroma of garlic and onions filled the immediate area as Jim put in an appearance with their entrees. Moo Goo Gai Pan with chicken, shrimp, and vegetables was set in front of Ryan. The server placed a covered silver tray in front of Keir and removed the lid, presenting a dish of crispy slices of fresh fish in a Sichuan sauce, decorated with stir-fried vegetables.

"Dig in," said Ryan as he scooped a portion of the fish onto his plate. "Do you want a taste before I devour this?"

Her lips pursed as she considered his food, and then she reached for the serving spoon, planning to add a bit of his fish to her plate. "Sure."

Instead, Keir speared a piece of fish and swished it in the sauce before bringing the tasty morsel to her lips. "Here you are. Eat up."

Surprised, Ryan opened her mouth. The Sichuan sauce added a spicy twang to the wonderful piece of tender sea bass. A dab of sauce covered the corner of her mouth. Ryan captured it with the tip of her tongue as Keir's hot gaze followed the gesture with more than the usual interest

Recovering swiftly, Keir asked, "Good, isn't it?"

"Mm-hmm. Do you want to try some of mine?"

He considered her question for a nanosecond and then nodded.

Ryan deposited some garlic-seasoned chicken and shrimp into his open mouth.

"Yours is good, too. Next time I'll order it." Keir waved his fork over his plate. "Feel free to get more if you want."

"Thanks. But I think I have enough here to keep me busy."

Nodding, Keir concentrated on the food in front of him, and Ryan did the same. "You said you went to school in New York. Is that where you met your husband?"

Her heart slammed against her chest. Another ticking time bomb had just been detonated. She knew they might enter this emotional territory, but she refused to think about her husband and marriage in connection with this new relationship. "Actually, I met him here, at a travel club outing."

"Travel club?"

Ryan drew in a deep breath and explained. "I like to check out different locales, and so did Galen. We hooked up during a one-day excursion to Mexico."

"That's a different way to meet. How long were you married?"

"Three years. What about you? How many years were you and your wife together?"

Keir put down his fork and pushed his near-empty plate away. "Together two. Married thirteen. Total of fifteen years."

"I'm sorry."

"No need. I think our divorce was the right thing to do." A faraway gleam entered his eyes, and Ryan got the impression his next words weren't directed at her. She felt as if Keir might be sorting the situation out in his mind by voicing his concerns out loud. "Although I miss my kids, Shannon and I are not the same people we were when we got married. Both of us want and need different things."

Reaching out to him, Ryan agreed. "That happens sometimes. I think the smart and truly brave people realize this and get on with their lives."

"If I'm treading on territory that's too painful for you, tell me. I know you're a widow. What happened to your husband?"

Taking a moment to compose herself and decide on the proper words, Ryan said, "Something utterly avoidable. Galen liked to cycle to work every morning. He was on his bike when a lady on a cell phone hit him with her car."

"I'm so sorry."

"Me, too. Sometimes I wonder if I could have saved him." Her voice softened as the painful memories played in her mind like a video recording. "Kept him at home five minutes longer. Stopped nagging him. I don't know. Done something that would have changed the outcome of that day. Needless to say, I get real antsy around people that do everything with a cell phone attached to their ear."

Keir nodded. "I understand. Do you mind if I take us in another direction?"

"Not at all." She took a sip from her water goblet as she struggled to get her emotions under control. In this moment she felt as if she'd revealed too much about her past. "I think I need it."

"Where do you see yourself going from here? Any big plans for your future?"

"Do you mean like an Oscar?" A shadow of a smile appeared and quickly disappeared from her face.

"Something like that."

"Again, I sort of fell into this career. So, I'm not sure. Sometimes I think I know where I'm headed, and other times, I'm totally lost."

"Is that why you don't want anyone to know you're out with me?" Keir asked seriously.

"A little bit. I've worked hard in this business. And I think, for a woman, your reputation is your greatest asset. I don't want to lose mine."

"And you feel going out with me will taint your rep? Put a black mark on your record?"

"That's not what I'm saying at all."

He leaned closer to her, and his voice took on a hard edge. "Then what are you saying, exactly?"

"Two things. First, I've got a rep of coming in, getting the job done, and leaving all the other mess behind. I like it, and I want to keep things that way. Being involved with someone from the studio blurs those lines, causes all manner of problems that I don't want attached to my reputation."

"Tell me more," he encouraged.

"I'm sorry, normally, I don't allow myself to get involved on the job. I work for you. That's the beginning, middle, and end of it."

"Actually, it's not. You see me socially. So we're more than employer and employee."

"I know. And I'd like to keep that aspect of my life away from the eyes and ears of my gossiping colleagues."

"Mm. Interesting."

Ryan felt compelled to explain a little more. "I prefer to keep my work and private life separate."

"Is that why you were hesitant to go out with me?"

"Partly. When I hired on to the show, Glo made it very clear that she didn't approve of on-the-job romances. She feels they kick up way too much drama."

"Glo works for me."

"And so do I," she added, playing with the diamond stud in her right ear. "But you're not my immediate supervisor. I have to work closely with Glo. Life could be really difficult if I piss her off. I'd rather stay on her good side. It makes everything easier and more pleasant."

"Answer a question for me." Pursing his lips, Keir pulled on the lobe of his ear.

Shrugging, Ryan replied, "If I can."

"What happens if we get closer? Where will I fit in your life? I don't think you'll be able to hide your feelings or our relationship. You won't be able to completely separate the two areas of your life. What will you do then?"

"I don't know. All I know for sure is I plan to do the best job possible wherever I work."

"I'm going to say this, and then we'll put the whole issue on the shelf for the time being. I don't want to increase your stress level at work. So, I'll go along with remaining low-key at the studio. For now."

Her sigh of relief quickly turned to apprehension with his next statement.

"I like you, and I plan to get to know you better. If we take a step to a closer relationship, we're going to have to revisit this issue, possibly change the rules."

For the present, that would have to do. She didn't know where they were headed, so the future would have to take care of itself.

"Tonight, you're not my employee. You're my date," Keir continued. "And I'm going to ask you a very important question. What about dessert? Are you up for The Great Wall of Chocolate?"

Giggling, Ryan shook her head. Keir was full of surprises, fun and happy surprises. "Great Wall? What exactly is The Great Wall of Chocolate?"

"Six layers of chocolate fudge cake, chocolate frosting, with raspberry sauce. We can add a scoop of vanilla ice cream to keep things legal."

"I hear a commercial," she teased. "It sounds really good. But I couldn't eat that much cake alone. Want to share?"

Keir's gaze slid over her, warm and enticing. "Yes, indeed."

Chapter 5

After sharing a delicious slice of chocolate cake dubbed The Great Wall of Chocolate and a double scoop of vanilla ice cream, Keir and Ryan left the restaurant. As they waited for the valet attendant to retrieve the car, a gust of wind whispered through the trees and swirled across the front of the building, causing Ryan to shiver. Chilled, she drew her jacket more snugly around her body.

Keir's gaze slid over her. His eyebrows knitted into a frown. "Cold?"

She nodded.

He moved closer, wrapping an arm around her and anchoring her against his body.

The valet attendant pulled the silver Jaguar to the front of the building and then jumped out, with the engine still running. Keir helped Ryan into the passenger seat before taking his place behind the steering wheel and popping a CD into the player. The sultry sound of Marion Meadows's saxophone filled the confined space. Seconds later, the Jag shot into the late-evening traffic.

Feeling full and mellow from good food, great conversation, and pleasant company, Ryan snuggled into the black leather bucket seat, swaying slightly to the music. Her thoughts returned to the evening she'd just spent with Keir. Who would have thought she'd have such a wonderful time? Dinner had been many things—fun, humorous, and full of surprises. They had exchanged their aspirations about their careers and feelings regarding their families. Ryan had seen a side of him that she really liked and she wanted to see more of.

Conversation was kept to a minimum as they sped through the night. Thirty minutes later Keir pulled into Ryan's driveway and cut the engine. He opened his door, hopped out of the car, and ran around the hood to the passenger door. With a hand at her elbow, Keir helped her from the vehicle, and they slowly strolled up the walkway to the porch.

Nervousness assaulted Ryan. It had been a while since she'd been out on a date, and she felt rusty about the proper end-of-evening etiquette. Did he expect a kiss? Possibly more? Would he morph into a beast with twelve hands? Up to this point, Keir had behaved perfectly. But Ryan's concerns were mounting as they reached the porch and started up the stairs. Her belly twisted into knots.

At the door, Ryan turned to Keir, then said stiffly, "Thank you for a lovely dinner and the excellent company. You were right. Going out was a great idea."

Ohmigod. She cringed and then whined silently. *I sound like a total idiot.*

He bowed his head slightly and muttered good-naturedly, "Told you."

Laughing lightly, she teased, "And you're just so humble."

Grinning, Keir shrugged. "When I'm right, I'm right."

The mood shifted, and tension reared its monstrous head. She glanced into his eyes and quickly looked away.

All of Ryan's earlier insecurities manifested themselves anew. Was she ready for this?

Ryan focused on another problem. The last thing she wanted to do was tangle with a man expecting something more. Unfortunately, good manners dictated that she invite him in. She wished she didn't have to. Ryan's mother, Elizabeth Brown, had raised her children with proper manners.

Ryan fished through her purse for the key, unlocked the door, and opened it a crack. "I really enjoyed tonight. Thanks again."

Keir smiled down at her. "So did I."

"Would you like to come in for coffee?"

"No," he answered decisively. "I should be getting home. Tomorrow's a workday. Maybe another time."

Relieved, Ryan let out an audible sigh and held out her hand. "Good night. Drive safely."

Forehead crinkled into a frown, he gazed at her hand, studying it. "No."

Confused, Ryan examined her hand and then turned to Keir. "No? I don't understand."

Amusement lurked in the depths of his green gaze. "Mrs. Mitchell, I am *not* shaking hands with you."

Mrs. Mitchell! Where had that come from? Two could play this game. "I'm sorry, Mr. Southhall. You've lost me."

"Tonight I've told you all of my deep, dark secrets. We are well past the hand-shaking phase."

Ryan lowered her voice to a husky whisper, enjoying the gentle sparring between them. "Do you have a better idea?"

"Yes, indeed." Keir planted his hands on Ryan's hips and tugged, bringing her near. "This."

Anticipation made Ryan's pulse leap with excitement, while heat warmed her blood. Keir slowly drew her into his arms, providing ample opportunity for Ryan to resist.

With a deft move of his hand, he cupped the side of her face in his large palm and nibbled on her bottom lip, tasting and exploring. His kiss was slow and thorough. Ryan melted at the sweet tenderness of his touch while drinking in his unique flavor and scent.

The knot in her belly uncoiled as pleasure shot through her. Eyes drifting shut, Ryan nibbled back while resting her hands on his arms. Keir framed her face with his hands, parting her lips as his tongue met hers, savoring the nectar.

Changing direction, Keir lifted his head and seared a path down her throat, sucking softly on the tender flesh at the curve of her neck before retracing the route and recapturing her lips. Seconds later, he broke the kiss and stepped away, taking in a deep breath of air. Keir removed his key ring from his pocket.

"You come up with the best ideas," she complimented.

"I thought you might enjoy it. I know I did."

Touching her lip, Ryan admitted, "So did I."

"I'll see you tomorrow," Keir promised, smiling gently at her before leaning down and brushing another brief kiss across her lips. He bounced down the stairs and crossed the yard to the Jag. The roar of the powerful engine echoed through the quiet neighborhood as he backed out of the drive and sped into the night.

Exhausted yet exhilarated, Ryan shut, locked, and then leaned against the front door. Her fingers stroked her bottom lip as she relived the wonderful connection of mind and body that had flowed between Keir and her.

Did she want to go out with him again? Absolutely. Should she accept a second date? Probably not. There were far too many issues standing between them. Like the fact that Ryan's immediate supervisor disapproved of on-the-job romances and dating the boss could cause a lot of conflict and drama on and off the set. Plus, there was the problem of his children. She didn't feel emotionally strong enough to cope with Keir's children; dealing with kids meant opening her heart to the whole package, and Ryan wasn't sure she was ready for that.

Ryan giggled softly. Here she stood, contemplating the future with Keir when he hadn't asked her out for a second date.

On her way through the house, she paused at the desk situated in a corner of the living room, dropping the keys in a golden dish. The telephone display indicated two new messages. She dialed in the code and listened to the gregarious voice of her big brother.

"Hey, you. What's going on? It's almost eleven o'clock. Don't you have to go to work tomorrow?"

She scoffed. "Tony the protector" took his role very seriously. Since she was a small kid, he'd always stepped in and taken charge of any situation where she might get hurt or needed help. Actually, both of her older siblings, Tony as well as Helen, believed it was their job to watch over Ryan.

"I just called to check on you," Tony continued. "Dinner was good Sunday. Thanks again for having us over. It's my turn to return the favor. Why don't you come by my place Saturday afternoon for chicken and ribs? Take a load off, and have a meal on me. That's what big brothers are for, right?" He chuckled. "Anyway, are you okay? Give me a call. You've got the number."

The second message was from Glo, informing Ryan to come into the studio at noon. There were a few technical problems, and their day would start a bit later. *Cool,* she thought, returning the telephone to the cradle. After her evening out, it would be nice to sleep in Tuesday morning. The flip side of that situation meant she would probably be on the set much later than expected.

Humming Anita Baker's "Giving You the Best That I've

Got," Ryan proceeded to the kitchen, filled the tea kettle, and placed it on the range. She removed a mug from the cupboard, a spoon from a drawer, and searched for a decaf tea bag. Her thoughts returned to her brother's question about her well-being. Ryan laughed out loud, still feeling the tingling sensation from Keir's touch and his taste of her lips. Thinking of Keir and their kiss, she muttered softly, "I'm more than okay."

Chapter 6

"Move camera three. I want the east angle." Palms open, Keir spread his hands wide. "A shot of Simon when he makes his entrance is what I'm going for. His image should be silhouetted against the sunlight. Got me?"

The cameramen nodded and then began to move around the room, making the appropriate adjustments as per the director's requests.

"Good." Keir studied his watch for a beat. "Once you've finished, take a fifteen-minute break."

Silently, Ryan placed a series of photographs in bronze frames on the set's coffee table. She added a plant to an end table and fluffed black pillows with gold, green, and red threads on the sofa and chairs as the sound of Keir's husky drawl made her tingle all over.

For the past three weeks, Ryan and Keir had been inseparable outside the studio. Meals, visits to the park, evenings watching television, and Sunday morning strolls through the farmers' market had replaced Ryan's solitary existence. Although their relationship hadn't stepped over the intimacy threshold, it was coming. The level of desire Ryan and Keir shared made it almost impossible for them to keep their hands off each other in private. Honestly, Ryan wondered how they kept things together at work and managed not to reveal the depth of their feelings for each other.

With a great deal of effort, Ryan maintained her role as the perfect employee during work hours, distancing herself from the personal issues of her coworkers in order to handle her own problem.

Glo Kramer remained the dark spot on Ryan's happiness meter. Glo's warning regarding fraternization worried Ryan. Granted, being fired didn't really concern Ryan, but the damage to her reputation and career could be irreversible. Her boss had the power to make life a living hell and to tarnish Ryan's pristine work record. Heads of movie studios were a small group, and the wrong word ended careers quicker than a zit on an actor's nose.

Butterflies waltzed around in Ryan's belly, and her Keir radar kicked in. She turned and found him standing directly behind her.

"Good morning, Mrs. Mitchell. How are you today?"

"Oh, Mr. Southhall. I didn't see you there. I'm fine. And you?" Ryan replied, with a hint of humor in her voice, loving this game they shared. Since their first date, Keir had teased her by calling her Mrs. Mitchell when they were at the studio. The teasing note in his voice had convinced her to return the gesture; using their surnames while exchanging pleasantries had become their subtle way of communicating.

"I'm doing great. Do you have time for a cup of coffee? I'd like to talk with you about the scene I'm shooting tomorrow."

Always cautious, Ryan gazed around the room, searching for her boss. She wanted to go with Keir, but they needed to be careful. There had been several near misses where Glo had appeared in a room when they didn't expect it. Ryan didn't want a hint of impropriety to touch her. Finding the area Glo Kramer free, Ryan nodded, and they started down the long, narrow corridor to the cafeteria.

As they turned the corner away from the set, Ryan found herself instantly swept into Keir's arms. Loving the feel of his strong, hard body against hers, she caressed the strong column of his neck while he nibbled on hers. "I'm having an attack of Ryan withdrawals," he joked, licking the side of her neck. Her knees went weak. "I need sustenance."

Sanity returned when Ryan opened her eyes, noting how the corridor opened into a large hallway, where anyone could happen upon them in this compromising position. She stiffened, hunching her shoulders as she pushed at his chest and hissing, "Stop!"

He lifted his head and gazed around, drawing her closer. "Nobody's here. Don't worry."

"We don't know who's around the corner," Ryan whispered frantically, fighting to get out of his embrace. "We agreed. No messing around on the job."

Eyes narrowing, Keir dropped his arms to his sides. "Nobody cares." The husky tone he normally used carried a frustrated edge.

Ryan continued down the corridor. "I care. People love gossip. Keir, think about it. You're the boss. Everyone wants to know the intimate details of your life."

Forehead wrinkled into a frown, Keir followed at a slower pace. The pair halted inside the cafeteria door. Glo sat at one of the long cafeteria-style tables, with a cup of coffee and a batch of sketches in front of her. Ryan shot Keir an "I told you" glare before heading to the set director's table. Hearing them approach, Glo lifted her head, examining Ryan and then focusing on Keir. A hint of suspicion burned bright in her blue eyes. It was quickly extinguished, replaced by a huge, friendly grin. "Hey, you two."

Keir guided Ryan to where Glo sat. "Do you want a cup of coffee, Glo?" he asked.

"No thanks." Glo lifted her paper cup. "I still have half a cup left."

Nodding, he headed to the vending machines and returned with a cup of coffee in each hand. He glanced at Ryan. The expression in his eyes said, "See. I'm trying to work with you."

"What are you up to?" Keir asked as he handed a cup to Ryan and then took the empty space next to Glo.

"Sketches for episode thirteen," replied Glo.

"Don't you have an office for this?" asked Keir.

"Yeah, I do. But, there's more room to spread out in here. Plus, most times it's quiet. No phones or people asking questions." Glo glanced at Ryan, with an inquiring gleam in her sharp gaze. "How's the set coming?"

Uncomfortable, Ryan shifted on the park-style navy bench. "We're all done." She jabbed a thumb in Keir's direction. "Mr. Southhall invited me for a cup of coffee to discuss tomorrow's sets."

"Excellent," said Glo. Nodding, Glo returned to the work in front of her.

Ryan glanced at Keir. Now that they had arrived here, what exactly were they going to discuss?

Glo reached inside her portfolio and withdrew an embossed envelope. "I received this in the mail this morning. It's nice. I think it's a good idea."

Keir hunched his shoulders. "You know me. I always want people to know how much I appreciate their efforts. I told Phil that I wanted to do something big after we got episode eleven completed."

Glo removed the invitation and read the printed card. "The Hyatt. Elegant. Ryan, I know you're new to our little family here, but you should come. Get yourself a date, and have a good time."

"Yeah. You should bring a date," Keir parroted.

Where's mine? Ryan wondered silently. "I'll think about it," she hedged, giving Keir the evil eye.

Glo glanced at her watch and then rose from the table. "Excuse me. It's time for me to move on. Phil and I are meeting at three. I'll see you guys later."

Ryan sipped her coffee as Glo packed up her stuff and left the room.

Keir turned his attention to her. "I held off on sending your invitation because I wanted to talk to you about it first. And now that Glo brought it up, this is a good time to discuss the Hyatt party."

"What about it?"

"I want you to go to the celebration with me."

Ryan drew in a deep breath and let it out slowly. She didn't want to have this conversation. "Keir, I can't do that."

"Why not?"

"What do you mean, 'why not?' I thought we agreed to keep our relationship away from the gossipmongers. I can't jeopardize my career."

"Nobody said you had to."

Annoyed, Ryan shut her eyes, reaching for a way to describe her fears. Facing him, she said, "Keir, I really like being with you. But my career is very important to me. Just like yours is to you. When we started seeing each other, you agreed to stay low-key. Now you want to change the rules."

"You are right," Keir said, taking her hand. "I did agree. But, I also said we'd revisit this subject if things changed. That's happened and we're revisiting."

"Don't!" Panicked, Ryan shook off his hand and placed hers in her lap.

Frustration was etched into his normally pleasant features. He grabbed her hand and held it tightly. "The situation has changed. Our situation is different. I'm not going to pretend anymore. Why should we act like teenagers worried about how our friends and parents will react? This isn't Romeo and Juliet. We're too damn old to play games, and I don't live that way. And I'm not going to."

"I can't do this."

"Sure, you can. Look, I appreciate how important your job is to you. I understand. Truly, I do. But you and I can't go on this way."

"Keir, you have nothing to lose. The big producer/ director. Your reputation will be fine regardless of what happens. I, on the other hand, have to think about my next job. What they think of me. What they have heard about me."

"That's not true, Ryan."

She shook her head and said, "Maybe we should quit before things go too far."

"Now you're running from your feelings. Is Glo that scary?"

"No. She's not," Ryan replied.

"Are you afraid she'll fire you? Because the studio is a business, and you're under contract."

"No, but—"

"Then what is it? I'm not feeling you right now." Keir swallowed a mouthful of coffee and then demanded, "Help me understand."

"I am afraid of what gossip may do to my career. Maybe I was wrong to think I could have a relationship on the job and work for you, too."

"Stop. Stop. Stop. You are blowing this way out of proportion. I'm not saying you have to confess before the preacher on Sunday. It's time for you to decide what you want." His voice dropped to a husky purr that melted her insides like butter over a hot burner. "There's nothing in the rule book that states you have to choose between me and your job. You can have both. Me and your career. Just take a stand on what's important to you."

"Glo," Ryan mumbled.

"Ryan, look at me," he demanded.

She lifted her head and looked directly at him, letting Keir see the confusion and worry in her eyes.

"Ry, our relationship doesn't concern Glo. She's not part of it. This is about you and me. Us. Ask yourself a question. Do you want to be with me? Someone would have found out eventually. That's the way things happen. You can't keep a secret like this hidden forever."

She sat silently, taking in everything he said.

"I can't make your decision for you," he continued. "But I have to be honest with you. I care deeply for you, and I want you in my life. You have to accept we are involved in an adult relationship, and we're moving toward the next step." He rose from the table, dumped his cup in the trash, and left the room, leaving her to contemplate his parting shot.

Her mind swirled with a mass of conflicting images. What was she doing? Did she really want to be the subject of her coworkers' bathroom and dinnertime gossip? And Glo. How would she react? What would she do? Ryan didn't see that situation working out like the happy endings on the last frame of some movies.

On the other hand, the past three weeks had been the happiest in her life since Galen died. Did she want to return to the sterile, lonely existence she called a life before Keir swept her into his world?

Keir brought fun, a good time, and laughter into Ryan's life. The muscles tightened at the base of her neck when she thought of exposing her private life to the entertainment industry. Could she truly have them both? Keir and her career? The only way to find out was to go for it.

Tony's old slogan popped into her head. *No guts, no glory.* Ryan wasn't a coward, although her behavior recently had made her feel and act like one. If it didn't work out, she'd find a way to wiggle out of her contract and move on. First, she needed to give this relationship the chance it deserved.

Chapter 7

Ryan gazed at the stars bathing the deep purple hues of the sky as they made their way to the Hyatt West Hollywood. Keir sat behind the wheel of the car, weaving in and out of traffic like a NASCAR driver headed for the finish line. As they sped along Sunset Boulevard, the fifteen-story hotel loomed on the horizon, large and foreboding. Ensconced in the passenger seat of the white Corvette, Ryan silently admired the efficient manner in which Keir handled the powerful car, while listening to Kenny G's mellow saxophone tune.

Keir took his eyes off the road and glanced Ryan's way. She knew what he saw. A woman nervously pleating the hem of her dress. He lifted a hand from the steering wheel, placed it on top of Ryan's hands, and squeezed reassuringly, effectively putting an end to her fidgeting. "Relax."

"I can't."

He returned his attention to the road before adding, "Yes, you can. It's only dinner with people you already know."

"That's easy for you to say."

"No. It's not. I don't like seeing you so upset. This is a celebration, and we're here to have fun." He grinned, running an admiring eye over her. Ryan felt flattered by the appreciative gleam in his gaze. "Besides, you look too good to worry about what others may think. Mrs. Mitchell, it'll all work out."

"Aren't you the optimist, Mr. Southhall."

He bowed his head slightly. "Only where you're concerned."

Gently smiling at her date, Ryan felt confident in her decision to attend the party, but uncomfortable with the whole idea of divulging their relationship, their brand-new relationship, to the employees of One Leaf Studio. At times the gossipers were brutal, and what they didn't know, they enjoyed making up. Ryan dreaded exposing her life to the public eye.

Keir brought the Corvette to a roaring halt at the valet booth, climbed out, and then tossed the keys to the uniformed attendant. A second employee opened Ryan's door and extended a helping hand. She accepted it, swung her legs from the bucket seat, rose, and stood at the hotel entrance as Keir strolled purposefully around the hood and stopped at her side. With easy grace, he slid his fingers between Ryan's and steered her through the sliding doors and into the Hyatt's lobby.

The urge to run like a scared rabbit filled her. *Come on, girl. You made your choice. Now live with it.*

Ryan's fingers fluttered around the gold clasp of her evening bag, betraying her nervousness. She found it impossible to let go of the idea that attending this party as Keir's date amounted to professional suicide. More concerned about her career than she'd ever been in her life, Ryan ignored her fears and walked purposefully at Keir's side.

From this point forward, their lives would be intertwined. Everything would change. Ryan acknowledged her job was secure. But, what she currently worried over was the way her friend's and colleague's attitudes might change. After all, Keir owned and ran One Leaf Studio.

Interaction with her colleagues was bound to change and Ryan didn't want that. Plus, she didn't want to create a reputation of sleeping around. She liked her quiet, unassuming image and blending into the woodwork made it easier for her to do her job.

They crossed the vast, elaborate reception area and stepped into the waiting elevator. Keir punched the button for the Sunset Ballroom before leaning against the opposite wall.

For the second time she felt his admiring green gaze slide over her small frame like a light caress of his fingers, causing her to grow warm all over. Dressed in a scarlet spaghetti strapped dress with a tightly fitted bodice, the garment flared into a full short skirt and stopped mid-thigh. A matching red handbag swung from her shoulder on a long gold chain and red sandals covered her feet.

"You look gorgeous," Keir whispered, leaning close and planting a soft kiss next to her ear. His compliment sparked a gentle fire inside her.

Warmed by Keir's words, she answered, "Thank you."

Ryan turned her attention to the man next to her, examining him from head-to-toe. He looked magnificent. Dressed in black silk trousers with a matching leather jacket and hand crafted black leather loafers, a pale gray crew neck sweater peeked from the folds of the jacket. Keir oozed power and success. He represented the ultimate successful Hollywood director/producer.

Leaning closer, Keir stroked a finger along her bare arm, drawing delicate circles on her soft skin. "Take my advice, go with the flow and everything will be fine. Remember, you're with me. And I run this show."

Right. Ryan thought. *It's not your reputation going down the drain. It's mine.* She offered Keir a less than convincing smile. Laughing at her expression, he took her into his arms and held her close. The warmth of his body mixed with his unique scent soothed her riotous emotions. Rocking her to and fro, Keir nibbled on the side of her neck. "This is going to be fine. An hour from now you'll be wondering why you felt so apprehensive."

Slowly Keir lowered his head. His lips brushed against hers as gentle as a whisper, creating delicious sensations. The warm, sweet kiss left her weak for more. Ryan returned his kiss, lingering, savoring every second.

The elevator bell chimed and a soft computer generated voice announced, "Sunset Ballroom."

He lifted his head, whispering, "Well, Mrs. Mitchell, let's show them who you are."

With a daring toss of her head, Ryan squared her shoulders, mustering all the courage at her disposal. "Absolutely, Mr. Southhall." Displaying more confidence than she actually felt, Ryan turned to the door, linking her fingers with his. The choice had already been made. She could do this.

The doors opened and they stepped off the elevator to music, people, and the appetizing aroma of food. Several curious gazes turned their way. With a hand at the small of her back, Keir guided her into the buzz of the ballroom.

Awed, Ryan studied the beautiful room. Submerged in a mellow evening light, ceiling-to-floor windows offered a panoramic view of Sunset Boulevard, submerging it in a gentle evening light. A disc jockey manned his station near the dance floor, providing light, generic elevator music that wafted through the air. Black cushioned chairs surrounded tables decorated with gold metallic tablecloths and napkins. Couples milled around the room, parading their evening finery with plates of food and tall mixed drinks. Ryan spied a set of glass double doors leading onto an outdoor patio. Beyond the doors she noted multi-colored deck chairs where additional studio people sat.

Gently tugging on her hand, Keir led her further into the room. She glued a friendly, confident smile on her face and preceded Keir, stopping here and there to chat with her co-workers as they made their way through the maze of tables. Although there were a few raised eyebrows and curious stares, Ryan didn't encounter a snide remark or any unpleasantness.

Phil Bergen rose from the head table and waved a hand in the air. Nodding, Keir steered her in a different direction. He leaned close and whispered in her ear, "We're supposed to be with the hot shots. Personally, I'd like to find a place where we can be alone."

For a beat she examined his handsome earnest face and then revealed what she felt in her heart, "So would I."

They strolled to the table where Phil sat beside his 20-something trophy wife.

The happy greetings and friendly gestures boasted Ryan's fragile confidence. Everyone seemed so friendly. It looked as if she'd worried herself into a frenzy for nothing. Keir was right. Nobody cared about her personal life.

Facing Keir, she gave him a big "you were right" grin.

Maybe she had overreacted. Or her ideas regarding the entertainment industry were greatly exaggerated. All her fears had been in vain. Hopefully, she could continue to work with these people without changing the status quo of her existence at the studio. Phil stuck out his hand. "Hey, my man. I thought you decided to skip your own party."

"Nah. I can't have that." Keir turned to Ryan. "I think you know some of these people. Let me introduce you to their better halves," he joked, pointing a finger at different couples as he introduced the administrative team of One Leaf Studio and their spouses. Finally he turned to one additional member of the team. Her insides were twisted into a mass of clenched stomach muscles as she turned to her boss.

Relief washed over the knots and untangled them. Glo sat smiling at Ryan and Keir. There wasn't a hint of anger in her expression.

Keir knew what he was talking about. Ryan had nothing to fear. Happy to have this drama finished, she took the seat he offered and settled down for an enjoyable evening.

The guests at the table chatted pleasantly while drinks and dinner were distributed. Ryan enjoyed the sparkling wine and the excellently prepared Steak Diane.

Deep in conversation with Phil, Keir caressed Ryan's hand under the table. Once she finished her meal, she leaned close to Keir's ear and whispered, "I'll be right back."

He nodded and rose as she left the table and headed for the ladies room. As she stood at the mirror reapplying her lip gloss, the bathroom door opened and closed. She turned toward the entrance as the sound of sharp, clipped heels hitting the tile floor grew louder.

Glo appeared around the bend.

"Hi." Ryan waved at her boss.

"Mm," was Glo's response. "So how long have you been seeing Keir?" Glo's tone surprised Ryan. The happy expression Glo had displayed for everyone at the table had been wiped away, replaced by a suspicious gleam of betrayal and hostility. Had it all been an act?

"Are you all right?"

Glo's blue eyes glittered with suppressed anger. "No. I'm not."

"Please, I'd like to clear the air and tell you how things happened between Keir and me." Ryan fumbled with the clasp on her evening bag.

Glo braced her hip against the sink and folded her arms across her chest. "Would you now? And why is that?"

Ryan bit her lip, choosing her words carefully. "Glo, I don't want my relationship with Keir to interfere with us. We have to work together."

"You should have thought of that before you went out with our boss. Interesting. Now you're concerned about how we'll work together. All you have to do is tattle to your new boyfriend. I'm sure he'll take care of any problems with me."

"You know me. That's not my way. I wouldn't do that."

"Actually, I don't know you at all. I warned you about getting involved with Keir. Yet you did exactly that. You lied to me. What happened to 'I'm not involved with anyone'?"

"No. It wasn't like that. Trust me—"

"Trust you? I don't think so."

"I didn't plan to get involved with Keir. It sort of happened. And I promise, I won't allow my relationship with him to come between me and my work."

"Please. Either you're very naïve or the best con artist in the state. Of course, things will be different. You're sleeping with the boss."

Not yet, Ryan thought, but kept that comment to herself.

Ryan reached out to touch Glo's arm. Her hand halted when Glo pierced her with her hard blue gaze. "I understand that you're angry. But, you and I have to work together. We share an office and have to do some assignments together. We have to work in harmony."

"No. All I have to do is be in the same room with you

for short periods of time. I don't have to do anything more. You have to do what I tell you." Fuming, Glo ranted on. "I've got two things to say to you. If you're after my job, I'm not going down without a fight. I've got tricks that you know nothing about."

"No. No. Of course not," Ryan denied. "I love working for you."

"Hmpf."

"Look, Keir and I happened. I didn't plan this. If I'm honest, I liked things just the way they were. He's the one that pushed me into admitting that there's an attraction between us."

"I don't care about any of that. Remember, from this point on, we do everything according to the book. No special treatment, coming in late, or leaving early."

"I've never taken advantage of our situation. Why would I start now?"

"I don't care about anything you have to say. Do your job. That's all I expect from you. I won't bother you, and we'll be okay."

Glo stormed out of the ladies' room.

Ryan started to call her back but stopped. Her hands shook as she dropped her lipstick back in her evening bag. Obviously, the situation wasn't going to be resolved tonight. With a little finesse and time, Glo would understand that Ryan didn't intend to make her feel like Boo-Boo the Fool, and hopefully, they would return to the pleasant camaraderie they had previously shared.

Chapter 8

At the conclusion of the evening, everyone filed out of the ballroom and onto elevators and spilled into the hotel lobby. Keir wrapped a warm arm around Ryan and guided her out the sliding doors into the evening air. Huddled under the Hyatt's awning, Keir, Ryan, and a number of their colleagues waited for their cars to be delivered by the valet attendants. The Corvette came to a roaring halt in front of the couple, and Ryan settled into the passenger's seat seconds before Keir pulled away from the curb and merged the 'Vette into traffic.

The crescent-shaped moon sat high, illuminating the sky. A whiff of cool air caressed Ryan's face as gently as an infant's touch as they sped through the night.

Earlier, they had agreed to stop at Keir's house for a drink and some quality time alone. As he maneuvered the car in and out of traffic, he reached across the transmission gear and linked his fingers with Ryan's. Keir brought her hand to his lips for a tender kiss. Ryan turned to him and smiled, feeling like the most precious person in the little world they'd created.

The landscape slid past, and Ryan's thoughts returned to the evening they'd shared. Tonight had been a roaring success. The decision to attend the party had strengthened the bonds between them. If she put aside the tense moments with Glo, everything else had run smoothly. After a moment of stunned surprise at the pairing, the staff and their guests had been welcoming and friendly. Beyond the initial murmurings, Ryan's coworkers really hadn't paid much attention to her or Keir.

Keir's thumb stroked back and forth across the back of her hand, stirring a gentle fire deep within her. Tonight was a night for change. Tonight was a time for new beginnings.

She felt strong and confident for the transition. At the same time, a tiny part of her felt like a traitor to her husband and his memory. In her heart, Ryan knew Galen would have wanted her to move on and enjoy and experience all that life had to offer.

Keir sped through the gated community, cruising through the subdivision until he stopped outside an attached five-car garage. He hit the remote and zoomed inside after the garage door rose to its highest point. Once he brought the car to a complete stop, Keir climbed out and ran around the hood of the car to help Ryan from the vehicle. She glanced around and then turned to him, with a mischievous grin on her face. "You like cars, don't you?"

Embarrassed, he looked away. "It's one of my hobbies."

"Mm-hmm." Ryan peeked inside a wine-colored four-door Hummer. "Jaguar, Hummer, and Corvette. Expensive hobby."

"It can be. But I want what I want." Shrugging, he took her arm and guided her toward the door connected to the house.

Ryan patted Keir's shoulder. "Of course, you do."

"There's no reason why I shouldn't have it." Keir turned the knob on the oak door and reached inside, switching on the lights. Ryan followed him into the house. She gasped.

The kitchen was gorgeous. The Food Network would love to tape their shows from this room. Ryan strolled around the kitchen, taking note of the top-of-the-line appliances, cooking sinks located next to the stove, furniture-style cabinetry, and wine storage.

"Boy! You must love to cook," she teased.

"Actually, I do," Keir answered, with a smug gleam in his eyes. "Wait until I prepare a meal for you. You'll be impressed and swept away by my culinary skills."

"Really," Ryan replied. "What about your other talents?"

"What do you mean?"

"Does you expertise run to other areas that will impress me?"

He nodded, and his voice turned soft and seductive. "Oh yeah. Only my very special friends get to experience those things firsthand."

Taking a step closer to him, Ryan drew invisible circles on his chest. Keir's cologne, mixed with his unique scent, wafted under her nose, adding fuel to her flame of desire. "I hope you consider me one of your special friends."

"Absolutely." Keir pulled her into his warm embrace.

Softly moaning, Ryan muttered against his lips as she returned his kiss. "I like that."

Slowly, his gaze slid downward. The smoldering flame she saw in his eyes gave her a jolt. Lightly fingering her bangs, his hand slid down her neck to her shoulders, gently caressing the tight muscles before softly settling loosely on her hip.

Keir pulled her against him. He radiated a vitality that drew her like a magnet. His unique scent swirled around her. Powerless to resist, she melted into his loose embrace, and he lifted her head and tasted her lips.

Reluctantly ending the kiss, Keir smiled down at Ryan and wrapped an arm around her waist, drawing her against his side. Panting softly, he rested his forehead against hers. "Let me show you the rest of the house." Dazed, Ryan slipped her hand inside his.

Good. She needed a break to get her emotions under control. They strolled down a long marble hallway to the front of the house. A marble staircase led to the second floor. Keir led her away from the stairs and into a sunken great room. The room was completely empty. She turned to him, with a smirk on her lips. "Lived here long?"

He hugged her close and kissed her forehead. "Ha. Ha. Maybe you should be in front of the camera. Have you thought about a career change?"

Grinning, she did a saucy twist of her shoulders, gazing at him with a false expression of innocence in her eyes. "It's a possibility."

Keir glanced around the empty room. "Seriously, I haven't got around to looking for furniture." He tugged on her hand and headed down a second hallway. "I think you'll like this room better."

He opened the door to a home entertainment center. "Come on in. This is the room I call home. I live and work in here."

It was a beautiful spot. Ryan entered the room and sank into lush, thick carpeting. Pearl-colored walls and matching carpeting gave the impression of spacious elegance. A flat-screen plasma monitor was mounted on one wall. An encased fireplace was surrounded by a cream wall. Olive and cream leather furniture was strategically placed throughout the room for maximum viewing potential.

"Make yourself comfortable." He waved a hand at the sofa. "I'm going to get a bottle of wine."

Nodding, Ryan moved around the room, stroking the soft leather and admiring the simplicity of the setup before taking a seat on the sofa. She glanced around the room and shook her head, giggling softly. Her little house would fit in this one room. A tall glass-top sofa table loaded with framed photographs and a gold statue caught her eye, and she hurried over to take a look. Four handsome faces filled the first frame she picked up. Keir sat with his daughter on his knee. An attractive strawberry blonde, with an arm wrapped around a young boy, snuggled against Keir. *This must be his wife, Shannon, and his son, Adam.* It felt a wee bit eerie seeing Keir's wife's photo in his house. *No, ex-wife,* Ryan corrected silently.

She returned the frame to the table and glanced at the remaining photos. Separate shots of the kids stood proudly next to a group scene with him. His greatest professional achievements were also captured on film. There were pictures of Keir receiving his Oscar, as well as his college degree.

Minutes later, Keir reentered the room, with an open bottle of wine and two long-stemmed glasses. He filled each glass, handed one to Ryan, and then slipped into the spot next to her.

"This room is beautiful," Ryan said as she sipped her wine. "It's the perfect setting for someone like you."

Keir saluted Ryan with his glass, saying, "Here's to us and new beginnings."

She touched his glass with hers and then said, before sipping the wine, "To new beginnings."

Once they finished their drinks, Keir plucked the glass from her hands and placed both glasses on the table in front of them. He took her face between his large hands and held it gently, gazing into her eyes. Ryan's eyes drifted shut with the first touch of his lips on hers. Keir's tongue parted her lips and tasted the sweet nectar of her mouth, sending a warm shiver coursing through her.

One kiss ended and another began. Their hands wandered, caressing and stroking exposed skin as they explored each other.

He pulled away. "Please stay the night."

Ryan nodded.

Keir took her hand, leading her from the room and up the stairs to the second floor. At the landing, he guided her inside the first door. The huge bedroom ran the length of the house. A custom-made king-size bed decorated with a tan and chocolate comforter dominated the room.

Awed, she said, "It's beautiful."

"Thanks. Come in and make yourself comfortable."

Butterflies fluttered in Ryan's belly. She took a deep breath and strolled across the room to the bed and sat gingerly on the edge, watching Keir move around the room. He took his time, drawing the heavy drapes, dimming the lights before popping an Alex Bugnon compact disc into the player.

Keir strolled to where Ryan sat, leaned down, and kissed her. A spark of excitement surged through her at the prospect of making love. Gazing into his green eyes, Ryan smiled.

Keir's fingers lightly traced the curve of her neck, gently settling on her shoulders as the kiss went on and on. His nearness made her senses spin out of control and wiped away her fears and reservations about making love with him.

Ryan's busy hands were on a journey of their own. They slipped under Keir's sweater and caressed his hot skin, tracing the muscular curve of his shoulders and chest before finding his nipples. She rolled the hard pebbles between her fingers. He moaned softly into her mouth.

Carried away, she failed to notice Keir easing the spaghetti straps off her shoulders. Once this task was completed, he drew the bodice of her dress toward her waist, freeing her breasts. Keir urged her to her feet, and the red silk glided to the floor, pooling around her ankles. A red thong, thigh-high stockings, and high-heel sandals exposed her nakedness to his appreciative gaze. Her nipples puckered from the coolness.

"You are gorgeous," he whispered, stroking his thumb back and forth across her delicate nipple. Keir lowered his head, and his warm breath fanned her breast as he flicked his tongue across the nub. Seconds later, he sucked strongly on the nub, sending a current of heat surging through her and settling between her legs.

Between moans of delight, Ryan muttered, "You're not playing fair."

He lifted his head, gazing at her with confused green eyes. "What?"

"You still have on clothes."

Her breast warm and moist from his tongue, Keir grinned at the picture she presented. "Sorry." He slowly pulled his sweater over his head and tossed it on the floor. "How's that?"

Pleased, Ryan ran her hand over the broad, hard planes of his shoulders. "Better. But no cigar," she whispered appreciatively while sketching an invisible line down his chest and halting at his belt. She undid his buckle and unzipped his trousers, pushing them away from his hips. The trousers bunched around his feet. Keir kicked off his shoes and stepped out of the garment, standing before her in a pair of chocolate shorts.

"I think we're even now," he said.

Unable to resist, she ran a finger along the slit in the boxers, enjoying the way his flesh twitched, straining against the silk. "Much better."

"I'm glad you approve." He held her in his arms and covered her mouth possessively.

Gently easing her back onto the bed, he fondled one round globe, watching approvingly as the nipple hardened. Keir worked his fingers under the straps of her thong and pulled it down her body, tossing the scrap of fabric on the floor with the rest of their clothes.

Focusing on her mound, he separated the slit and began to stroke her sensitive nub. His finger rubbed against the swollen nub, moving back and forth. Unconsciously, she pushed against his finger, swaying to the rhythm of it.

"That's it," Keir whispered into her ear. "Let it happen."

The sensations grew stronger within Ryan as Keir moved faster, increasing the pressure. Her skin prickled with the heat of his touch. She never dreamed his hand would feel so warm and enticing.

Her breath came in short pants as she felt the first tug of her orgasm. Involuntary tremors followed. Within seconds her body throbbed out of control. "Keir!" she cried, arching against his hand. Wave after wave of ecstasy surged through her.

"That's what I want to see. You look so beautiful," murmured Keir.

Sweetly drained, Ryan floated back to earth.

Limp as a dishrag, Ryan lay on the bed, trying to recover. Keir rid himself of his underwear, opened his nightstand drawer and removed a condom. He tore the packet open and quickly rolled the latex over his shaft before stretching out next to her. She felt the heat and length of his erection against her side. Curious, she slid her hand between their bodies and curled her fingers around him. Enjoying the sense of power it gave her, she began to stroke his pulsating, condom-covered flesh. Keir moaned.

Kissing his cheek, she offered softly, "Babe, I want you inside me."

"That's where I want to be." Panting, he pushed into her, fighting the natural resistance of her passage. Giving her time to adjust to his size, Keir lay still for a moment, deeply embedded within her. Then he slowly began to move, withdrawing several inches before sliding deep within her.

The hot tide of passion raged through both of them, and he pumped into her hard and fast. Keir's hand lifted her hips off the bed. Meeting his thrusts, she wrapped her legs around his waist, pulling him deeper into her. Ryan moaned as her orgasm hit, sweeping away all coherent thoughts. She clenched her muscles around him, holding him tightly within her hot, liquid walls.

Keir gasped, burying his face against her neck. She felt his release as his body trembled over hers, triggering her third orgasm.

Floating back to earth, Keir wrapped his arms around her and held her close, saying, between shaky breaths, "Thank you."

Barely breathing, she muttered, "You're welcome."

Chapter 9

The bright morning sun peeped between the slit in the drapes, crept across the bedroom, and stroked Ryan's cheek, nudging her to wakefulness. Her eyes fluttered open, and she remained quiet, listening to the steady, strong beat of Keir's heart against her ear as she lay across his chest.

Last night had been wonderful. They had shared a beautiful evening, which had culminated in hours of fantastic lovemaking. For Ryan, it had meant so much more. This had been her first sexual encounter since her husband died. She couldn't have been more pleased.

Because of that, Ryan felt a bit awkward waking up in another man's bed. She eased from under Keir's possessive arm and rose from the bed, making certain she didn't disturb him. Moving quietly and swiftly around the room, she grabbed her clothes and headed out the room, closing the door softly behind her.

Now what? Ryan wondered, standing nude in the hallway before checking out the first empty bedroom. Beyond the bed, she made out a bathroom. *Ah*, she thought. *A shower! Yes!*

After turning on the water and stepping under the showerhead, Ryan took the soap between her hands and lathered her body. She sighed, eyes drifting shut as she enjoyed the warm water and relived the glorious moments spent in Keir's arms. Her skin still tingled everywhere he'd touched her.

Without warning, the shower door slid back, and Keir stood, large and naked, staring at her. "Why didn't you wake me?"

"I didn't want to disturb you," Ryan answered feebly.

"No bother." He stepped inside the stall, behind her, and shut the door. His hands settled on her hips, pulling her back against the hard planes of his body, as his lips sought the shell of her ear, tracing the shape with the tip of his tongue.

Water cascaded over them, showering the pair with gentle, pulsating wetness while Keir stirred a fire in the lower regions of her body. She scooted against him, feeling the hard outline of his erection against her butt. He wrapped his arms around her waist and held her tightly. Ryan tilted her head to the side, inviting his kiss. He accepted her offer, kissing her lips and allowing his tongue to slide between her lips. He tasted of toothpaste and the sweet essence of Keir.

This was wonderful. Being here with Keir was exactly where she wanted to be.

Keir released her lips, trailing a hot path down her neck to her shoulder. Turning her to face him, his hands moved lower, fingering the brown tips. After a moment of this delightful torture, his mouth replaced his hands. He kissed her taut nipples, rousing a melting sweetness between her legs.

The sensations were too intense, and Ryan trembled. Moaning, she tilted her head back against the tile wall as she breathed his name.

One hand left her breasts, skipped over the tight muscles of her stomach, circled her belly button before dipping between the slit between her legs. His fingers toyed with the nub, causing her passage to grow wet.

"Here, let's try something different," Keir suggested in a husky, tempting whisper while urging her to face the tile wall, with a gentle hand. "Hold on a minute." He stepped out of the shower and returned a few seconds later.

Ryan turned her head to see what he was doing. Keir shook a foil packet at her before covering his erection in latex.

Anticipation shot through Ryan, palms flat against the wall. Her legs barely held her upright. The thick head of his erection brushed against her entrance, causing fire, hot and intense, to spread through her.

"Ohmigod!" She felt her passage grow wet, readying itself for Keir's invasion. His hands holding her in place, he pushed his thick, hard shaft into her waiting wet sheath, inch by delicious inch.

Ryan gasped. Her muscles clenched around him, enjoying the feeling of having him throbbing inside her.

Keir withdrew the barest breath before thrusting completely inside her, over and over, filling her with his flesh. He took a long slide in and then a slow withdrawal, leaving enough of his flesh inside her to make her scream for more. Nothing mattered except the feel of Keir inside her.

Nerves dancing, body quivering, Ryan matched the primitive beat of his lovemaking. Their labored breathing rose above the pulsating head of the shower. Eagerly rocking back against him, Ryan met each thrust of his hips. The first tremor hit her, followed by another and another as she drew closer to the inviting oblivion of completeness.

His arm came around her waist, hauling her back against him as he began a steady rhythm of intense movements. "I love being inside you," he muttered, changing the tempo of his strokes.

"I love having you inside me," Ryan admitted, pushing against him to meet each thrust of his hips.

Small explosions radiated through Ryan's abdomen and down into her legs. Collapsing slightly against the tile wall, Keir followed her, relentless in his thrusts. Another, more urgent, wave swept through her.

"Come on, babe. Give it to me," he pleaded in a hoarse whisper.

Her body shuddered in the throes of a tsunami of sensations. Before Ryan could form a single word, her orgasm overtook her, and she screamed her release.

Keir stiffened, groaned, and made a series of fierce strokes. Pulsating, he swelled within her canal, and then he toppled toward the wall, pressing Ryan into the cold tile as his hips made a few additional thrusts.

Trembling, Keir slid over the edge into bliss and came inside her. "Ryan!" he cried, pouring himself into her.

Hours later they stretched across the bed, gently caressing, stroking, and kissing in the afterglow of lovemaking. Head resting against his chest, she drew miniature circles around each nipple while listening to the steady beat of his heart. It reassured her and made her feel safe.

Unfortunately, she couldn't spend the rest of her life in this bed. Although it was a delightful idea, she needed to get up and get going. Monday was a workday.

Sighing contentedly, Ryan turned on her back and snuggled against Keir's side. "I guess we should think about moving."

"Probably." His hand glided over her breast and caressed the nipple.

"I mean"—she paused, lifting her head and squinting at the clock—"it's after two. I do have to go home sometime."

"Why?"

She kissed his lips. "The only clothes I have are the ones I wore last night. I can't wear that dress to work tomorrow. Plus, I don't have any underwear. I'm pretty sure nothing you own will fit me."

He growled, licking the side of her neck. "Clothes are our enemy. Let's stay in bed a while longer. Do a bit more exploring and then get up and have some breakfast."

"Breakfast! Honey, look at the clock. I'd say lunch or dinner is more appropriate."

"Okay. Dinner."

Ryan lifted her head and gazed at him. "That has possibilities. Don't forget you still have to take me home."

Keir grinned. "I've got another option. You can stay the night, and I'll drop you at home in the morning. You can go into work a little late."

No, that idea didn't work for Ryan. Glo's disapproving expression and ugly words flashed through Ryan's head. Wandering into the studio later than expected would stir up a hornet's nest of new problems. "I don't think so. But I don't have a problem with exploring some more before I head home. Maybe next time."

"Woo! I like the sound of that. You want to get together next weekend?"

Grinning up at Keir, Ryan said, "With the right incentive, I might be persuaded to consider it."

"That works for me. I do need to tell you that my kids will be visiting next weekend. Maybe we can get together so you can meet them."

Ryan stiffened and then calmed herself, willing her body to relax. She didn't want to do this yet, and staying the night while his children were in the house was impossible. Keir and Ryan were just getting to know one another, and adding children to that mix didn't seem the right thing to do. They needed time together alone and a chance to get comfortable with one another.

"Are you sure, Keir?"

"Mm-hmm. Why?"

"Us as a couple is pretty new. What if you and I don't make it? Wouldn't it be bad to introduce me to your kids and then I disappear?"

"First of all, I don't see any reason why we won't be getting along. Do you?"

A little embarrassed, she answered, "No."

"Glad to hear it. They're part of my life, and so are you. So, I feel you should meet."

"You have a point," she answered. Keir's explanation didn't make her feel any better. Ryan didn't want his children to get too attached to her. If they broke up, it would be like losing a parent again. Their lives had been disrupted enough.

"Don't worry about that. My kids will love you."

I don't want them to love me, and I don't want to love them. At least, not yet, she thought.

Ryan made one final attempt to convince Keir. She didn't know how to make him understand her anxieties. "I really think we should wait."

He turned her to face him. "Why?"

She didn't want to cause a rift between them. But the words had to be said. "I need to get used to having you in my life, and now you want to add in children. Don't get me wrong. I want to get to know them. Maybe later."

"Honey," Keir began, drawing her into his arms. He gently kissed her lips, saying, "You'll be great together. Trust me on this."

Holding him close, Ryan pleaded, "It's not about trust."

"Tell me what it is," he said.

"I'm scared."

He frowned. "About what?"

She felt so uncertain about their relationship. Her whole life had been turned around with the start of it. She didn't know how to add children, and she didn't have any confidence in her abilities to work with them. "I need a little more time to get used to us."

"I'm still lost."

"You and me together." She swallowed loudly. "And then kids."

"How much time are you talking about?"

"Not long. Keir, you have to remember, this is all new to me. Bear with me."

Sighing, he bit his lip and studied her. "Okay. I can do that."

Grinning, she answered, "Good."

"But remember this. Any relationship I have comes with two kids. If you can't accept that, then we'll both need to rethink our situation."

"I understand."

With a sigh of relief, she turned to him. All she needed was a little more time before the intrusion of children changed their lives. In a few weeks, she'd be ready to take on the added responsibility of Keir's family. But not yet.

"When you take the man, you take the family," her mother had always said. Ryan knew her mother had been right, but she wasn't sure she wanted to add Adam and Emily to their relationship just yet.

Chapter 10

As the weeks passed, the relationship between Glo and Ryan went from bad to worse. Each time Ryan tried to explain how she and Keir got together, her boss refused to listen, changed the subject, or found a reason to disappear. No matter what Ryan said, Glo remained obstinately opposed to listening to Ryan's explanations.

The anger and mistrust radiating from the older woman made it almost impossible for Ryan to work in the tight little space they called an office. Consequently, Ryan found excuses to escape the oppressive environment and stay on the studio floor.

Unfortunately, the stack of paperwork requiring her attention grew daily as it sat untouched on her desk while she waited for a quiet moment and an empty office away from Glo's accusatory glare. Those times were rare. Glo nested in the office, barking out orders to the staff, including Ryan, which explained Ryan's off-hour visit to One Leaf Studio on this Saturday afternoon.

Soon after they became lovers, Keir began to talk about introducing his children to Ryan. Tiptoeing around the issue, she gently declined, stating that they needed time to get used to the relationship before adding children to the mix.

The truth be told, Ryan didn't want to meet the kids yet. Although it had been a while since their parents' divorce, Ryan felt certain the kids still held on to a spark of hope that their parents would work through their issues and get back together. She didn't want to confuse the children by having Keir introduce a woman into their small world.

Dressed in a comfortable pair of denims, a white long-sleeve sweatshirt, and white sneakers, Ryan strolled past the empty set toward her office. There was an eerie quality about the silent sets. She smiled. *Obviously, I like it when things are jumping. There are certainly more interesting goings-on to catch your eye when the studio is busy.*

As she approached her office, a sliver of light from under the closed door caught her attention. The guard hadn't mentioned anyone being here when she signed in. Maybe the cleaning crew forgot to turn out the light last night. Shrugging, Ryan removed the office key from her purse and inserted it into the lock.

The door swung open. Keir stood in the center of the small room, shaking a finger at Glo. "Just do it," he commanded in his sternest tone.

"Oh!" Ryan muttered.

Surprised, he grabbed Ryan's arm and drew her into the room. "Hi," he said.

"Hi yourself," replied Ryan.

The tension in the room was thicker than fog in London. Ryan glanced from Keir to Glo. *What's going on here?* Ryan wondered. Powerful emotions were bouncing off the pair. Had they been arguing? And if so, about what? She felt as if she'd just stepped into the movie theater in the middle of a film and was trying to figure out the plot.

"I'll come back later," Ryan said. Pointing a finger at the hallway, Ryan retreated a step.

"No," Keir objected, taking her hand and leading her into the office. "Come on in. We're almost done."

"Are you sure?" asked Ryan.

"Of course. This is your office," said Keir. Smiling down at her, Keir brushed a finger across her cheek. "What are you doing here? Isn't this your day off?"

"Yes," replied Ryan.

Beyond him, Glo, who sat at her desk, scoffed and turned away. *Great.* There went any peace Ryan expected to have today.

Ryan headed across the office to her desk and dropped her straw bag on the surface. "I thought I'd get some paperwork done today. How about you?"

"I came to pick up next week's script," replied Keir.

Nodding, Ryan turned to her boss. "Glo, how are you?"

"Fine," Glo answered curtly, immediately turning toward the window and away from the couple.

The sound of feet pounding against the concrete floor drew Ryan's attention. Before she asked who else was there, two children pushed into the office and gazed at its occupants.

"I thought I told you to stay in the cafeteria until I got done," Keir admonished.

"We got tired," the boy answered.

The little girl added, "It's scary."

"The movie ended," Adam added.

"Okay. Give me a minute," said Keir. "We'll get the DVD player on our way out." With an arm stretched across the shoulder of each child, Keir added, "Let me introduce you to a friend of mine." He pushed the boy forward and said, with pride, "This is my son, Adam. Mrs. Mitchell, this is Adam. Adam say hello to Mrs. Mitchell."

"Hi," Ryan said as she held out her hand. The boy

shook it after a moment's hesitation. His direct gaze unnerved Ryan.

Adam was a handsome kid. He shared the same wavy hair, green eyes, and skin coloring of his father. "Hi, Miss Mitchell."

Keir lifted the little girl into his arms and tickled her tummy. "This little munchkin is my daughter, Emily. She's five. Say hello to Mrs. Mitchell."

Avoiding direct eye contact, the youngest muttered, "'Ello."

Ryan tried to catch her eye. "Hi, Emily."

The child stubbornly gazed beyond Ryan's shoulder, refusing to look at her. After a moment, Ryan gave up. She didn't want to make the little girl feel uncomfortable.

Emily was a beautiful little girl, with dainty features that must have come from her mother. Dark hair feathered across her shoulders, thick and curly. She didn't have Keir's green eyes. Instead the child's were a light brown, with a hint of gold sparkling from their depths. *Keir better get prepared.* Emily Southhall was going to be a knockout when she hit her teens.

"We're on our way to lunch. Why don't you join us?" Keir suggested to Ryan, placing Emily on her feet and taking her hand.

"Oh no. I don't want to intrude. Besides, I came in today to work." Work would have to wait. Ryan didn't want to get stuck in the office with her boss. She planned to make her escape as soon as Keir and his family left the building.

"I insist." Keir took her arm. He leaned close and added, "This is a good opportunity for you to get to know my kids. Come on. Come with us."

Ryan took another quick peek at Glo, noting the sour expression on her face. Ryan's stomach twisted into knots. She didn't want to be left behind with Glo.

Smiling, she grabbed her bag and started toward the door. "You've convinced me. Glo, see you later."

"So long." Glo waved.

After much debate and a volley of suggestions, Keir, Emily, and Adam settled on Red Lobster. Emily and Adam wanted to go to Bob Evans. Keir vetoed that idea within seconds of the request and suggested they have lunch at a place where everyone could find something they liked. During this major discussion, Ryan remained silent. She didn't want to call attention to herself, or make any demands that might put the kids on edge.

Once they arrived at the restaurant and were seated, their server brought paper place mats and crayons for Emily and Adam. Ryan and Keir relaxed in the busy nonsmoking section, with glasses of Piesporter wine, and talked about their plans for the rest of the day.

The kids ordered chicken fingers, french fries, and sodas. Keir and Ryan decided on grilled trout, baked potatoes, and salad. As they waited for their meals, Adam talked to his father about his baseball league team and the playoffs at the end of the season.

Ryan spent more time listening than talking. She was the interloper, and she wanted to remain silent and neutral.

Once the server placed their food in front of them, Keir tried to draw Ryan into the conversation. He asked if she'd ever played softball on a league. She shook her head. The one thing she knew about baseball was that she enjoyed listening to the Los Angeles Angels on the radio as she cleaned her house.

Throughout their meal, Emily and Adam stole quick glances at each other whenever Ryan made a comment. Each time Ryan asked a question, they were always polite but never initiated any discussion with her. She understood neither child felt ready to let her into their lives or wanted to share their father. The only person that didn't seem to notice the uncomfortable situation was Keir. He prattled on about things as if they were one big, happy blended family. Keir set the tone, giving her an opportunity to keep her low-key profile.

Over dessert Emily dropped a forkful of chocolate cake on her dress. Crumbs and chocolate icing stained the bodice of the white sundress. Ryan rose from her chair and held out her hand. "Come on, Emily. Let's take care of that before it stains your pretty outfit."

Ignoring Ryan's outstretched hand, the little girl skirted the edge of the table and skipped ahead to the ladies'room. Sighing heavily, Ryan followed at a slower pace, keeping a sharp eye on the child's location. It seemed Emily didn't plan to make this easy for Ryan.

Ryan pushed open the ladies' room door to the sounds of running water. "Emily?"

"Yeah?" The little girl sat on top of the vanity, twisting the faucet handles. Water sprayed the entire countertop, soaking the front of her dress.

"Emily, what are you doing? Honey, your dress is wet."

Ryan lifted Emily off the marble counter and planted her on her feet in front of the vanity. Ryan reached for the faucet handles and turned the water down to a steady trickle.

"Here, let me see," Ryan said as she considered the front of the dress. "You're going to be a little wet for a while. But we need to work on the stain. Hold still." Ryan snatched a paper towel from the dispenser, added a drop of liquid soap and water, and then dropped to one knee in front of the child. She gently dabbed at the spot on the delicate white lace.

Shifting from one leg to the other, Emily brushed a hand at the dark smudge.

Ryan caught Emily's busy fingers in her hand. "Honey, wait. You'll have water everywhere if you don't keep still."

The angelic little person morphed into a demon—claws, horns, and more. "You don't tell me what to do. I don't have to listen to you. You're not my mother."

Stunned, Ryan rocked back on her heels as if the child had struck her. "I just want to help."

"My mommy said you'd probably pretend to be my friend. I don't know you, and I don't want to."

This was why Ryan hadn't wanted to get involved with Keir's children so soon. They weren't ready to befriend her, and she wasn't certain she wanted to get to know them, at least not yet. Standing, Ryan softened her voice. "I'm only trying to help you."

"My mommy says you'll act nice because you want my daddy to like you."

Shaking her head, Ryan stated, "That's not true. We need to get to know each other before we can become friends."

"You don't want to be my friend. You're just pretending."

Ryan let out a hot puff of air. She hated being put in this position. Grimacing, she massaged her temple. This encounter wasn't going well.

"Emily, why would you say something like that? I just met you and your brother. I don't know you very well yet. But I don't have any reason to trick you."

"My mommy told me to watch you. That all you want is my daddy. That you'll act real nice so he'll think that you like us. But you don't."

Ryan wadded up the soggy paper towel and tossed it in the trash. "So far, I do like you."

"Adam and I don't need you." With the air of defiance that generally belonged to teenagers, Emily stuck her nose in the air and left the ladies' room.

Dumbfounded, Ryan stood there watching the child leave like a royal diva.

Chapter 11

The tantalizing aromas of grilled margarita chicken, sautéed broccoli and carrots, and smashed baked potatoes peppered the air in Keir's kitchen. Seated at the cocoa-colored marble top counter, swirled with beige, orange, and silver flakes, Ryan sighed contentedly, pushing her empty plate aside before pulling a half full glass of white wine closer. Her fingers stroked the moisture from the long stem of the glass.

"Dinner was delicious. You are one fantastic cook." Ryan patted Keir's shoulder and leaned close, inhaling his unique scent, giving him a leisurely kiss on the lips. A hint of garlic and the tangy taste of lime lingered.

He tilted his head in silent acknowledgment. "Thank you and I told you so."

"As I've mentioned before, you're so humble."

He chuckled softly, spinning the liquid in his glass.

"I'll get the dishes," she added. She slid off the chair and lifted the dishes from the dark counter.

"Works for me. Don't bother with the pots and pans. There's only a few. I'll take care of them tomorrow."

Nodding, Ryan moved past the custom-built solid-wood cabinetry, stainless steel range, and wall oven. She crossed the marble flooring to the dishwasher, placed the dishes and cutlery inside the machine, and shut the door before returning to the spot next to him.

"Do you think I can come back tomorrow for another meal?" she asked.

He lifted her hand to his lips and kissed the palm. "Mrs. Mitchell, you're welcome anytime."

"Thank you, Mr. Southhall. I might take you up on it."

"Do."

Surprised, she studied Keir's expression. He was perfectly serious.

Ryan sank deeper into her chair, thinking about how her life had changed in such a short time. After three years of cutting off her emotions and focusing exclusively on her work and career, Ryan felt alive and eager to explore every angle of this new relationship. Weeks ago she was alone. Now she had a wonderful man in her life, with similar interests.

Stroking his cheek, Ryan asked, "What are you going to do when we shut down next week? Are you planning some sort of getaway with Adam and Emily?"

"They're in a summer program at school. I'm not going to bother them. What about you?" Keir sipped from his glass.

"Eight days without going to work. It's going to be heavenly. I thought I'd clean my dirty house and then work in the garden." With a devilish little smirk, she added, "The producer on this show I work for is a difficult taskmaster. He keeps everyone so busy. I haven't had time to do anything."

"Is he now? Maybe I should talk with him on your behalf."

Her face scrunched into a playful frown. "I don't think it'll do any good. He's one serious slave driver."

"There has to be something I can do." Keir stroked his

cheek as the twinkle in his eyes grew brighter. "Let me think a minute. After all, we're in the same business."

Ryan folded the chocolate cloth napkins into perfect squares and placed them on the marble surface. Keir didn't need to know all of her plans. There were a few personal things related to her husband and marriage she needed to conclude.

He draped an arm around her shoulders, pulled her against his side, and kissed her forehead. "Poor baby. You need a real vacation."

"Mm-hmm." She pouted remorsefully. "I'm so overworked and underpaid."

"I can't help you there. You signed a contract."

"Spoilsport." Ryan poked a playful finger at his chest.

Chuckling, Keir said, "What about a trip out of town?"

"What about it?"

"Some exotic locale with lots of sun and sand," he suggested, massaging her shoulder with one hand.

Gazing at Keir, Ryan teased, "You're talking the talk. I don't see you walking the walk."

Without a word, Keir rose, circled the island, removed an item from a drawer, and tossed it on the counter in front of her. It hit the surface with a distinct thump. "How about a vacation to Hawaii?"

Gasping, Ryan slowly inched her hand across the counter. A thick orange, black, and white Fodor's guide of Hawaii, a Sheraton Waikiki brochure with a list of the amenities, and two round-trip, first-class plane tickets sat on the marble surface.

"Well? How about it?" he asked impatiently.

Elated, Ryan hopped off the chair and rounded the island, flinging herself into Keir's arms. "Yes! Yes! Yes!" She punctuated each yes with a kiss. This man was wonderful. How had she gotten so lucky?

Keir ran the back of his hand across his forehead,

wiping away imaginary beads of sweat. "You had me scared for a minute."

"No, I didn't. You knew I couldn't resist a trip like this," Ryan responded between quick, light kisses.

"It was touch and go for a minute." He wrapped his arms around her and drew her against his warmth.

Laughing softly, Ryan flipped through the pages of the brochure, studying the hotel confirmation. All of the good cheer of a moment ago evaporated. A heaviness in her heart replaced her previous excitement. *No!* she screamed silently. "Eleven days! Wait a minute. I can't go away for eleven days. Shutdown is only eight."

"Yes, you can," Keir stated in a certain voice.

"Seriously, I can't." She shoved the sheet of paper between the brochure's pages. Guilt was added to her feelings of disappointment. "The construction crew works for a couple of days before the rest of the studio returns. Generally, Glo expects someone to stick around to answer questions. If they're working on my designs, then normally I show up, and Glo does the same."

Disbelief dulled Keir's green eyes. "What?"

"I can't go."

"Oh yes, you can, Mrs. Mitchell. I've planned this trip. We are getting on that plane Friday morning."

Ryan sighed sadly. "It's not that I don't want to go. I have obligations on the set of *your* show."

"Are you saying you'd rather be at work instead of with me?"

"No. No. Of course not. But I don't want to cause any problems or major upheavals at the studio with the people I work with."

"Sounds like you're trying to find a way out of going with me."

"Keir, Hawaii is my dream vacation. And I'd outrun you to the airport to hop on the plane. But I have to do the right thing at my job. Glo has to okay the extra days."

"Want me to talk to her?" he volunteered.

"Absolutely not."

"Why not? It's my company."

"True. But Glo is my immediate supervisor," Ryan pointed out. An image of Glo's angry face as she accused Ryan of trying to steal her job flashed through Ryan's head. Keir's two cents would make things worse. "Promise me, you'll stay out of it."

"Come on, Ry."

"I mean it," she uttered in a soft, menacing tone. "Promise." She waited.

"I won't bother your boss."

"Thank you."

Hugging her close, he kissed her long and hard. Ryan responded with all the emotions in her heart.

"Ry, we need this trip. Our lives are so busy. It's hard to devote the time to a relationship that we deserve. I don't want to ignore your needs. That was my mistake with Shannon. I plan to do much better with you."

At that moment she realized how important Keir had become in her life. He wanted her to be happy, and he was actually making the time for them to be together so that they could solidify their relationship.

She wrapped her arms around his neck and drew his head down for a "thank you" kiss.

When the kiss ended, Keir asked, "What was that for?"

"For being so good to me. For understanding that we need time alone together. Most men don't see that as a problem."

"I've got kids who require a lot of my time, and you're truly understanding about that aspect of my life. I want you to know that I appreciate you and the things you do to make our lives better."

"I'll talk to Glo on Monday. After that, we'll know how much time I have. Okay?"

"Do I have a choice?"

"No."

Hours later, Ryan snuggled against Keir's hard, warm frame. The earlier euphoria had faded, and her restless mind refused to shut down. She mentally struggled with a volley of options about their trip and how it would effect the people in their lives.

Although their relationship was no longer a secret, Ryan still found it difficult to be open in front of her coworkers. She didn't plan to live her life in the public eye. No matter what Keir did, she deserved, and refused to give up, her privacy. To that end, Ryan continued to maintain a low-key existence.

Her first problem was Glo. Had Keir told the set director about the trip? Ryan hoped not. Things were difficult enough between Glo and Ryan. This trip might rub salt into the open wound and create more destruction. Most days Ryan tiptoed around Glo, but she didn't know how long that would last before her boss found some reason to turn up the heat and cause a ruckus.

Adam and Emily were another issue. Ryan didn't want the kids to feel as if she was taking their father from them. Leaving town might heighten their anxiety.

Ryan shifted on the mattress, searching for a comfortable spot and a way to turn off her restless thoughts. Keir pulled her closer to him and whispered into her ear. "You're worried, aren't you?"

"Little bit," she answered honestly.

"Why?" He teased her arm with a gentle caress of his fingertips.

"The whole Hawaii thing."

"What about it?"

"You haven't made an announcement, have you?" Ryan asked. "Told the people at work?"

"No. But, you've got to remember that I'm the producer, as well as the creator of the show," he reminded. "I can't disappear for eleven days without leaving a number where I can be reached. Sometimes quick decisions are required. The studio needs to be able to keep in touch with me."

"I know."

"What are you suggesting?"

Ryan scrunched up her face, and her body tensed. It was going to be hell at work until Glo got over this bit of news. "I don't want the studio to think that I'm taking advantage of my relationship with you."

"That's not a problem. You don't. As far as I know, you do your job and keep everything under control without a lot of fuss. So let's cut through the crap. Tell me what's really rolling around in your head."

"Your kids and my boss," Ryan answered promptly.

"Glo. What about her?"

"She can be real intense at times. There are days when she expects me to be at the studio even when there isn't anything going on. A good example is the construction crew coming back after shutdown. Generally, one of us stays on-site while the crew works. I don't want to put on airs and make her think that I'm too good to do these things."

"You keep forgetting that I'm the boss. I can do what I want when I want. Don't worry about her. Glo is not going to be a problem."

Ryan scoffed silently. *Famous last words.* When the notion hit Glo, she could be the biggest pain in the butt. Again, Ryan didn't want to resurrect Godzilla. What went on between her and Glo remained in their office and nowhere else.

Kier's next question broke into her thoughts. "What else is on your mind?"

"Your kids."

"Emily and Adam? Why?"

"Do you think it's too soon for us to be taking trips without them? I mean, they just met me, and it's going to take a while for them to get to know me and for me to find my place in their lives. They might think I'm trying to take you away from them by going away on a long trip."

Keir kissed the tip of her nose. "Honey, you have too many thoughts. The kids are fine. Don't worry about them. This is our time. We don't need to clutter it with imaginary problems."

There was something else that Keir wasn't aware of. Emily hated her. Each time Keir brought his children around her, Emily defied every request the new woman in her father's life made. The little girl always ended with, "You're not my mother." Ryan didn't want to upset Keir. But there had to be a way she could reach the kids without bringing Keir in to play the role of the heavy. She didn't want polite little robots who hated her.

There were so many issues involved in taking time off for this trip. "We can talk more about the kids later. Let's get back to Glo," Ryan suggested. "How did she take the news about the trip?"

Keir was silent for several seconds. "Okay. Glo's part of my team. I had to tell her. She found it utterly romantic."

Yeah, right, Ryan thought. *Maybe you can sell me the Golden Gate Bridge while you're at it.* She didn't believe it at all. Or maybe she did. Glo always played pleasant in front of Keir. Whenever Keir came into the cubbyhole they called an office, Glo and Ryan put on a happy show. The game ended the moment he left the room.

"For lack of a better phrase to describe our relationship,

I know we're out of the closet. But I still like to keep my private life to myself."

Sighing, Keir turned on his back and ran a hand through his wavy hair. "What are you saying, Ryan?"

"Nothing bad," she hastened to assure him. "I love the idea of a vacation. But does everyone at the studio need to know that we're going?"

"I have to leave a number. This is still my production company."

"I don't have a problem with that. But do you have to tell everyone else? Can we keep the information in the hands of your administrative assistant?"

"Sure."

"Thank you."

"Anything else?" he asked.

"No. Monday I'll talk to Glo, and we'll settle everything after that."

Keir kissed her ear. "Good. Let's go to sleep."

Chapter 12

Armed with her leave request form and a prepared speech, Ryan drove onto One Leaf grounds at 5:00 A.M. She intended to persuade Glo to agree to a few additional days off, without offering details about her trip.

Unfortunately, Ryan didn't have much time to consider the problem once she reached work. Her day started with a bang and quickly shot into super speed. In anticipation of the weeklong shutdown, multiple scenes were being shot at the same time—some at the studio and others on location. Ryan worked on location with the assistant director and stayed off-site all day.

The nonstop pace came to an end after 6:00 P.M., when the crew returned to the studio. At the end of the shooting day, Ryan searched for Glo, spotted her, and started her way. Before Ryan reached her boss, the older woman had disappeared down another hallway.

Exhausted, Ryan dragged herself to the cafeteria for a minute of quiet and a cup of coffee before tackling the work for the next day's shooting schedule. On the way there, she picked up her pace; if she hurried, she might reach home before *American Idol* started. She pushed the heavy cafeteria door open and was shocked to find Glo sitting on one of the park-type benches, with a sandwich, a Pepsi, and a sketch pad in front of her.

Now that her opportunity had presented itself, all of Ryan's concerns about Glo and Glo's anger over what she'd considered Ryan's duplicity came back with a vengeance. Would the older woman take this opportunity to cause trouble? Reject Ryan's request for time off? Use the need for a set person to be on call to interrupt Ryan and Keir's plan?

Ryan shook off those notions and started across the tiled floor to the vending machines. Her sneakers made squeaking sounds as she moved. Ryan stood at the vending machines, chewing on her thumbnail. She glanced back at her boss, mentally working on the best way to handle Glo. The direct approach had always worked best for Ryan. Dishonesty always caused additional lies and problems.

After purchasing her coffee, Ryan added sugar and cream and then headed to where her boss sat. With her belly in knots, Ryan fidgeted with the white plastic lid of her coffee cup and offered a nervous hi.

Glo glanced at the younger woman and then refocused on her work. "Hey."

Ryan cleared her throat and asked, "Are you busy? Can I talk with you for a moment?"

Without looking up from her sketches, Glo waved a hand at the empty bench. "Sure."

Ryan slid into the spot opposite her boss. "Do you know when the construction crew will be returning once the studio reopens?"

"They're expected back the Friday before we all return," Glo answered absently, studying the pages. "Why?"

Well, it was now or never. Ryan pulled the leave request form from her back pocket and pushed it across the table.

Glo glanced at the triplicate form and asked, "What's this?"

"Leave request. I know we always have someone stick around while the construction crew works, but I really would like a couple of extra days off."

"Why?"

Ryan bit her bottom lip. She didn't want to talk about her trip. It might create new problems. Having Keir step in was out of the question. She didn't want him to use his role as a studio exec to force Glo into giving her the time off. Ryan wanted to be granted the time off because she earned and requested it. "I'm going out of town and would like to stay a few extra days, if possible. But one of us always sticks around when the crew is here, and I was hoping I wouldn't have to."

Pursing her lips, Glo picked up the form and examined it. "Is this about your trip with Keir?"

Shocked, Ryan blinked. "What?"

How did she know about the trip? Oh yeah, Keir had mentioned Glo seemed interested and happy about their plans. Ryan held her breath. Was this the point where Glo stuck it to her?

"Keir mentioned you two were going away."

Feeling as if her head were full of cotton, Ryan tried to get her bearings. "Yeah. Umm. It is."

"Don't worry. It's not often you get a trip like this one. I mean, Hawaii. Wow! Have a good time."

For a moment, Ryan questioned what she'd just heard. *Who are you, and what have you done with Glo Kramer?* Since the party at the Hyatt, Glo had never failed to show her disapproval of Ryan's relationship with Keir. Ryan didn't understand why Glo hadn't used this perfect opportunity to stick it to her.

"I talked with Phil, and we're going to switch the schedule so that your scenes will be shot this week, and then you won't have to be here with the crew," Glo said as she looked directly at Ryan. "Will that help?"

"Yes! Thank you."

Smiling at the younger woman, Glo added, "There really isn't a reason for you to be here. I'll handle anything that comes up. Go enjoy your trip."

"Are you sure?"

"Mm-hmm."

Ryan let out a sigh of relief.

Glo reached across the table, signed the leave request form, and separated the middle pink copy from the original and yellow copies. Then she tucked the pink copy inside her sketch pad. "Make sure you get the white copy to Human Resources. You'll want them to process your check as soon as possible."

"Okay."

"Also, talk with George. Make sure he understands how we want the sets to look. They'll be working late tonight to get everything done for tomorrow. He won't have you to discuss this with, so he needs to be clear on the details."

"I'll talk to him and leave my number if he needs to call."

"Before the end of the week, you need to bring me up to speed. Just in case there's a delay or two. We should go over everything you're working on."

Ryan nodded. "I really appreciate this."

"No problem. Enjoy. I'll see you tomorrow."

Ryan felt strangely let down as she rose from the bench and started for the door. After hyping herself up for a major battle, she felt as if the war had been won without a single shot being fired. Expecting a series of snide remarks and cutting quips, Ryan had been pleasantly surprised to have a decent, professional conversation with her boss. Ryan wasn't sure how to handle Glo's change of attitude. Heading for the door, she dropped her empty paper coffee cup in the trash.

Glancing back at the woman sitting at the table, Ryan wondered, *What just happened here?* After weeks of simmering anger, Glo had politely given her the okay to take a few extra days on the tail end of her vacation.

Why didn't Ryan feel victorious? Instead, her instincts told her the mousetrap had sprung, and her tail was caught in Glo's trap.

That had almost been too easy. Ryan strolled from the cafeteria and started down the hall to her office. There was still plenty of work to do before she called an end to her workday. Ryan halted and glanced at the closed cafeteria door. Glo had been her old self. The person Ryan had loved working for before the evening at the Hyatt, the lady that had offered advice and praised Ryan's work. Ryan continued on. Halting outside her office, she did a mental check of her conversation with Glo. It had been like talking to Dr. Jekyll after weeks of living with Ms. Hyde.

Could Glo have finally realized that Ryan was harmless? All she wanted to do was work and go home at the end of the evening. Granted, she went home with Keir, but she wasn't trying to upset any plans Glo had for her career.

Her boss's understanding deserved a little special something. While they were on the islands, Ryan intended to pick up a little thank you gift for Glo. Present the gift as her special way of showing Glo that she appreciated her help. There had been a major shift in Glo's thinking, and Ryan was very grateful. It would make the return to work easier.

Once she got home this evening, she'd call Keir and let him know that everything was on for their trip. Ryan smiled as anticipation coursed through her. Eleven days in a tropical location with a handsome, sexy man. She could hardly wait.

"Ladies and Gentlemen, this is Captain Elliott speaking. We've been cleared for landing, and unless there is an unforeseen delay, we should be on the ground within the next fifteen minutes. Thank you for flying American Airlines. We hope you'll fly with us again, and have a wonderful stay in Hawaii. Flight attendants, please prepare for landing."

Keir watched Ryan's face light up. She could hardly stay in her seat. He smiled, loving her enthusiasm. At that moment, he made a silent promise to give her the most exciting, romantic vacation within his power. Ryan deserved the best.

Honestly, he couldn't wait to experience Hawaii with Ryan. He wanted to see the whole trip through her eyes.

Ryan turned to him, with a smile on her face. "I can't wait until we land."

Keir chuckled, leaned across the armrest, and kissed her leisurely. "Me, too. What's the first thing you want to do, Mrs. Mitchell?"

"Explore the island," was her immediate reply.

"Sounds good to me. Once we settle in at the hotel, let's check out Waikiki."

She linked her fingers with his and muttered in a soft drawl, "Well, thank you, Mr. Southhall. I think I'd enjoy that."

The plane started its descent, and Keir offered her a stick of gum. "Make me a promise."

Frowning, Ryan glanced his way. "What is it?" Her voice held a hint of concern.

"While we're here, if there's anything that you want and don't have, or if there's a place you want to go to, tell me. Don't hesitate. I want to know because I want you to have a perfect trip."

"This is perfect. You don't have to do anything more—" Ryan began, but Keir cut her off with the firm pressure of his lips on hers.

"This is our dream vacation. Our first vacation together. I want everything to be perfect for you."

Kissing the back of his hand, Ryan said, "It already is."

Once they landed, things moved very quickly. Keir escorted Ryan from the plane and through the airport. As they approached the luggage carousel, a man dressed in a dark suit stopped Keir and led them to a black limousine. While they waited in the air-conditioned car, with the motor running, the driver emerged from the airport with their luggage. He stored the bags in the trunk and quickly got behind the wheel of the car. Again, Keir watched Ryan, enjoying her wide-eyed enthusiasm.

Ryan snuggled into the crook of Keir's arm and laid her head on his shoulder as the landscape flew by. Palm trees, plenty of sand, and the sun represented the best of Hawaii. All too soon the limo pulled into the circular drive of the Sheraton Hotel. Like the prearranged limo, the check-in process took less than ten minutes, and Ryan and Keir were soon on their way up the elevator to the penthouse suite.

At the door to their suite, Keir swung Ryan into his arms and swept her through the double doors. "Welcome to Hawaii, sweetheart."

Laughing softly, Ryan clung to him. "Oh, Keir. It's beautiful."

The living room was decorated in muted tones of beige, crème, and brown. Keir's sandal-covered feet sank into the plush beige carpeting. Ryan slipped to her feet in front of him as he wrapped an arm around her waist and led her to the balcony.

Pushing the glass patio door open, they stepped out into the crisp, fresh air and got their first glimpse of the spectacular view of the beach and ocean. They sighed, overwhelmed by the scenery.

"This is so beautiful," she said.

"Once our luggage gets here, we can go out and explore," Keir suggested. "But first, let's check out the rest of the suite."

Taking him by the hand, she pulled him along behind her. "I'll have to claim my side of the bed if I want to have any peace while we're here."

"What makes you think I'm going to let you rest?"

Turning to him, Ryan batted her eyes coyly. Her voice turned deliberately seductive. "Why, Mr. Southhall, did you bring me on this trip so that you could have your wicked way with me?"

"Absolutely, Mrs. Mitchell. I plan to ravage you at every opportunity."

"I hope so." Ryan laughed out loud and shook her head. "You are so bad."

They entered the bedroom together. A bottle of chilled champagne, a tray of assorted cheeses and crackers, and fresh fruits adorned a portable trolley. A king-size bed with a light bedspread dominated the room. An armoire and dresser completed the furnishings.

The glass patio doors in the bedroom connected to the living room patio. It stretched across the suite.

Ryan took Keir's hand and led him onto the patio. "Thank you," she said.

Keir wrapped her in his warm embrace, holding her close. Ryan rested her head against his chest, listening to the strong, steady beat of his heart.

"You are welcome, sweetheart." They stood together for several minutes before returning to the bedroom.

Ryan lifted her head, silently inviting him to kiss her.

He took Ryan up on her offer and covered her lips with his. Sighing, Ryan wrapped her arms around the tight cords of his neck and leaned into him, enjoying the feel of his solid frame against hers.

A heated thought feathered in and out of her mind as she stroked his tongue with her own, loving the taste of passion and desire on his lips. *This is heaven.*

Chapter 13

The heat of passion played heavily in the bedroom. Desire, pungent and thick, filled the air. Ryan couldn't get enough of Keir. One kiss fed into the next as tension built.

At the first tentative tap on the suite's door, Ryan stiffened. "No!" she moaned against Keir's lips.

The second, more insistent rap caused Keir to break away, saying regrettably, "That's probably our stuff."

Pouting, Ryan dropped her arms to her sides, and she stepped back a pace, staring with longing at him.

"Let me take care of this. I'll be right back." He leaned close and brushed an all too brief but sweet peck on her lips before heading out of the bedroom.

Her heart gave a jolt, and her pulse pounded. Sighing, she saluted his back with a wave of her hand. "Hurry back."

From her vantage point, she found herself studying Keir's profile as he opened the door and greeted a young man.

The hotel employee waited in the hallway, dressed in a red jacket with black and gold braiding wrapped around one shoulder. Raven-colored trousers and a pair of sturdy walking shoes completed his uniform. A gold badge with the word GENE written in black letters was pinned to his chest. Their luggage sat on the floor at his side. "Mr. Southhall?"

Keir nodded.

"Your suitcases."

"Thanks. Please take them through to the bedroom."

Struggling with three bags, the bellboy entered the suite and made his way to the bedroom. Ryan moved to the sliding patio doors, watching the young man enter the room and place the bags side by side on the bed.

Smiling at him, Ryan said, "Thank you."

"You're welcome." He bowed slightly and offered a quick, tentative smile and then headed into the living room.

Waiting at the door, Keir stuffed a ten-dollar bill in the bellboy's hand and ushered him out of the suite. Seconds later, Keir strolled into the bedroom, crossed the carpeted floor, and halted in front of her. He stood so close, she felt the heat from his body. His hands quickly circled her small waist, drawing her against the hard planes of his body.

Keir's gaze roved over her face before traveling lower. When his gaze returned to her face, something intense flared between them. A tingling started in the pit of her stomach, intensifying the craving for his touch.

Grinning, he asked, "Where were we?"

Ryan settled into his embrace, wrapping her arms around his waist, and lifted her head for his kiss. Keir didn't need a second invitation. His tongue met hers, sliding over it, exploring the delectable recesses of her mouth. Instantly, he transported her back to the heaven they'd shared before the bellboy interrupted them.

He lifted his head and ran a finger across her moist lips. "Beautiful," he complimented and covered her mouth again.

She moaned, drinking in the heady aroma of soap and the special scent of Keir. His tongue felt erotic, and his taste so unique. Ryan couldn't get enough of him or the pleasure.

As one kiss ended, another began. They continued like this for several minutes, tasting and teasing each other until need overwhelmed them.

Groaning, Keir released her lips, leaning his forehead against hers. He held her loosely against the warmth of his hard body. "Maybe we should get unpacked before we do anything else," he said. "Besides, I've got to check in with my assistant. She needs to know how to get in touch with me."

"Spoilsport."

In response, Keir swatted her on the butt and then headed to the desk and flopped into the chair.

Although she would have denied it, if asked, Keir had a point. Their gear completely covered the bed. Until they cleared away their belongings, nothing interesting or fun would happen.

She unzipped her suitcase and removed her toiletries, moving between the bedroom and bath as she stored them. Once she finished that task, Ryan unfolded her dresses, shook out the wrinkles, and hung them in the closet, and then filled the dresser with her lingerie.

"Ry?"

"Hmm?" she muttered, without looking up.

"Look at this chair. It rocks."

"Does it?"

"Yeah."

Ryan turned to the desk and watched Keir for several seconds. She giggled. The owner of a multimillion-dollar business sat rocking back and forth in the executive chair like a child who'd just discovered a new toy.

A flicker of an idea ignited in her mind. She strolled

toward the chair. Along the way, she pulled out the edges of her T-shirt and undid the snap on her knee-length brown shorts.

Ryan halted in front of Keir and kicked off her sandals. Eyebrows stretching toward his hairline, Keir remained silent, watching her. She cupped his face in her hands, leaned down, and slid the tip of her tongue between his lips, inviting more.

He accepted her invitation and touched her tongue with his, swirling around hers, and settled into a deep kiss.

Dazed, she drew away.

Keir's eyes glowed with sensual fire that matched the flame brewing in her. "Am I being seduced?" he asked in a husky tone.

"What do you think?" She sucked on his bottom lip. Her hands spread over his chest, stroking the muscles and lovingly circling his pebble hard nipples through his brown Polo shirt.

Moaning, he muttered, "There's a possibility."

"Maybe," she uttered softly, moving to his ear. She traced the shell pattern with her tongue.

"Aren't you amorous, Mrs. Mitchell?" He swept a hand gently over the curve of her ear.

The soft caress caused Ryan to shiver with delight. "No, Mr. Southhall. Just horny."

"Well, we need to do something about that." Smiling up at her, Keir ran a finger across her moist bottom lip. "I aim to give you everything you need while we're in Hawaii."

"How about a few of my wants." She feathered light kisses along his neck.

Keir stroked her breasts, asking, "Anything in particular?"

"You."

"Anytime. Anyplace," he answered, slightly panting.

"Good. I agree with that sentiment one hundred per-cent. I don't think you need this anymore." Ryan pulled the shirt from his slacks, removed it, and tossed it on the floor. She fumbled with his belt, undid the buckle, and lowered the zipper. A budge filled the front of his briefs. Ryan ran a finger along his stiff ridge, teasing, "Is this part of the welcome wagon?"

Keir's eyes drifted shut while he swayed to the movements of her hand and moaned softly. "Oh yeah. All for you."

Not satisfied, Ryan reached inside the slit in his briefs and freed his throbbing erection. She ran fingers up and down the soft skin, fascinated by the way he felt. Craving more, she took his lips in a fury of tiny kisses as her hand stroked his rigid flesh, enjoying the feel of hard steel covered by warm, pulsating flesh.

Keir sucked in his breath. Ryan gave his hot, slick, and pulsating erection a few quick strokes, wishing he was inside her.

After a moment of this exquisite torture, she took a step back, quickly removing her clothes, adding them to the heap. Bare of everything except her bra and panties, she returned to his embrace.

"Do you mind?" he asked as he popped the front tab on her bra.

"Be my guest," she responded, watching as he did the honors. He removed the bra and worked her panties down her hips and off her body. She kicked them into the growing pile of clothes and then helped him out of his briefs and reached for her purse. Ryan removed a condom, tore it open with her teeth, and rolled it onto him.

Ryan quickly offered the man a tantalizing brown nipple. Keir circled it with the tip of his tongue, leaning back to examine his handiwork. Smiling, he blew on the bud, causing it to harden, before focusing on the other breast. He sucked on the hard pebble as if he were receiving nourishment, while continuing to stroke the other. The heavenly sensation increased the ache and wetness between her legs.

After several minutes of this torture, Keir wrapped his arms tightly around her waist. "Come on, baby. Let's take a ride," he whispered. With his hands on her hips, he guided her onto his pulsating flesh. Inch by inch she took him into her greedy passage until he filled her completely.

Moaning softly, Ryan rose and slid back down on him. Her eyes shut as she experienced the feeling of having him fill her. Keir guided her, with his hands on her hips, as she moved up and down on his thick shaft.

With her hands on his shoulders to steady herself, Ryan rode him hard and long, moaning and sighing at the tantalizing feelings. Her eyes rolled back, and a groan escaped her as she enjoyed the exquisite sensations.

Panting, Ryan grunted, "Ohmigod, Keir! This feels perfect!"

"Yeah, it does." He thrusted upward, meeting her movements so he was deeply sheathed within her.

Keir's breath came in hot gushes as he locked her within his embrace and rose from the chair. Bodies connected, he swirled around and pinned her small frame against the desk beneath him. The telephone, notepad, and pen dug into her skin. She didn't care. She needed, wanted, all of him inside her.

Frantically, he pumped into her, rocking his hips against hers as he buried himself in her over and over. Her muscles worked, clenching and releasing, as he plunged and pulled back.

Trembling, Ryan arched her back, taking him as far into her body as possible. She shuddered as completion flowed through her in waves of heat and pleasure. A second later, Keir tightened his hold on her, went stiff, and arched, crying out her name. His hot seed spurted.

Together, they floated back to earth. Keir recovered first, tenderly kissing her on the lips. "Well, Mrs. Mitchell, that was wonderful. Want to try it on the floor?"

Fighting to catch her breath, she panted, "Anytime, anyplace."

Chapter 14

Hand in hand, Ryan and Keir took a leisurely stroll through downtown shopping district on the island of Maui. After a quick plane hop from the big island to Maui, they had boarded a bus for a spin to the island's highest point to visit an active volcano. A thick coat of ash had floated through the air as their driver drove higher into the mountains. Their tour guide had retold the tale of misfortune awaiting anyone with the courage or gall to smuggle away a precious stone from the volcano site.

Momentarily distracted by the crystal blue water, Ryan had gazed longingly at the boats docked at the pier. Lifting her face toward the sun, she'd felt warm, fresh air caress her skin as they admired the beautiful blue sky and ocean. Taking an appraising peek at Keir, she'd wondered if he might be persuaded to rent a boat so they could cruise the waters.

Now they were back in the downtown area, strolling along while occasionally stopping at a shop window to admire the merchant's wares. Ryan sighed contentedly. Keir had promised her a dream vacation, and from the minute they'd stepped off the plane, he'd delivered.

Two more days were left on this vacation, and she wanted to do a little shopping before they returned to the big island. Maui, with its rows of shops and street vendors, seemed the perfect place to pick up something for everyone. There were still a few items needed for her family and Keir's. T-shirts would work for her family.

Adam and Emily were a different matter. Unfortunately, Keir's children required spectacular presents. Glancing at the stores ahead of them, Ryan felt confident she'd find the appropriate gifts at the Warner Brothers store. Some trinkets the kids wanted that their parents hadn't purchased for them.

Ryan also wanted to buy something special for Glo. The unselfish way her boss had rearranged the shooting schedule deserved a special treasure.

She slowed and then halted outside a small jewelry store. Ryan studied the expensive pieces in the windows before coming to a decision. "I'm going in here. Do you want to come with me?" she asked Keir.

With a mock scowl on his face, Keir teased, "I don't know. A jewelry store is a mighty dangerous place. What are you planning to do in there?"

"I'm not going to use your money. I've got credit cards."

"Good," he teased. "I was worried."

"Ha. Ha. You are so funny. Really, I want to pick up something for Glo."

Now Keir's forehead crinkled into a frown. "Glo? Why?"

"She understood our dilemma and put forth the effort to help so we didn't have to change our plans." Ryan laid a hand on his cotton-covered chest. "I want to do something nice to show her how much I appreciate her help."

"That's not necessary. That's part of her job," he retorted, shoving his hands into the pockets of his shorts.

"Well Mr. Slave Driver, I think it's important. And I'm going to."

"Why don't you buy something for yourself? I don't think you have to waste good cash on Glo. She was doing what she was hired to do."

"Are you coming in with me? Or are you going to wait out here?"

Snarling, Keir followed her into the store. "I don't believe this is necessary. Spend your money on yourself."

Ryan ignored him while she selected a gold bracelet with intricate hieroglyphs etched into the gold. She added Glo's name to the inside of the piece of jewelry.

Keir didn't know about the tension between Ryan and Glo. Truly, she didn't want him to know. But, Glo made this trip possible and Ryan had decided to take Glo's change of heart as a good omen. Ryan believed it was her turn to make their work environment comfortable.

After purchasing the bracelet, they made their way down the street, stopping to check out several stores. Ryan picked up several T-shirts with palm trees and the word "Maui" written in glittery multicolored letters. On a whim, she added T-shirts for herself, Keir, Adam, and Emily to the stack.

Her mission wasn't complete. Adam and Emily still needed their wow presents and for that she planned to stop at the Warner Brothers or Disney Stores.

They reached the Disney store first. When she stepped into the store, Ryan immediately felt like a kid again. All the glitter and music, plus the videos of old Walt Disney classics, tickled her.

A short search uncovered the perfect presents.

After lunch, they stood on the sidewalk trying to decide what to do next. Ryan leaned close and gave Keir a quick peck on the lips.

Surprised, he tilted his head to the side and smiled at her. "Why did you do that? Not that I'm complaining, but it was unexpected."

"For being so good to me, and for this wonderful vacation." Grinning broadly, she added, "For understanding a woman's need to shop."

Keir mocked her remorsefully. "Those are the trials of being involved with a beautiful, sexy woman. Besides, everything has benefits."

"Benefits?" she asked, with a lift to her voice.

"Mm-hmm. How grateful are you?"

"Very."

"Good. How about we head back to the hotel and you can show me."

"Aren't you the subtle one?"

"No. But that's okay."

Keir swiped the key card through the slot and waited for the green light to flash. He opened the door and slowly danced Ryan into the suite. The door automatically shut behind them. Bathed in semidarkness, Keir and Ryan entered the living room.

They'd shared a meal at the Sheraton's five-star restaurant, followed by dancing in the nightclub. With an arm wrapped around her waist, he'd then led her from the hotel, and they'd strolled along the beach, enjoying the romantic evening, complete with a full moon.

"So far you get all As," she complimented once they were in the living room. "What's your plan for the rest of the evening?"

Hands on Ryan's hips, Keir pulled her against him. She felt his long, hardened flesh against her stomach. His hot breath brushed against her skin as he whispered in her ear. "How about I escort you into the bedroom, and we spend the rest of the night making love?"

The suggestions sent her spirits soaring as a ripple of excitement surged through her. Yes, making love was exactly what she wanted to do. Grinning, she wrapped her arms around his neck. "Good call."

Keir lifted her into his arms and strode through the suite to the bedroom. Her body melted against his. He set her on her feet in the center of the bedroom.

"I'm all yours," she whispered.

"I hope so." He dropped to his knees and lifted one delicate foot, caressing her ankle as he removed her sandal. "Here, let me help you."

Ryan rested her hands on his shoulder, balancing on one foot. Shivers of delight followed when he kissed her ankle and sucked on her toes. Ryan thought she would faint from pleasure.

After slipping the sandals off her feet, he rose and hooked his fingers under the spaghetti straps of her top, slowly drawing them across her shoulders, down her arms, and off her body. The sheer top hung loosely around her breasts, offering Keir a delightful display of her round flesh. He pulled it off her body and removed her skirt.

Keir turned her into his arms as his lips closed hungrily over hers. Ryan tasted a hint of the wine they'd shared at dinner. He broke the kiss as his lips sought the curve of her neck, kissing the pulsing beat at the base of her throat.

His lips followed the path of his finger, and she squirmed, needing more of him. Keir's touch was light and painfully sweet.

Moaning, Ryan gave herself freely to the passion of his possession. Another kiss sent the pit of her belly into a wild swirl.

She shut her eyes, riding out the series of sensations his touch evoked. His lips started with a taut brown nipple, explored her soft caramel flesh, switching breasts as he gave each a quick lick. He caught the warm globes in his hands, circling the nipples with his fingers and added his tongue to one breast and then the other. A fire raged within her.

His hands slid across her silken belly. His busy fingers slid the silk thong aside as his thumb rubbed the throbbing nub between her legs. He palmed her mound. His fingers separated the springy curls and found her nub, rubbing the sensitive flesh. Ryan whimpered.

His finger flicked back and forth across her flesh. The pleasure was so intense. She matched his rhythm, pushing herself hard against his probing fingers.

Moments later Keir dropped to his knees in front of her, pushing the scrap of fabric off her body. Ryan gasped, arching her body hard against his thumb. His expert touch sent her to even higher levels of ecstasy. Keir replaced his thumb with his mouth, licking and sucking at her until she thought she would die from the pleasure.

Her back arched and she moaned as he sucked harder. Unable to control herself, Ryan's thighs shook and she cried out, trembling against his mouth, exploding in a downpour of fiery sensations. Climaxing, she went limp. Unable to stand, she dropped into a puddle like a cooked noodle.

Keir caught her and rose to his feet, swinging her into the circle of his arms. He crossed the room and placed her in the center of the bed. Without wasting a precious moment, he stripped off his clothes, added a condom to his engorged sex before laying down next to her, pulling her back into his arms for another searing kiss.

She tasted herself on his lips, finding the experience unique and exciting.

Without additional foreplay, he thrust into her slick, wet passage. Her breath came in long, surrendering moans as her hips rose to meet his. Together, they found the right tempo and soared higher.

Ryan couldn't control her cries of delight. Her body trembled against his, taking him as far into her as possible. Waves of ecstasy throbbed through her as she shattered into a million pieces. Keir climaxed a split second later. Ryan held him close until the tremors subsided.

Spent, they lay together, wrapped in each other's arms. Ryan was the first to speak. "Thank you."

He chuckled. "Thank you?"

"For tonight. For every night we've been here." Ryan snuggled close to him as their legs became intertwined.

Keir faced her. Winking down at her, he brushed a hand across her breast and then moved lower, fondling the wet curls protecting her opening. Her nipple immediately responded to the caress. "We're not done yet. Didn't we say something about anytime, anywhere?"

Chapter 15

The day following their return to California was busy. Ryan spent the morning emptying her suitcases and doing her laundry. Wednesday marked her return to work, and she wanted her home in order before she set off to the studio. As she rinsed and put the last glass in the dishwasher, the phone rang. She picked up the receiver on the third ring. "Hello?"

"Hi, Ry," Keir greeted.

Happiness spiked inside Ryan. She loved hearing from him. Smiling, she answered softly, "Hey."

"You busy?"

She glanced around her kitchen and answered, "No. Why?"

"The kids and I are out taking care of some stuff, and I wanted to see you. Is it okay for us to drop by?"

A soft gasp of surprise escaped Ryan's lips as she listened. Glancing down at her dust-covered T-shirt and stained denims, she wondered cynically, *What can I say? No, I'm cleaning my house. I look like hell. Maybe another time.* That would really spread the love between them. Caught like a rat in a trap, Ryan responded, "Sure."

"Great! Thanks, sweetheart. We'll be at your place in thirty minutes."

After a quiet good-bye, Ryan hung up the phone and moved across the kitchen to the refrigerator. What did she have to serve to kids? She had one half hour to come up with some sort of refreshment and make herself look presentable. Since the kids weren't her best friends, Ryan wanted this visit to go better than their last meeting. She hoped they had finally warmed to the idea of their father having a friend.

Since the trip to Hawaii, Ryan had come to realize how much her relationship with Keir meant to her. Emily and Adam were part of the package. Being involved with Keir meant having a relationship with his children and maybe even his ex-wife.

Her mother had always preached to her girls, "When you take the man, you take the family." When she chose Keir, she'd agreed to the complete deal, whether she wanted it or not. Although she felt certain her relationship with Keir didn't hinge on whether his kids liked her, things would be easier if they got along. Determined to build a link between herself, Adam, and Emily, she began to plan their visit.

The doorbell rang as Ryan snapped the dishwasher door shut and started it. She emerged from the kitchen with a tray of goodies. Dressed in a clean short-sleeve top and violet shorts, she hurried to the front entrance. With a smile planted on her face, Ryan opened the door and greeted her guests. She welcomed Keir with a soft kiss on the lips, while his children tolerated quick hugs.

"Hi, Adam," Ryan said, noting his blue and white T-shirt with RAPTORS printed in blue letters and denim pants. The princess had on a pink dress with the face of Dora the Explorer on the bodice. "Emily, you look so cute. I love your dress. Come on in."

Because their father stood at their side, the boy and girl smiled pleasantly.

"Come on in, " Ryan repeated, leading the way to the living room and waving a hand at the tray sitting on the coffee table. "Have a seat. I have sliced fruit, peanut butter and jelly sandwiches, and chocolate chip cookies for you guys. Help yourself. Keir, I thought you might appreciate something a bit different. How about a cup of coffee and a cinnamon roll?"

"Sounds good. Thank you." Keir slipped into the chair across from the sea green sofa and watched his kids. "Go on, enjoy," he told them.

Ryan strolled into the kitchen, returning with two mugs of coffee and a small plate of rolls. She placed the treats on the end table between the two crème and jade green chairs, noting neither child had touched the food on the tray.

The rhythmic rumble of the dishwasher filled the silence. The tension in the room felt uncomfortable, so Ryan decided to do something about it. Fixing a pleasant, welcoming smile on her face, she asked, "What have you guys been up to today?"

Keir crossed the ankle of one foot over the knee of his other leg as he sipped his coffee. "We had breakfast at the farmer's market and then picked up some fruits and vegetables before coming this way. There's stuff for you in the car." Keir produced his keys and tossed them to his son. "Adam, go out to the car and bring in that bag of food for Ryan."

The boy caught the keys in one hand and hurried from the house. Minutes later, he returned with a large brown paper bag. Ears of corn, a loaf of Italian bread, and carrots stuck out the top.

Ryan rose from her chair and took the bag from Adam's arms. "Thank you." She took the food into the kitchen and stored it in the refrigerator.

Upon reentering the living room, Ryan noted that the

children sat as quiet as adults on the front pew in church on Sunday. This was so unlike children who played together. Concerned, Ryan glanced Keir's way, with a question in her eyes. He hunched his shoulders.

This felt so awkward. The kids didn't want to be at her house, and they didn't feel comfortable. Neither did Ryan. There had to be a way to break the ice and ease the tension in the room. At the very least, she wanted to get along; anything was better than this oppressive silence.

Searching for something to say, Ryan decided to give them the gifts she and Keir had purchased while on vacation. "While we were in Hawaii, I picked up a couple of things for you guys. Let me go upstairs and get them. I'll be right back," she promised, heading for the stairs.

The children were sitting exactly where she had left them when Ryan returned. Handing a colorfully wrapped box to each child, Ryan said, "I hope you like them."

Both children glanced at their father. Keir nodded approvingly. Adam tore the paper off the box.

Adam's face sprang to life the moment he opened his box. "Wow!" he exclaimed, removing an iPod nestled between white sheets of tissue. "This is awesome!"

Ryan slipped around the coffee table and sat next to the boy, pointing a finger at the headsets and armband. "I was worried that you already had one. But your dad assured me that it was something you had been begging for."

Adam nodded and slid the iPod into the armband. "Yeah."

Smiling at the boy, Ryan tapped the side of the box. "You're not done. There's something else in there."

"Oh, man!" Adam withdrew decks of baseball, Yu-Gi-Oh, and Superman trading cards from the recesses of the box. He tore the cellophane wrappers from the cards and quickly shuffled through the decks. Grinning, he turned to Ryan and asked, "How did you know I wanted these?"

"I guessed. But it looks like they're a hit with you. I'm glad you like them," Ryan answered, touching his arm.

"Adam," said Keir. Keir's stern tone and the slight lift of his eyebrows achieved the proper response.

Shamefaced, Adam muttered, "Sorry. Thank you."

Keir nodded.

Ryan hugged him. "You're welcome."

Emily sat with her box on her lap. She made no move to open it. This little girl was a hard sell, and Ryan understood her loyalties to her mother. All Ryan wanted was a little place in Keir's daughter's life. "Honey, why don't you open your gift? I'm sure you'll love it," said Ryan.

Responding to the prompt, Emily tore the box open. She lifted the first item from the box and glanced at it. The Bratz doll was dressed in a sparkling outfit with rhinestones. Unlike Adam, Emily didn't express any surprise or delight at what she found in the box. Keir rose from his chair and put his empty mug on the table before sitting beside his daughter. Smiling at his daughter, he asked, "What do you think?"

Grinning at her dad, Emily answered, "Pretty."

"We hoped you might like her," said Keir. "But go back to the box. There are some other things in there."

Emily dug inside the box and brought out several outfits for the doll.

For the next few minutes, the kids played with their gifts as Keir talked softly with Ryan. "How about dinner tonight?" he asked.

"You'll have the kids, won't you?"

He nodded.

Ryan glanced at the sofa, where Adam and Emily played contentedly, and shook her head. "I think they've had enough of me for one day."

He tapped her leg with the back of his hand. "Come on."

"No. I'm serious. You've been away for eleven days.

They need your undivided attention for a little while. Give it to them. Devote some time to your kids. Besides, I don't want to be in their faces every time they come to visit you. They come to spend time with you, not me."

"You're part of my life," he reminded, taking her hand.

"Yes, I am. But"—she removed her hand from his— "they were here long before I came in the picture. And if I disappeared tomorrow, they'd still be here, needing your time and guidance. We'll all do things together, but not yet and not all the time. They need to get to know me gradually, and hopefully, they'll grow to like me. It's not fair to them to shove me down their throats every time they are with you."

Keir grimaced. "I hate it when you're right."

"I know you do."

"But you've made a good point."

"Thanks for listening." Ryan tilted her head toward the sofa. "Go spend the rest of the day with your family. I'll talk to you later, and we'll see each other on Wednesday."

He fished the keys from his pocket, saying, "Maybe I'll take them to the beach. They'll like that."

"That's a plan. It sounds good."

Ryan rose.

"Emily, Adam. It's time for us to go," Keir said as he turned to Ryan and took her hand. "Thank you for having us over."

"You're always welcome." Ryan accompanied the Southhalls to the door and waited as the kids raced down the stairs and hurried to the SUV. Leaning close, Keir kissed her lips softly. "I'll talk to you after they go to bed tonight."

"That works for me." She stood in the entrance, watching Keir back out of the driveway and steer the SUV down the street, before shutting the door and returning to the living room to gather the dishes. She sank into the soft folds of a sofa cushion and then shot off the sofa. "Ow!" Something hard and sharp had jabbed into her butt. Ryan separated the cushions and found the Bratz doll jammed between them. *Emily must have forgotten her doll,* Ryan reasoned. *No, she didn't. The girl had deliberately left the gift.* At closer inspection, Ryan found Emily's gift box stuffed under the sofa.

Ryan sighed sorrowfully. She felt so helpless against Emily's stubbornness.

She tossed the doll back in the box and picked up the tray of food, making her way across the living room to the kitchen. Ryan placed the tray on the counter and opened the dishwasher and began to empty it. She knew Keir's daughter wouldn't be easy to get close to. Ryan had hoped the gift would help her cause. It was beginning to look as if she might have a tremendous battle of wills on her hands with the five-year-old.

What to do? What to do? This wasn't a situation that she could talk to Keir about. He would be concerned for Ryan's feelings and upset by Emily's duplicity. After punishing her, Keir would demand that the child apologize. Complying wouldn't make their lives easier. It would add more fuel to an already burning fire.

She'd keep the doll and stay quiet about it. There might be a time in the future where the situation would change and they could become friends. But today wasn't that day.

Returning to the living room, Ryan took the toy upstairs. She placed the box in her mother's room and then shut the door after herself. When Emily wanted her Bratz doll, it would be here waiting for her.

Chapter 16

Like one of those nonstop action flicks, Ryan's first day back to work was hectic and busy from the minute she drove onto One Leaf Studio grounds. Although the director ran her ragged, it felt good to be back to work.

Around six in the evening, Ryan escaped the crowded set and returned to the cubbyhole known as her office to take a breather. Sighing contentedly, she sank into the chair at her desk and gave the floor a tiny kick with her sneaker-covered foot, sending the chair into a slow spin. She stretched her arms wide, and finger combed the hair at the back of her head. As Ryan righted the chair, the phone rang. She reached for it and recited in a singsong voice, "Set department. Ryan Mitchell speaking."

Without any greeting or preamble, Ryan's older sister asked, "Where have you been for the past two weeks?"

Grimacing, Ryan scrunched up her face and stomped her feet. Why hadn't she stayed on the set? "Hello to you, too, Helen."

"Your brother and I have been worried. You haven't answered your phone in days," Helen said.

Ryan rolled her eyes. Guilt, the mother of all emotions.

Her sister used it like an assault weapon. She cradled the phone between her shoulder and ear as she continued to finger comb the hair at her nape. "I went out of town."

"Really? By yourself?"

Ryan giggled softly. Her older sister didn't have a subtle bone in her body. When it involved her family, words like "privacy" didn't register in Helen's vocabulary. As the senior member of the Clemons family, Helen felt she had earned the right to question her siblings on any topic that popped into her head. She acted like those grandma types who used their age as an explanation to say and do things that would normally be taboo.

"How have you been?" Ryan switched the subject. "How are your kids and Larry?"

"They're good. Andre and Gee are involved in summer programs. Gee's working on her game. She wants to apply for a softball scholarship. Andre's taking some science courses this summer so he can get into advanced placement courses in the fall. And my dear husband is working 24/7 so that he can make partner."

"Everyone in your house is busy. What about you?"

"I'm fine. Although there are only five weeks left before I have to be back to work."

Stalling, Ryan rocked back and forth in her chair, muttering, "Ahh, the life of a teacher. You guys have it so good."

"Look who's talking, Ms. 'my job has been closed down for almost two weeks.' You deal with a class of thirty-five seventh graders for nine months out of the year and see how you fare. Believe me, it gets old really quick. Hormones to the left and hormones to the right. They want to be adults one minute and break down in tears like babies the next. Deal with that on a daily basis and see if you don't pull your hair out by the roots."

"No thanks," Ryan answered firmly. "I've got big kids

to deal with. I'll trade you fifteen seventh graders for one temperamental television star any day."

"I'll take my kids."

Smiling, Ryan responded, "That's what I thought you'd say."

Ryan shook her head. An eighteen-year veteran of the public school system, Helen knew how to work people and get the information she wanted. One thing about her sister, she didn't let anyone or anything deter her from her course of action once she decided on it.

"So, what's going on Ryan?" Helen asked. The seriousness and concern in her sister's voice touched Ryan's heart because she knew her family cared about her well-being.

Before she fully realized it, Ryan admitted, "I went to Hawaii."

"Hawaii! Wow! You should have told me. Maybe I could have scraped up the money and gone with you, shared a room, and got to see the sights."

Smiling seductively, Ryan thought, *I had a roommate, and we definitely saw the sights. Some of the best from the inside of the bedroom. I love you, but I don't think I'd trade him for you.*

"What about your husband? What would you have done with him and the kids?" Ryan asked.

"Sold them as a package deal for a dollar."

"Very funny." Ryan laughed, knowing full well Helen absolutely adored her husband, Larry, and her children.

Helen continued to prattle on. "Did you guys shoot on location? Is that why you were on the island? Was there any downtime to explore? Wow! It sounds so wonderful."

For a moment Ryan debated letting her sister believe that she'd gone on the trip for work. But the honest part of her refused to keep lies between them. "Actually, no. I didn't go for One Leaf."

A long pause followed, filled with a valley of unasked questions. Ryan waited, knowing an explosion or interrogation was next.

"Who did you go with?" asked Helen.

That's my sister, Ryan thought, admiring how calm and focused her older sibling stayed, although she knew Helen wanted to demand answers to very different questions.

Ready to explain, Ryan opened her mouth to tell her. The door burst open, and Glo strolled into the room, with her cell phone attached to her ear. The sounds of the studio followed Glo into the room as the scent of Elizabeth Arden's Red Door wafted through the air. She gingerly stepped around Ryan, heading to her own desk.

Saved by the boss, Ryan thought as she eyed her boss. "Helen, I've got to go. We'll talk later. Bye."

Sighing with relief, Ryan dropped the phone in the cradle, knowing perfectly well she'd only succeeded in postponing the inquisition. Ryan opened a desk drawer and removed a navy velvet jewelry box. Silently, she waited for Glo to complete her telephone call. After a moment, the set director snapped her phone closed and slipped it into the slot on her belt. Ryan rose and moved across the tight space, dodging props along the way, and waited next to Glo's desk.

"Hey," said Ryan.

"What?" Glo asked.

Ryan passed the box to her boss. "I got this while we were on Maui. It reminded me of you, and I couldn't leave it. I hope you like it."

Glo stared at the box but didn't reach for it. "Why?"

"I appreciate everything you did for me before the trip. You got me a few extra days."

Glo pushed the box back into Ryan's hands. "Don't worry about it."

"Really. Please take it. It's a peace offering. A sort of new beginning for us after the problems we've shared."

Shaking her head, Glo rose from her chair. "Look—"

"Wait." Ryan opened the box, displaying the bracelet. Egyptian hieroglyphs adorned the ring of gold. An inscription lined the interior of the bracelet.

Glo gazed at the item. An indescribable expression molded her face.

Ryan didn't know what to make of it. She pushed the box at Glo for a second time. "I know I broke the trust between us when I started seeing Keir, but when you helped me work out my schedule, it made me think that you'd forgiven me, and we could start working like colleagues again."

Glo opened her mouth to say something, but a familiar and very welcomed voice interrupted her before the first word left her lips.

"Hi, ladies." Hands in his pockets and casually dressed, Keir strolled into the room.

All the noise from the studio dimmed. Surprised to find Keir in her work area, Ryan said, "Hi. You done for the day?"

"Almost. I thought I'd check to see who was still here before heading out for the evening," replied Keir.

"Oh," Ryan muttered.

Without saying another word, he examined Ryan's face before turning to Glo. "What's going on?" he finally asked.

"I just gave Glo the gift we found on Maui," said Ryan. "We were talking about how much I appreciated her helping us sort out the vacation mess."

Keir nodded, stroking Ryan's bare arm. As usual the sensation sent her heart into a gallop. "We both want you to have this," Keir told Glo. "Believe me, Ryan refused to leave the island until she found the perfect present for you. I had aching feet to prove it."

Ryan grinned at Keir. "Don't believe him. He loves shopping more than I do. Keir, Glo's giving me a hard time about it. She keeps insisting she doesn't need this. I disagree. What do you think?"

Keir removed the box from Ryan's hand and held it out to Glo. "Please take it. We both want you to have it."

Glo started to protest, but Keir instantly cut off her stream of words. "I won't take no for an answer. I insist," he said.

The two women stared at each other. After a moment, Glo smiled and took the gift. "Well, if you insist. What can I say? Thank you."

"Nothing," Keir teased. "Take your present gracefully."

The tone of Keir's voice made Ryan flinch. She put a hand on his arm, needing physical contact to dispel the feeling of unease coursing through her. For a second, Ryan sensed animosity, anger, even dislike, flowing between the two studio veterans. Before she could label it, the sensation was gone, and everyone had their happy faces on.

"Ryan, it was sweet of you. You didn't have to do it," said Glo.

"I wanted to," Ryan answered.

Taking the piece of jewelry from the box, Glo unsnapped the clasp and wrapped the item around her wrist. She admired the bracelet for a beat before saying, "It looks as if you guys put a lot of energy into finding something for me. I can't let all that hard work go for nothing." Smiling at Ryan and then Keir, Glo added, "Thank you. It was sweet of you to think of me while you were on vacation."

Ryan took a step closer to the older woman and said, "No. Thank you for letting old wounds heal. I promise, you won't regret it."

Chapter 17

Saturday loomed in the near future like a bright beacon after a week filled with a hard and fast shooting schedule. Tired and ready to escape the demands of her job for the day, Ryan was strolling across the set on her way to her office when she halted near camera three, giving full attention to the man holding court. She remained in the shadows, listening to the director drone on. Surrounded by the crew and actors, Josef Brennen was describing his philosophy, directing style, and vision for the next scene.

Dressed in a pair of denims, a green short-sleeve T-shirt, and sneakers, a woman detached herself from the group and approached the camera. With a coffee cup in her hand, she stepped close to the platform and said, "Excuse me, Ryan."

"Sorry, Sandi," said Ryan.

"No problem." Sandi, a camerawoman, climbed onto the stand holding the camera and accompanying equipment, sat down, and placed her cup in the holder before adjusting the lens.

As one of the few female camera people hired by the studio, Sandi handled the stationary cameras and equipment. The loud, jovial camerawoman got along with everyone. It never bothered her the way the men ogled her attributes. Sandi's engaging personality made it almost impossible to be around her without getting caught up by her infectious jokes and laughter.

Unfortunately for the male population of One Leaf Studio, Sandi lived in a committed relationship with her partner, one of the show's extras. She confessed to anyone who listened, and to a few that didn't, how fulfilling her life was. If Ryan's memory served her correctly, Sandi and her partner were planning to register as domestic partners this fall and have a baby.

Curious to see how Sandi handled the heavy equipment, Ryan took a step closer. Years of experience were apparent in how the camerawoman maneuvered the camera. As Sandi twisted one of the levels, adjusting the lens angle, the multiple bracelets hanging on her right wrist clanged together, creating a musical jingle, which drew Ryan's interested gaze.

Ryan's heavy lashes flew up, and she took in a gulp of air. *It couldn't be,* she thought frantically, watching Sandi wave her hand in the air.

Sandi glanced at Ryan. "You okay?"

"Yeah. I forgot something I need to do," Ryan explained lamely, dismissing the incident as her imagination playing tricks. She turned away and started for her office. But the nagging voice in her head forced her to do a U-turn to take a closer, second look. She knew of only one way to find out who the bracelet truly belonged to.

The question gnawed at her insides. Filled with a sense of dread and uneasiness, Ryan retraced her steps.

She tapped the camerawoman on the shoulder. Sandi turned. Surprise registered on her face. "I thought you had left," Sandi said.

Ryan drew in a deep breath. *Here we go.* "No. Your jewelry caught my eye. That gold bracelet is really unusual."

Smiling, Sandi wriggled her wrist, displaying all of her bangles and chains. "It is different, isn't it? Believe it or not, I found it in the trash."

Shocked, Ryan's mouth dropped open. *Come on, girl. Pull yourself together.* "No way!"

"Yeah." The camerawoman poked a finger at the hallway. "I worked the late shift Wednesday night, and I went down to the cafeteria for a cup of coffee. I accidentally dropped my change from the vending machine in the trash. So, I had to go Dumpster diving to search for my money. Instead, I pulled this bracelet from the can. After I got it home and cleaned it up, I realized I'd hit the jackpot."

Voice trembling, Ryan asked, "May I see it?"

"Sure." Sandi unhooked the clasp and handed the bracelet over.

With fear in her heart, Ryan ran her finger across the hieroglyphics on the curved outer surface. She turned the piece of jewelry over and glanced inside, checking out the inscription, written in Greek letters.

Ryan felt like crying. Unfortunately, breaking down in front of a bunch of One Leaf stage employees didn't seem appropriate. Gossip always concerned Ryan. She didn't want her colleagues to suspect the depths of her emotions. Ryan forced a smile from somewhere deep within her and handed the bracelet back to Sandi. "Thanks. It's really unique."

The camerawoman hooked the clasp and shrugged. "Yeah. I put a note up on the board in the lounge, but nobody has claimed it so far. I figured I'd wear it and see what happens."

Ryan glanced at her watch and started to back away from the set. "Wow! Look at the time. It's time for me to get back to my office before I'm missed. Talk to you later."

Dazed, Ryan moved along the hallway to her office. Why had Glo tossed the gift in the trash? She didn't strike Ryan as a cruel or malicious person, but this went beyond anything she could understand.

The obvious answer rested with Glo. What was bothering her?

Ryan had questions, plenty of questions. Only one person had the answers. With purposeful strides, she marched down the hall to her office. When she entered the small space, her gaze immediately flew to her boss's desk. It stood empty.

Maybe Glo was in Phil's office. They seemed to be together a great deal these days. The rumor mill had proclaimed the two were in the thick of a torrid affair. As usual, folks got things wrong, but that didn't stop them from adding to the growing list of gossip tidbits they shared.

Glo strolled into the office, with her cell phone attached to her ear, as if Ryan had conjured her boss from her imagination. She gingerly stepped around Ryan and moved to her desk, sinking into her chair and spinning it away from the door toward the window. Her conversation turned low and soft.

Ryan waited silently at her desk. Although she didn't like conflict, especially at work, today's turn of events needed an immediate explanation.

After she hung up, Glo sat watching Ryan, with an inquiring lift of her eyebrow. "Are you all right?"

Ryan focused on Glo "Actually, no, I'm not."

Surprise flared in Glo's blue eyes and then quickly disappeared. "Really? What's going on? Is there something I can help with?"

"I think so."

Ryan stood, hooked her thumbs inside the front pockets of her slacks, and moved across the tightly packed

office to Glo's desk. Perching on the edge of the wood surface, Ryan rubbed a hand across her face, working out the
proper words in her head. "I just came from the set."

"Everything okay?"

"The set is fine. I was talking with Sandi. You know her,
don't you?"

"The camerawoman?"

Ryan nodded.

"What about her?"

"She had on a bracelet similar to the one Keir and I
gave you."

Glo's eyes darted away, and she ran a nervous hand
through her hair while maintaining her silence.

"When I asked her about it," Ryan continued, "she said
she found it in the cafeteria trash can."

"Oh! That's too bad. Someone must've lost their jewelry."

Tension built between the two women. Ryan didn't
like making accusations like this, but she had to know
the truth.

"Are you sure it's the same? Maybe it's a duplicate,"
added Glo.

"I'm sure. Sandi let me see it. It had your name in-
scribed on the inside."

"Well, I don't know how that happened."

"Actually, I think you do." Standing, Ryan gazed
steadily at her boss. "Why did you throw your gift in the
trash, Glo?"

Glo rose from the chair and towered over Ryan. "How
could you say something like that to me? Of course, I
didn't throw your present away."

"Then explain to me how it ended up on Sandi's wrist.
I can understand it not being to your taste, but to toss it
in the trash, you must have hated it."

"Oh, what the hell! Maybe I can finally get rid of you
and get the department moving in the right direction."

"What?" Shocked, Ryan blinked. Glo's switch from her boss to a shrew caught Ryan off guard.

"I'm tired of playing nice with you. Hate is too strong a word to describe my feelings for you. You're a pain that I want gone."

"Gone! Why?"

"Because you come with a boatload of problems, starting with Keir and ending with your lies."

Confused, Ryan shook her head. "What are you talking about? I haven't done anything."

"Yeah. Right. We had to rearrange the whole shooting schedule so that you could have three extra days of vacation."

"Three days didn't kill anybody."

Glo chuckled unpleasantly. "Spoken like a person who didn't have to do the work. When I tried to explain how losing you would effect the department, Keir didn't care. It's all about you."

Ryan tossed her hands in the air and then let them fall to her sides in a tired, frustrated gesture. "Now this is all my fault because I'm involved with Keir? I thought we had resolved that problem."

Glo laughed. The harsh, biting sound ground against Ryan's ears. "Since you hooked up with Keir, there's been one problem after another. Yeah, I put your bracelet in the trash. I don't want anything from you. It almost gagged me to accept it, and I wanted that bracelet out of my sight as soon as I could get rid of it."

Now that the admission had been made, Ryan found it almost impossible to accept. A small part of Ryan wanted to believe it had all been a mistake, a misunderstanding that required a simple explanation. Glo had been angry with her when she first learned of the relationship between her and Keir, but Ryan believed all of that had been resolved.

"Glo, I thought we were okay."

"You were wrong."

"I don't understand. Why did you take the gift if you didn't want it?"

Snorting, Glo said, "I acted nice because of Keir. I need my job like everyone else."

It felt as if someone had taken a sword and shoved it through Ryan's heart. "I don't understand," Ryan began. "What have I done to make you hate me so much?"

"Miss Goody Two-Shoes. I've had it with you. You want the truth. Let me give it to you. Every rule that applies to the studio employees had to be broken to accommodate you."

"What?"

Laughing bitterly, Glo shook her head. "Come on, girl. You can't be that naïve. You've worked at, at least one other studio. We do shut down every year. And all of the employees come back at the same time. When has anyone rearranged the shooting schedule for a set designer?"

Cringing, Ryan was beginning to realize how bad this situation must look to her coworkers.

"And Keir made you do it?"

"Finally, the lightbulb switched on," Glo stated.

"So all of your goodwill gestures were just an act for the boss?"

"Didn't you ever wonder why he always seems to pop up? Be close?" Glo shook her head. "Pitiful."

For the second time today, Ryan felt like crying. But she needed to know everything. "What did I walk in on the Saturday Keir's kids were here?"

Glo scoffed. "Oh, that day. Keir made it clear that you were supposed to get whatever you asked for. Extra days off, if you requested it. He wanted to keep you happy."

Ryan's head hung in shame. There were no words to express her feelings.

"When you came back with your little present, I tossed it in the trash because I couldn't bear to take anything from you," Glo added.

There were so many emotions swirling inside Ryan. Betrayal led the pack. Keir had lied. He'd promised to steer clear of any involvement with Ryan on the job. Good or bad, Ryan didn't want him sticking his nose in her business.

No wonder her boss hated her. Every request Glo had made had been countered by Keir. What a nightmare. Ryan was caught in the middle of it, with no way out.

Chapter 18

Swamped with paperwork, Keir sat behind his desk, with a cup of cooling coffee. The Bose stereo system played mellow jazz while he skimmed through a stack of future scripts. Grunting, he closed one of the scripts and leaned back in his leather chair, running a frustrated hand back and forth across his forehead. Lips pursed, he considered the writers' concept of how to wrap up the season. Keir's vision of the first season's cliff-hanger bumped heads with the teams'.

From the hot mess the writing team had handed him, it didn't look as if the team knew or shared Keir's dream. It was time to step in, take charge, and get the writing team back on track. If his schedule permitted, Keir planned to write and direct the final episode himself.

Refocusing on the work, Keir picked up his ink pen. He was running a large red *X* through several pages of screwed-up dialogue when the telephone rang. Annoyed with the interruption, Keir grabbed the receiver and growled out, "Southhall!"

After a slight pause, Ryan asked hesitantly, "Keir?"

Stunned, Keir's head snapped back as he sat up straighter in his chair. Ryan never made contact with him in the office, preferring to catch him at home or on his cell phone. Heart pounding against his chest, Keir thought, "*Something's wrong. Very wrong.*"

"Ryan?" he asked.

"Yes." She cleared her throat. "Do you have a minute? I need to see you."

Her question added an additional element of concern to his growing list. She never came to him for help. Whatever the problem, she stood alone and found a way to handle it.

Without a doubt, Keir planned to make this time different. If she trusted him with her concerns, he'd find a solution. Whatever the situation, he intended to provide help and meaningful support.

It must be important; Ryan never drew attention to herself in any way at the studio. She kept meetings between them businesslike and to a minimum to reduce any murmur of impropriety the rumor mill might latch onto. Needless to say, the eagle-eyed gossipmongers hated it when they were thwarted so effectively.

He swallowed loudly and asked, "Everything all right?"

"We should talk. Is this a good time?" The slight quiver in her voice deepened his anxiety.

Keir closed the script and tossed it into his out-box. "Yes."

After hanging up the phone, Keir rose from his chair and strolled to the window, searching for Ryan's animated form. An image flashed in his head of the first time he noticed her from this vantage point. As Keir waited, he surfed through a mental list of issues Ryan might have encountered that required his attention. Immediately, his thoughts turned the investigative spotlight on Glo Kramer. That was where most of the tension in Ryan's life fell. Ever since Keir and Ryan had gone public with their relationship, Glo and Keir had been on opposite sides of every matter involving Ryan. Glo countered each request, making it necessary for him to pull rank.

He rejected the idea almost as quickly as it filled his head. Glo knew better. She'd been in the entertainment business for decades, and Glo knew when to keep her mouth shut. No, it wasn't her. It must be something else.

Leaving the window, Keir formulated a plan. He strolled to the coffee station and tossed the used grounds into the trash before adding a new filter and fresh coffee. Once he made her feel comfortable in his office, he'd get to the heart of the matter.

So what could it be? Keir wondered as he poured water into the coffeemaker. The strong aroma of coffee filled the room. Whatever the issue, he'd put things right. Maybe someone on the set was hassling her. Smiling, he nodded, confident he'd hit on the problem.

Once Ryan got to his office, Keir intended to be understanding and kind. After he learned who or what had upset her, he'd find the culprit, summon him or her to the Eiffel Tower, and resolve the problem "Keir Southhall" style.

With that plan firmly in hand, Keir poured a fresh cup of coffee and returned to his desk. Minutes later, Ryan knocked on the door. He rose, crossed the carpeted floor, and opened the door.

Ryan stepped into the office and shut the door after herself, leaning against the wood panel as if her strength had been zapped. Her face was drawn. It nearly broke his heart to see her this way.

Disappointment and rage stared back at him. Ryan looked as if her world had crumbled into dust. Her sparkling brown eyes were empty, staring past him instead of at him. Normally, Ryan's eyes sparkled with merriment. The natural curve of her beautiful, delicate mouth was set into a grim line.

"Hi," said Keir. Keir's hand cupped her elbow to lead her to a chair. She stiffened and hunched her shoulder to dislodge his hand and then moved away from him. Brows crinkled into a frown, he studied her. "Would you like coffee or anything?"

Ryan shook her head and took the visitor's chair opposite Keir's.

Slowly moving back to his desk, he said, "This is the first time you've called my office. What's going on?"

Silently, Ryan examined the floor, wringing her hands together. After a moment, she seemed to notice and placed them in her lap. "I, uh, was down on the set a little earlier." She seemed to gather her strength and continued. "Sandi, you know her, don't you?"

A mental picture of a tall, red-haired camerawoman came to mind. He needed more information, so he nodded at the appropriate pause and waited.

"Anyway, she was near the set, working on one of the cameras," said Ryan. "You remember the bracelet we bought Glo in Hawaii?"

Okay, so how did these two topics come together? He'd expected to hear something totally different. Humoring her, Keir answered, "Yes."

"Sandi was wearing it."

Confused, he shook his head. "What?"

"You heard me. The woman had it on her wrist! When I asked her where she got it, Sandi told me a story about finding it in the cafeteria trash can."

Again, he asked, "What?"

"The bottom line is Glo threw it away. I went back to our office. When Glo came in, I asked her about it. At first, she denied knowing anything about the bracelet. After a few minutes, she admitted throwing it away." Ryan's voice broke, and she studied the ceiling, fighting back tears. "I asked her why. She admitted she was sick of dealing with me. Everything had to be changed to accommodate me. Extra days for our trip to Hawaii and the rearranging of the shooting schedule were all done for me. Keir, is that true?"

Keir maintained a calm exterior, but his insides were in turmoil. He'd figured wrong. Dead wrong. This was *all* about Glo. What was wrong with that woman? She'd always come through when he needed her, except this time.

Keir swept his tongue across his dry lips. "Ry."

For the first time since entering the room, she looked directly at him. "Is it true?"

Hedging, he ran a hand across his forehead. "Well . . ."

"Is it true?" she asked in a solid, determined tone.

"I only did it so that we could have our vacation. Remember? The trip of a lifetime." Instinctively, Keir knew he couldn't hide what he'd done any longer. He focused on the belief that he could fix things. If Ryan gave him a chance, he felt certain he'd put things right between them.

Nodding, she rose and started for the door. "That's what I thought."

Keir jumped from his chair, following her across the room. At the door, he placed a gentle hand on her shoulder. "Wait."

Ryan stiffened, shoving his hand away. "For what? You lied to me."

"It's not as bad as it seems. Come back, sit down, and we'll talk about it."

Ryan swirled around. Anger and pain flashed across her beautiful face. Her voice was tight and low. "Talk about what? How you fixed everything? You made Glo and Phil Berger rearrange the whole week's shooting schedule so that I wouldn't have to come back with the rest of the crew. I work here. Do you know how much trouble this little arrangement caused? Is that what you want to talk about?"

He'd never seen her like this before. Keir didn't know

how to explain the situation so Ryan would understand that he'd done this for them.

"Listen," he muttered urgently, taking her hand and trying to lead her back to the desk.

Ryan shook off his hand. "No. I can't trust you ever again. You made a promise to me, and you broke it. You said that you would never interfere with my job. We could have a relationship, and my job and reputation would be safe. You lied. You did cause trouble. Big trouble! How could you?"

"Are you willing to throw away everything that we have because I made a mistake?"

"You did."

"I was only trying to help."

She sighed heavily. "You overstepped your authority. I didn't need or want it."

Feeling desperate, he tried a different approach. "I did it for you, to make your life easier."

A nasty, almost hysterical chuckle rose from her throat. Ryan shook her head. "What you did was crap in my backyard. You undermined my credibility and made me look like a fool. Is that how you make my life easier?"

"That's not it at all."

"Really? Then what is it?"

"I care about you, Ryan. Us as a couple and you as an individual. Next to my kids, you are the single most important person in my life. I didn't want anything to affect your job here."

She leaned her forehead against the door and whispered so low, he barely heard her. "You affected my job. You caused all kinds of grief, and now you want me to believe you did it for me? The truth of the matter is you interfered in my life to make yours easier."

"It wasn't just mine. You benefited from everything I did," he said.

"Yes, I did. But you didn't offer me any choices. You took it upon yourself to just take over and make decisions in my life."

"You enjoyed it at the time," Keir reminded her in a low, almost accusatory tone.

"You are correct. But it doesn't change the fact that you lied." Ryan whipped open the door and left.

Chapter 19

Fresh from the shower and dressed in a pair of loose-fitting chocolate-colored sweats, Keir headed through the house to his entertainment room. Faced with the prospect of a solitary evening, he picked up the remote and switched on the high-definition television, listening to CNBC as he wandered aimlessly around the room. Unable to concentrate on the woes of the world, Keir channel surfed until he found a music station to fit his mood. B.B. King, Lucille, and the blues fit the bill.

Groaning in frustration, he rotated his head from side to side, working out the tension building in his shoulders. Today had been a bitch. Glo had blown everything to hell by opening her big mouth and talking to Ryan about their deal.

Antsy, Keir paced the length of the floor before changing course and heading for the bar. He opened the liquor cabinet and selected a bottle of scotch, splashing a large portion in his glass. Keir swallowed a third of the drink and then refilled it before heading to the sofa.

He needed to concentrate on Ryan, work out a plan to fix things between them.

What could he do to appease her? His head on a

platter might make her do the "happy dance." In the short time they had been together, he'd never seen her this way. Ryan's emotions jumped from calm to hurt and then to betrayal and a few more, which were so fleeting, he didn't get a chance to name them.

There had to be a way. If he begged for forgiveness and promised to never interfere again, would that help? Would Ryan believe him? Keir didn't believe so. Could he do it? He wasn't sure.

Somewhere in the house, the cordless phone rang. He rose from the sofa and followed the sound to the great room. Absently, he picked up the receiver and depressed the ON button. Anchoring the telephone between his ear and shoulder, Keir took a good swallow of scotch, rolling the expensive liquor around his tongue, and returned to the entertainment room. "Southhall."

"Well, you're finally home. I've been calling all afternoon."

Blood pumping through his veins, Keir stood straighter. Had something happened? "Shannon, are Adam and Emily okay? If the kids need me in a hurry, why didn't you call on my cell phone?"

"I wanted to talk to you away from the studio."

"Shannon, are Adam and Emily okay?" he repeated.

"They're fine."

Relaxing, he flopped onto the soft cushions of a chair and picked up his drink, sipping the scotch as he contemplated the reason for her call. Keir and his ex-wife weren't on the best of terms. Although their separation had been a mutual agreement, the divorce had changed them both. Out-and-out warfare wouldn't be a true assessment of their current relationship. Shannon never missed an opportunity to land a punch or a TKO at Keir's expense. His ex-wife enjoyed making him bleed. Today had been brutal, and he didn't feel up to a verbal game of "let's see who can score the most punches."

Exasperated, Keir sighed, scratching the side of his neck with his finger. No point in pussyfooting around. He might as well find out what she wanted and get rid of her as quickly as possible. "What do you need?"

Loudly laughing into the receiver, Shannon quipped, "Wonderful greeting. No 'how are you?' or 'are you doing okay?' You automatically assume I want something."

"Normally, you want something. Tell me how this time is any different?"

"Maybe I wanted to chat. See how you're doing. Or spend a little time talking about old times."

His tone turned rock hard. "Don't jerk me around tonight. I've had one hell of a day. I'm not in the mood."

"I'm pretty sure this talk won't improve your mood," she answered smugly.

"I don't have time for this, woman. Spit it out, or I'm hanging up." His eyes squeezed shut. *Damn!* After the day he'd had, a verbal sparring with his ex-wife rated lower than a California mud slide.

"Fine. The kids are both good. But I do want to talk with you about them."

Cradling the telephone between his chin and ear, Keir rose from the chair and returned to the liquor cabinet, adding a generous helping of scotch to his glass before returning to the chair. "So what's on your mind?"

"Your new lady friend."

Confused, he shook his head. "What?"

"Don't play coy. I know you're seeing someone. The kids don't lie. Although I must admit, they try to keep quiet about what's going on at your place."

What business was it of hers? Shannon had friends.

He cracked his fingers as he realized the kids must

have mentioned Ryan to their mother. After all, they had been to Ryan's house and received gifts from their trip to Hawaii.

Ready to take the smug tone out of her voice, he asked, "And how is my relationship your problem?"

"Relationship." She laughed. "That's an interesting name for it."

Instantly, his temper was roused. Generally, he'd jump in with both feet and let the argument take them both to a very ugly place. Tonight, the gentler side of him refrained from traveling down a road that was far too familiar and unpleasant. "Shannon, let's not play games. What do you want?"

"Keep my kids away from that woman."

"What kind of shit are you stirring up now, woman?"

"This is not about me. But I am concerned for my children. I don't know anything about *your* friend. Who is this woman?"

"It's none of your business."

Shannon continued as if he hadn't spoken. "What she does is a mystery to me. She may be a serial killer, for all we know—"

Keir cut in. "That's ridiculous."

"Don't even go there. Until I find out more about her, I don't want your lady friend around my kids."

"They're my kids, too. Ryan would never hurt them. She believes in family and putting children first. My turn to rant. What about the boy toy slipping in and out of your bed? I don't want Emily and Adam seeing that. Handle your own business before you start making demands on mine."

Jumping to his feet, Keir began to pace. He hated when his ex-wife brought him to this level. This verbal raping of each other caused more animosity between them.

"Don't go into my bedroom," growled Shannon.

"Then don't go into mine," Keir shot back.

"Whenever there are people in my house, I'm right there with the kids. Can you say the same? Where are you?"

"Standing next to Adam and Emily. We do everything together. There's nothing for you to worry about."

"Are you sure?"

With a return of calmness, Keir stated confidently, "Positive."

Voice sharp with agitation, Shannon added, "I mean it. Keep her away from Adam and Emily."

"Why? What do you have against her? You've never met her. She means nothing to you. Or does she? Jealousy maybe?"

"Don't be ridiculous. What if she wants you all to herself and she doesn't want the burden of kids from a former marriage? They're kids. Children are the most trusting souls, and anything can happen."

Keir couldn't keep the surprise out of his voice. "Are you trying to tell me you believe Ryan would hurt the kids to keep me away from them?"

"I don't know what she's capable of. So I can't say. But, it is my responsibility as a parent to watch over them. And that's what I plan to do."

"What makes you think that I would let anyone come between me and my kids? If I saw the slightest problem, I'd nip it."

"I think something else is being nipped, and the kids might just come in a poor second. You might be ignoring the signs."

Keir opened his mouth to deny her claims, but Shannon rushed on.

"You don't know her that well. The kids told me that you two went to Hawaii together, and that she's been around maybe a month or so. I say, until you're completely sure of her, don't have her around my children."

He didn't need this. His day had been difficult enough without adding his ex-wife to the mix. Besides, he didn't want her to know that Ryan might never be near the kids again if he didn't fix the problem plaguing them.

"Look, I appreciate your concern," said Keir. "First, I would never take my kids around anyone that I didn't feel was safe. Second, Ryan is the most gentle, caring woman I know. She'd never do anything to hurt anyone, including Adam and Emily. When I wanted to introduce her to them, she didn't want to cause any confusion, so she kept suggesting we wait and get on a better footing. Don't worry about her. She's a good woman."

Shannon laughed. "You? With a good woman? I don't think so. Your taste in women runs to bimbos and starlets. When did you get some taste?"

For a moment, he wanted to laugh. Ryan was so far from being a starlet that the description was hilarious. "Bite me."

"No thanks. Been there, done that. Don't want to do it again."

Same old Shannon. She had to have the last word. That was fine with him.

"Well. I've said what I set out to say," Shannon continued. "I'll talk to you again. I know you don't like what I've suggested, but I need you to at least give it a little consideration. Yes, you can do whatever you want when the kids are with you. But please keep their safety in mind. Bye."

Before he came back with a retort, Shannon hung up. He punched the button to disconnect and finished his drink. Crap kept coming from all angles tonight. First

Ryan, and now Shannon, had twisted his gut into knots that refused to untangle. Shannon could be ignored. What he planned to do about Ryan was still a mystery. One thing he knew for sure, he wasn't giving up on her or their relationship. It had become far too important to him.

Chapter 20

Ryan made the final check mark on her clipboard and then headed to set three. Determined to stay one step ahead of her cantankerous boss, Ryan intended to stop at each set and run down her checklist before leaving the studio. Standing on the edge of the set, Ryan compared the floor plans in her hands against the finished products.

Minus the blazing lights and sets crammed with actors, directors, and camera, sound, and technical people, the studio seemed quiet and still. Shivering, she pulled the edges of her navy knit cardigan around her shoulders and secured the top button. With the close of business, the harsh, hot floodlights had been switched off, leaving the soft, muted overhead lights. There was an eerie quality to the deserted set.

On her way to set three, she glanced in the direction of the Eiffel Tower, noting the darkened office. With a sense of relief, she sighed. *Good.* An unlit, empty room meant Keir had probably left for the day.

For the past week, Ryan had sidestepped discussions with Keir regarding the Glo fiasco. At one point, he'd demanded Ryan sit down with him and resolve their issues.

She'd refused politely, while maintaining the appropriate level of respect for the head of the studio. As she moved along the corridor, a lone figure detached itself from the shadows and followed her.

"Hey."

Startled, Ryan let out a little yelp and whipped around, clutching the clipboard to her chest. "Hell! You scared the crap out of me."

Smiling gently, Keir apologized. "Sorry."

Eyeing him suspiciously, Ryan sighed heavily before asking, "What are you doing here? I thought you had gone for the day."

Keir hunched his shoulders and then tapped the coffee brown leather briefcase with his free hand. "Had to come back. I forgot some stuff I needed to work on. What about you?"

"Checking the sets before I call it a night." She turned the clipboard so he could see it. "I want to make sure everything is in order for tomorrow's early morning shooting schedule. I'm almost done. Sets four and five need to be reviewed, and then I'm out the door."

He gave the clipboard a cursory examination before returning it to Ryan. "Mind if I tag along?"

"It's your studio," she tossed over her shoulder as she strolled down the corridor.

Grimacing at Ryan's comment, Keir slid into step beside her. "How has work been going?"

"Good."

"Any problems?"

Here we go again, she thought. He never knew when to leave things alone. Ryan halted and whirled around to face her boss, demanding, "Why?"

Hands raised in an act of surrender, Keir took a step away from the woman. "Whoa! I'm not trying to cause any trouble. It was a simple question."

Yeah, right. Ryan eyed the man. *A simple question you'd probably turn into a big problem. No, thank you.* "I'm fine."

"If there was a problem, you wouldn't tell me, would you?"

"No," she answered curtly.

"Thanks. Glad to hear it," he muttered sarcastically.

They resumed their trek to set four. After several silent moments, Keir said, "You know, I have a hard time letting go of control over things. It's that whole 'director in charge' thing."

"Mm-hmm." Where was he heading with this? Ryan wondered, watching Keir out of the corner of her eye as she proceeded to check the set.

"I believe it's my job to watch over the people I care about. To keep them safe."

"I can take care of myself," she assured him.

"There's no doubt in my mind that you can. But, part of me wants to be the one to protect you. Take care of you. Be the one you turn to when things go haywire. Can you understand that?"

"So that's why you lied to me? Made my boss and the studio revamp the entire shooting schedule so that you could make life easier for me? Am I getting this correct?"

"No. That's not why."

"Please explain it to me. Help me to understand why you did it after you promised you'd never interfere with my job."

"I made those changes for us. Can't you see that?"

"Yes, I can. But you lied."

"If I had let you handle the situation, you would have rolled over and played dead. Let Glo run over you."

"Glo's my supervisor, Keir. Believe it or not, I take directions from her."

Ryan turned away, heading to the next set. Keir caught her arm, holding it loosely. "Don't leave." After a pause, he added, "Please."

"We don't have anything else to say." She shook off his arm.

"That's where you're wrong. There's a lot of unfinished business between you and me. Let's talk about us. Can you at least consider listening to me?"

"Give me one good reason why I should," Ryan demanded.

"Because we're better together than apart."

"What?"

"You heard me. I believe you understand what I'm saying."

Ryan waved a dismissing hand in Keir's direction and turned away. "I don't understand you."

"You know exactly what I'm saying. Together we're whole. Complete. Separately, we flounder like fish washed up on the beach."

"Sex. You're talking about sex. Of course, we're better together. I don't have a lot of fun alone when it comes to sex."

"That's part of it. But there's more. In bed, out of bed. You and I function great together. We complete each other. I felt it almost immediately after we met. Didn't you?"

Yes, she did. Honestly, those feelings had been so strong that they'd frightened her, made her shy away from them. But Ryan didn't intend to tell him that.

Using her fingers to create quote marks, she said, "You're trying to play on the 'we belong together crap.' Let me tell you, it's not going to work."

Ryan was lying. She understood exactly what he was saying. There was a special something about them. They fit perfectly together, in a way she'd never felt with any man, including her husband.

Folding her arms around the clipboard, Ryan stood, with a sour expression on her face, hoping he couldn't see the hope in her eyes. "I think you're trying to sell me a boat-load of used goods. But, I'm going to give you a chance to convince me. Make me understand," she challenged. "You're not God, Keir. It's not your job to make decisions for the people you care about."

"That wasn't my intention. I want to protect you." Unconsciously, he placed his hands on her shoulders. After a week of no contact, it felt heavenly to feel the warmth of his touch. "I wanted to cut through the bull and do something special for you. What good is being the head of a studio if I can't help and protect the people I care about?"

"You can't control everything."

"That wasn't my plan. All I wanted to do was go on vacation with you. Spend time with you and enjoy your company. I repeat, what's the point in being the head of a company if you can't offer the people you care about a few perks?"

"Keir, why are you so intent on running things?" Ryan touched his arm. "You can't make our lives perfect. It just isn't possible. We're human beings, who make mistakes. What's really going on in your head?"

He rubbed fingers back and forth across his forehead and then admitted in a soft tone, "I don't want us to end up like Shannon and me."

Confused, Ryan opened her mouth to ask for more info but instantly shut it.

Keir continued. "When I married my wife, I planned to be with her until one of us died."

Ryan moved closer, sensing Keir wanted to reveal the truth. "Why aren't you together?"

"Most people believe we split because of some issues with infidelity. That's the last problem we had. I never cheated on my wife, and I never would. What really happened is I got so wrapped up in my work that I forgot to take time out and be with my family. I let them slip away."

She gnawed on her bottom lip before asking, "When you finally realized what was going on, did you try to change things?"

"It was too late." Shaking his head, Keir let out a shaky breath. "Shannon couldn't handle the stress of the Hollywood lifestyle. We'd get dressed up like dolls and attended premieres of movies she didn't know anything about. It was all too much for her. Stand here; smile pretty. Shannon hated it. Once the fighting started, it seemed as if we couldn't stop."

"What did you do?"

"Nothing. Worked more hours. Stayed at the office longer so that I didn't have to hear her mouth."

Ryan gently stroked Keir's arm. "It's not your fault. There were two people in your marriage."

"It was. I should have been more aware of what was happening in my household. We should have talked more. I should have been more available so Shannon wouldn't feel so isolated or alone. That's what really broke up our marriage."

"So you want to make sure we don't end up the same way? Am I correct?"

Keir nodded. "It's difficult to have this kind of career and maintain a family life. So much of my time is spent looking for production dollars, promoting a new idea or movie. I don't want you to think you are a second-class citizen in this relationship. We should be happy and spend time together. That's why I tried to smooth the way. Make things come out right for us."

"Honey"—she held his hand—"you can't control every aspect of our lives. You've got to go with the flow. There's only one way to do that. Talk to me. Offer your help honestly. Don't go behind my back. I've worked too hard to maintain a clean reputation. It's pretty much shot now."

"I was only trying to help."

"I know. But, Keir, you can't run my life or make choices for me. I won't live that way."

Frowning down at Ryan, he asked, "What are you saying?"

"Unless I come to you, don't step in. Let me sort things out for myself."

Keir removed the clipboard from her grasp and tossed it on a sofa, taking her hands between his. "Let's try again. I promise you won't be disappointed."

"I don't know. You put my career in jeopardy. Ignored my wishes. How can I trust you?"

"That's a good question. I think the only way you'll know for sure is to let me prove it to you. I admit, it's hard to let things happen without my guiding hand. But I'm willing to try, if you are."

Keir kissed her lips, touching her gently before stepping back. When she didn't protest, he moved closer, wrapping his arms around her waist and drawing her against him. Ryan let out a contented sigh. She loved being near him, taking in his cologne and unique scent.

Should she give them a second try? She'd already risked so much to be in this relationship. Did they deserve a little more time to see if it would work between them? Ryan wanted to. She missed him deeply.

Stepping away from the warmth of his body, she wagged a finger at him, threatening, "No more going behind my back. If you do, I swear, I'll end it with you, quit, and find myself another job."

He pulled her close and muttered into her hair, "We'll make it work. I promise."

Chapter 21

The sky was ablaze with a rainbow of bright colors as Ryan, Keir, and his children cruised along the highway on their way to Outback Steakhouse for dinner. Sunglasses perched on her nose, Ryan sank deeper into the Hummer's front passenger seat, fighting valiantly to ignore the bickering children in the backseat. From the scowl etched into Keir's face, it was clear that his tolerance level bordered near critical mass. If Adam and Emily didn't settle down real quick, they were headed for a severe reprimand.

After taking a quick peek at the pair, Ryan shuddered, wondering how Keir had persuaded her to accompany the trio this evening. The word "relationship" popped into her head, flashing in bold, neon letters. That was why she'd agreed to this evening. The need to develop a place for herself in Adam and Emily's lives was imperative.

Generally, unless Glo scheduled her for the weekend shift, Ryan reserved Friday nights to kick back and relax after the hectic pace of the week. She took a second peek at the pair and caught Adam snatching a handheld electronic game from Emily. The little girl let out a piercing howl of outrage, which vibrated throughout the Hummer, and then repeated her older sibling's gesture before scooting as far away from Adam as her seat belt allowed. Silently, Ryan admitted it might have been a good idea to pass on dinner, stay home, call for a pizza, and then finish off her evening with a chilled glass of wine.

So why had she agreed? The simple truth remained: if she planned to stay in this relationship, she must establish some level of friendship with the kids. That wouldn't happen if she didn't go on outings like this one. So here she sat, listening to Keir's children snipe at each other.

"Dad-dee." Emily shifted between the bucket seats to moan close to her father's ear.

"Sit back and snap your seat belt," Keir commanded.

Emily brought her hand to her mouth and whispered, "I got to go."

"Go where?" the clueless father asked, while keeping his eyes on the road. He expertly maneuvered the Hummer through the rush-hour traffic.

The five-year-old looked in Ryan's direction, and then she lowered her voice a notch. "You know. To the bathroom."

Keir flinched, and then a frown spread across his face. "Why didn't you go before we left Ryan's?"

Emily sighed and then replied, as if she were speaking to the town idiot, "I didn't have to go then."

Adam poked a finger in his sister's rib cage. "That's what you get for stealing my soda."

Emily used both hands to shove back, answering in a tone fit for a queen addressing an underling. "I did not."

"Yes, you did," exclaimed Adam.

Ryan rolled her eyes, feeling the first pulse of a headache forming between them. Hopefully, this wouldn't be the extent of adult conversation for the evening. Her gaze slid over the pair an additional time and then landed on Adam. Although the boy's attitude toward the new woman in his father's life had thawed, going from frosty to tepid, Adam and Emily remained a united team against Ryan.

"Can you hold it until we get to the restaurant?" Keir asked as he took his eyes off the road for a minute to study the child's face.

"No," Emily groaned. "I got to go now."

Sighing, Ryan pointed at the green highway sign, instructing, "Take this exit and loop around. We're not that far from my house."

"No," Keir stated. "Let her wait until we get to Outback."

"Please, dad-dee!" Emily begged like a child dying of thirst. "I need to go now."

Ryan gazed at the child's contorted face and wiggling little body and took pity on the girl. She placed an encouraging hand on Keir's arm, suggesting, "There's no point in making her wait. It's easier to go back to my place. We should still be able to make our reservation."

"Damn!" Keir hit the right turn signal and merged into the exit lane. "You're probably right."

Seven minutes later the Hummer rolled to a stop in Ryan's driveway. The little girl hopped out of the car once her father shifted the transmission into neutral and ran toward the porch. Ryan followed at a slower pace, digging in her purse for her keys.

Once Ryan turned the key in the lock and pushed the door open, Emily slipped into the house and stood dancing from foot to foot in the hallway as she waited for Ryan to give her permission to go to the second floor.

Ryan pointed at the stairs and directed, "Go on up."

Without a comment, Emily raced up the stairs. Seconds later a door slammed shut.

With nothing to do, Ryan took a seat on the sofa and thumbed through a copy of *Good Housekeeping* until an article about growing perfect roses caught her eye. Ryan forgot everything around her, focusing on the information. Once she read the final paragraph, she shut the magazine and glanced at the clock. It had been a few minutes since Emily went upstairs. What was going on? Chuckling softly, Ryan wondered if the girl had fallen into the toilet. Curious, Ryan dropped the magazine on the coffee table and headed to the staircase.

Some instinct cautioned her against calling out once she reached the second floor. Quietly easing down the hallway, Ryan halted at the open bathroom door. Emily was not in the bathroom. Puzzled, she started down the hall and stopped at an open bedroom door.

Emily stood before one of four curio cabinets, admiring the lit cases full of dolls. Slowly pushing the door open farther, Ryan stepped inside. "Hi."

Embarrassed, the girl whipped around to face the adult. Her eyes were as large as soccer balls. "I-I-I . . ."

Smiling reassuringly, Ryan moved into the room and stopped next to Keir's daughter. "Don't be scared. You're fine."

"Whose room is this?"

"My mother's."

"Are these her dolls?"

"Yes and no."

"What does that mean?"

"This was my family's hobby."

"How come there's so many?"

Wetting her lips with her tongue, Ryan said, "Collecting dolls was something we shared. Mom collected toys long before I was born. After a while, her interest turned to dolls. Once I got old enough, I joined in."

This had been her mother's passion and their hobby. Ryan stood directly behind Emily and took a look around the room. Dolls of every size, shape, and variety dominated the room. Barbie and Ken dolls through the ages filled two wooden curio cabinets. The third and fourth curio cabinets held dolls from around the world, and a series of Raggedy Ann and Andy dolls found a home on the bed, while the two windowsills were lined with Cabbage Patch dolls. All were perfectly cared for, maintained, and preserved.

"These were my sister's," Ryan said as she pointed at the Raggedy Ann and Andy dolls.

"You've got a sister?"

Ryan nodded. "And an older brother, just like you."

Emily moved to the bed and fingered the white lace on Raggedy Ann's pink dress. She smoothed the hair made of yarn and asked, "Does your sister live here?"

"No. She's got her own home and family."

Horror spread across Emily's young face. "Your sister left her dolls?"

Ryan wanted to laugh. But the child found this situation very disturbing. Nodding, Ryan picked up one of the Cabbage Patch dolls and straightened the blue jean overalls. "When she went away to college, Helen took her bears but left the dolls for me and Ma to take care of. I was so proud. My big sister left me in charge of her collection."

"They're all yours?"

Ryan considered Emily's question. "No. They belong to both of us."

Cautiously sitting on the edge of the bed, Emily grabbed one of the Cabbage Patch dolls and rocked it back and forth. "Does you sister come and see them?"

"Sometimes. We'll come up here and sit and talk while we comb the dolls' hair and fix their clothes. There are days where we gather them all together and take off their clothes so that we can wash them. And then we spend the rest of the day dressing and arranging them."

"What about your mom?"

Ryan rose from the bed, moved across the floor to one

of the curios. After opening the wooden door, she removed a classic Barbie doll. "My mother and I use to hunt for new Barbies. Every couple of months or so, we'd take the bus downtown and spend the day in the toy stores. It was our special treat. On the way home, we'd stop for waffle ice cream sandwiches. That was the best part."

She handed the doll to the little girl and returned to her spot on the bed. Emily followed, sitting next to Ryan. "Where's your mom now?"

"She died a few years ago."

"Do you miss her?"

The pain of loss still weighed heavily in Ryan's heart, and she never denied her feelings. "Mm-hmm. Yeah. A lot."

"I don't want my mom to go away."

"She won't," Ryan assured Emily. "Your mother loves you, and she'll be here for you." *Time for a distraction.* "What about you? Does your mother take you shopping to buy toys?"

"Sometimes. Not like what you do."

Ryan didn't know how long the little truce would last. She decided to make the most of it. She rose from the bed and removed the Bratz doll from the dresser drawer and placed the doll between them.

Emily was embarrassed, and her eyes grew large and round. Her gaze darted away, as she was looking at anything but the doll.

"I think you left this by mistake," said Ryan. She had decided to forgive her. Accusations would only put the child back on the defensive. She wanted to mend fences and develop a relationship with Emily.

Realizing Ryan had given her an easy way out, Emily picked up the doll. "I forgot."

"That's what I thought," Ryan offered in an understanding voice. "I kept it for you. I knew I'd see you again."

"Thank you," Emily said.

The pair sat quietly for several minutes, engrossed in their own thoughts. Ryan rose. "Your dad's waiting. We should probably go."

Emily rose from the bed and glanced in Ryan's direction. The kid's face creased into a frown as she contemplated something very serious. Leaving her to it, Ryan headed for the door.

"My mommy says you want to take my dad-dee from us. That you want your own family, not us."

This was a very touchy situation. The Southhall clan still considered her an interloper in many ways. Normally, little girls loved their fathers and didn't like any woman coming between them.

She didn't want to isolate the little girl any more than she already had. If Ryan said the wrong thing, she'd be calling Emily's mother a liar. Ryan didn't want to find herself in the center of a controversy with the Southhall family.

Ryan suspected that Keir's ex-wife felt threatened by Ryan and kept feeding her children this crap. The last thing Ryan wanted to do was compete with Keir's kids for his affections or fight with their mother.

"No. I don't want to do that," said Ryan.

"He's not the same when you're around. Dad-dee thinks about you, not us."

This is one perceptive child, Ryan thought, gnawing on her bottom lip. How could she put her mind at ease? "You and Adam are the most important people in your dad's life. You come first with him. But he also wants everyone to be happy."

Emily listened but didn't comment.

"I want to be friends with you and your brother," Ryan continued. She hoped her honesty would win the child over.

Shrugging, the girl remained silent.

"I'm not trying to come between you and your mother or your dad," said Ryan. "You can be friends with me and still love your mother. You're not doing anything wrong. I promise. Ask your parents. They'll tell you. We can do things together or not. All I know for certain is I want to be your friend."

"Why?"

This kid was a hard sell. "Partly because of your father. He'd want us to be friends. And I'd like that, wouldn't you?"

Emily plucked at the ribbon in the Bratz doll's hair.

Ryan probed. "Do you think we can be friends?"

She waited for the child to digest the info.

"Yeah," said Emily.

"I like you and your brother. I don't want to take your mother's place. But I think there's room for me, too. I want a place of my own in your life. Your mother will always love you. When you are here, I want you and Adam to feel comfortable at my house and with me."

"I'm sorry."

Confused, Ryan shook her head. "What?"

Studying the floor, Emily muttered softly, "I was bad."

Smiling, Ryan wrapped an arm around the girl and hugged her close. "Don't worry about it. You know what I'd like?"

"What?"

"I'd like us to do like my mom and me."

"Huh?"

"We can go to toy stores and start our own doll collection. Would you like to do that with me?"

Emily's head bobbed up and down.

"Good. While your dad and brother watch games on TV or do whatever men do, we can buy a curio cabinet and fill it with our own set of dolls. What do you say?"

"Yeah."

"Great!"

"When? When can we start?"

"I'll talk to your dad. Maybe we can start the next time you come over."

"Next week?"

Ryan shrugged. "Maybe. We'll have to work the details out with your dad."

The car horn blared. Ryan glanced out the window and found an impatient Keir standing next to the car. She stretched out a hand to the little girl. "Time's up. We better go. Your dad doesn't look too happy with us."

It was a calculated risk that Emily wouldn't take Ryan's hand. But, if Ryan planned to ever establish any bond between them, it had to start somewhere. Without a moment's hesitation, Emily slipped her small fingers in Ryan's larger hand, and they left the room together.

Ryan's heart swelled with possibilities. Maybe they could become friends and be the family that Keir wanted them to be.

Baby steps. She'd accomplished baby steps with Keir's daughter. Baby steps just might lead to much more.

Chapter 22

Two weeks later, Ryan stood at her kitchen counter, sprinkling garlic powder, Mrs. Dash, and rosemary on both sides of T-bone steaks prepared for the grill. Once the task had been completed, she added three table-spoons of Lawry's steak marinade to the steaks before snapping the lid on the container and placing it in the refrigerator to chill. Drying her hands on a paper towel, she took a moment to glance out the kitchen window.

Together, Keir, Adam, and Emily worked diligently to build a fire in the drum Ryan's parents had converted into a barbecue grill. Smiling, she watched Emily run around the side of the house and return seconds later, dragging the water hose. Keir stood at Adam's side, directing his son in the fine art of building a proper fire.

Laughing at the trio, Ryan took a moment to admire the small group. Since the heart-to-heart in her mother's room, Ryan and Emily had formed a pact. Emily began to soften toward Ryan, and a tentative friendship blossomed once Emily realized Ryan wanted to be friends. To date they had shared one treasure hunt for Bratz dolls. The trip had been a hoot. They didn't always see eye to eye, but Emily had created a place in her world for Ryan.

Yes, Keir's daughter was a princess. When the diva in training grew up, she would rule her land with an iron fist. Ryan felt sympathy for the poor soul who fell in love with Emily Southhall.

Humming to the theme song from the movie *The Fighting Temptations*, Ryan headed to the refrigerator and removed the ingredients for potato salad. She returned to the counter, peeled potatoes, and chopped eggs and onions.

It had been years since she'd enjoyed such simple pleasures . . . the constant and supporting presence of a man she cared for, maybe even loved, although she refused to look too closely at her emotions in that area. Yes, indeed, life had settled into a wonderful, happy pattern for her and her new family.

"Ry?" Keir called from the back door.

"Yeah?" Ryan answered.

Comfortably dressed in a pair of tan carpenter shorts and a ginger-colored T-shirt, Keir entered the kitchen. "We're almost ready for whatever you want to put on the grill. Maybe we should cook something for the kids to eat first?"

Keir crossed the tile floor to the refrigerator and filled a cup with filtered water from the fridge door. Facing Ryan, he watched her with a mischievous gleam in his green eyes while finishing his drink. He moved behind her and wrapped his arms around her waist, drawing her against his body. Keir made a beeline for her neck, kissing and licking the soft skin.

Ryan found herself melting against him until the first whiff of strong chemicals forced her to wrinkle her nose in disgust. "Oh!" She stepped out of his embrace.

Puzzled, he raised his head and asked, "What?"

Turning in his arms, she pinched the tip of her nose with her fingers. "You stink. Your clothes smell like charcoal and lighter fluid, my friend."

Hunching his shoulders, Keir admitted, "Well, yeah. Probably."

Ash and charcoal stains covered the front of his T-shirt.

"No probably about it. It's a fact. Do you have another shirt you can put on? This one's pretty much done in."

"I might have one upstairs." He strolled across the tile floor. "I'll just change."

"Wait. Leave that one here," Ryan suggested. "I'll put it in the washer, and when you get ready to go home, you'll have a clean shirt."

"Okay. But I suspect an ulterior motive for this 'take-off-your-shirt' stuff."

"Really? Like what?"

"You just want to see me naked."

"I want to do more than look," Ryan whispered.

"Are you interested in touching?"

"There's that," she answered, with a grin.

Doing a double lift of his eyebrows, Keir added softly, "Basically, you just want to see me strip. Am I right?"

Smiling leeringly, she answered, "Absolutely."

"I don't want to disappoint the lady of the house," he muttered, taking the bottom edge of the shirt in his hands and pulling it off his head. The T-shirt dropped on the floor, and he kicked it in Ryan's direction. "How's that?" He smiled seductively.

"Wonderful," she answered, sauntering to where he stood near the doorway. Standing on tiptoes, Ryan planted a kiss on his lips while her hands roamed over his chest. Instantly, his arms wrapped around her, and for the second time in less than five minutes, she found herself in his embrace.

Pleased with this turn of events, Ryan gave herself up to the taste of Keir's sweet lips as she lifted her arms to pull him against her.

The door bell exploded in the quiet of the kitchen,

pulling them apart. Ryan muttered, "Who is that on a Sunday afternoon?"

"I'll get it."

"Thanks, hon."

"Hey, anything for my lady."

Giggling, she answered, "Sweet talk will get you a whole lot tonight."

"I'm going to hold you to that," Keir tossed over his shoulder as he headed for the front door.

"Don't. You've got the kids this weekend."

He sighed. "Can I sell them and come back later?"

"Nope."

"That's all right. We'll make up for this delay later this week," Keir promised, strolling from the room.

Ryan tossed a dish towel at Keir's retreating back before turning to the kitchen window to check on the kids. She laughed out loud when she saw Emily point a finger at her brother and shout, "You better listen to me. I'm the boss of you. Do you hear me?" Ryan shook her head at the diva in training.

A familiar voice drifted into the kitchen. "Who the hell are you?"

Keir retorted, "Who the hell are you?"

There was a moment of stunned silence, and then Keir shouted, "Hey! Where are you going? Stop!"

Shocked, Ryan dropped the knife in her hand, wiped her hand on a paper towel, and started for the door. Too late. Helen had stormed into the room.

Keir trailed the woman. "I'm sorry, honey. This woman barged her way into the house. Do you know her?"

Too shocked to say a word, Ryan stood rooted to the spot, watching her older sister dominate the room. *Oh my God! What is Helen doing here?*

Arms folded across her chest, Ryan's older sister took her time studying Keir. Her gaze traveled from the top of his wavy dark hair down the hard planes of his bare chest, along his narrow waist, until she reached his feet. Helen turned to Ryan and asked, "Who is he?"

Keir gave Helen a taste of her own medicine. "Who the hell are you? What do you want?"

Helen addressed Ryan. "Answer the man's question!"

Finally finding her voice, Ryan said, "My sister, Helen Ford. This is my friend Keir Southhall."

"Friend?" said Helen. Immediately, Helen's eagle gaze focused on Keir, giving him a second sweeping glare. She let out a grunt of disapproval. The disdain in that one word made Ryan cringe. "I'd say there are other names for it."

"Helen!" cried Ryan.

"When did this happen?" replied Helen.

Halting her sister's tirade with a sweeping hand gesture, Ryan regained control of her voice. "None of your business. Now, what can I do for you?"

"You're my sister, and I'm here to protect you," said Helen

Shaking her head, Ryan began, "Helen—"

"Come on now," said Helen. She started across the ceramic tile floor. "You need your family."

Sighing, Ryan asked, "Why are you here?"

"Well, thanks for the warm welcome," replied Helen. "I came to see my baby sister and find out how you're doing. You went on vacation, and we haven't talked since that one time on the phone."

The back door opened and slammed shut. Emily, followed closely by Adam, raced into the kitchen.

"Dad-dee," Emily cried. "Come on. The fire's ready."

"Yeah, Dad. Check out the grill," said Adam.

Helen's eyes grew large, and her forehead crinkled into a frown. "Dad?" she muttered softly.

Ryan's heart pounded against her chest. This was not the way she wanted Helen to meet Keir or his children.

Unfortunately, what she wanted didn't matter anymore since the situation was out of her hands. She placed her hands on the kids' shoulders. "Helen, this is Emily and Adam. Kids, this is my older sister, Helen."

Emily broke out into a smile. "The doll lady?"

Nodding, Ryan grinned. "Yeah."

"Hi." Adam waved.

"I like your dolls," Emily admitted shyly.

"Thank you," said Helen.

Hurrying to the refrigerator, Ryan handed each child a container. "Keir, why don't you and the kids put the meat on the grill?"

Keir's gaze shifted from Ryan to her sister and back again. There was a question in his eyes. "Are you sure?"

"Mm-hmm. I'm fine," said Ryan.

"Okay. Emily, Adam. Let's go," called Keir.

The minute the group stepped out the back door, the older woman bombarded Ryan with questions. "What's going on here? What possessed you to get involved with a man with kids? Of course, you realize that children complicate things? Sweetheart, this is a recipe for disaster. I don't want to see you get hurt."

Sighing, Ryan returned to the sink and turned on the water, rinsing a green pepper and celery. "I'm a grown woman. I don't need you to burst into my home and save me."

The older woman stopped next to the sink and put a hand on her sibling's shoulder. "What are you doing?" Helen said in a conciliatory tone that made the hair on the back of Ryan's neck stand up. "Honey, you have a good head on your shoulders. Do you realize when you take the man, you also take his children?"

I already know about the pain in the butt stuff. Emily gave me a large dose of "I hate you" already. But she told Helen, "I know that."

"Are you sure? This isn't just about you."

"I didn't say it was," Ryan snapped.

"There are kids involved. You have to be careful."

"Helen, we're fine here."

"Okay. Tell me more about this Keir. Is he married?"

"No!" Ryan whipped from the sink, facing her sister. "Of course not. What kind of woman do you think I am?"

Helen laid a hand on Ryan's shoulder. "A good woman that may be making a bad mistake."

"Well, I'm not. Keir is divorced."

"With *two* children."

"I can count. I know how many children he has."

Nodding, Helen stepped across the kitchen to the cupboard and removed a glass. She filled her glass with cold water. "Can I ask you a question?"

"Why stop now?" Ryan answered.

"Where is their mother?"

"Shannon's around. Emily and Adam live with her. They share joint custody. The kids visit every other weekend and during the summer."

Swallowing the last of her water, Helen placed the glass in the dishwater. She returned to where Ryan stood at the window and rubbed the younger woman's shoulder. "Ryan, honey. I know your life has taken some unexpected and unpleasant turns, and you miss your husband. But, are you sure you want to make this big of a transition?"

"Of course. I've made the change."

"Have you really? Or are you using this man so that you won't have to think about what you've truly lost."

"Helen, enough."

"No. We're far from done."

"I'm done. Keir is part of my life, and so are his children. I know you think you're helping me. But you're not. Leave it alone."

"I love you. And I don't want to see you hurt. Please stop and consider what you're doing."

"Enough. Let's talk about something else. What's going on? Why are you here?"

Surprised, Helen stared at her sister. "You really don't remember, do you?"

"Remember what?"

"I came to support you. To be here if you needed me."

"Again. About what?"

"Galen's birthday. He would have been thirty-eight this week."

All of the fight went out of Ryan. She turned away, wrapping her arms around herself. How could she have forgotten her husband's birthday?

Tears formed, but Ryan refused to cry in front of Helen. She blinked rapidly, fighting back the tears. "Thank you for caring. I'm fine."

Helen asked, "Are you?"

"Yes."

"What about Galen? You're completely over him?"

Shocked, Ryan turned to her sister. "He was my husband. I can't dismiss him like a high school date. I loved him. Galen will always have a place in my heart."

"But you've moved on with Keir."

Ryan opened her mouth to respond and then closed it, without saying a word. Had Keir taken Galen's place? She glanced out the window at the man. Ryan didn't have an answer.

She couldn't let Helen see her this way. "How's your family? What's going on with Larry, Andre, and Gee?"

"Honey."

"No. Stop. I've moved on. Thank you for caring, but I can handle things now."

Helen opened her mouth, but Ryan cut her off. "I

mean it. This is my life. Let me live it my way. Just like you've always lived yours. It's my turn."

Ryan turned away from the hurt in her sister's eyes. Helen always made Ryan feel like one of her children. Ryan had been married, and Helen still wanted to treat her like a five-year-old.

Everyone had to grow up, sooner or later. It was Ryan's turn. "I don't need you to hold my hand. Keir is my support system now."

Chapter 23

Lips set in a straight, uncompromising line, Helen stared out the kitchen window, contemplating the South-hall family working together in the backyard. She turned to Ryan and stated in a dull, troubled voice, "Obviously, you don't need me anymore."

"Stop that." Ryan's heart went out to her sister. She understood how much Helen loved her. But it was time for her big sister to stop trying to run her life and protect her. Ryan reached out a hand to comfort her. "That's not true."

Shaking her head, Helen sidestepped Ryan. "I've gotten a totally different impression." Tears shimmered in her brown eyes. She turned on the heels of her loafers and marched out of the house, slamming the front door for good measure. The loud bang reverberated through the small brick house.

Guilt hammered at Ryan. Ryan hated seeing her sister suffer. After Galen died, Helen had remained at Ryan's side, helping her through funeral preparations and the dark period. Each year, Helen spent Galen's birthday and their anniversary with her younger sister. Ryan always felt grateful for her sister's support during that time.

She drew in a deep breath and let it out gradually.

Now things were different. Keir and his family were in her life, and that added a new dimension. Ryan returned to the kitchen counter to continue her dinner preparation. There would be time enough after everyone left to think about her husband and his birthday.

Ryan glanced out the kitchen window, observing Keir, Adam, and Emily. A sad smile raced across her face and disappeared. Helen had succeeded in destroying the happy mood. Everything was different.

Minutes later, Keir entered the house. Silently, he stood inside the back door, watching her. Ryan heard the door open and close. She ignored his presence, choosing instead to work at the counter.

"Hey," he said softly.

"How are things going?"

"We're almost done outside."

"Good," she replied.

"I saw your sister take off a minute ago," he stated.

Ryan nodded. Her hand shook as she sprinkled chopped vegetables over the chunks of potatoes before mixing in relish, Miracle Whip, and mustard.

Moving farther into the room, he stopped directly behind her. "Everything work out?"

No. Nothing came together. My sister's pissed off, and I wouldn't be surprised if my dead husband haunts me for forgetting his birthday. "Yeah. It's good."

"You all right?" Keir's hands rested on her shoulders, gently massaging the tight muscles.

Tears were very close to the surface, and she fought them back with superhuman strength. She was far from all right and felt Keir sensed it. But Ryan refused to discuss or take a closer look at her feelings. Not yet. Not until she was alone.

The urge to lean against him and forget the events of the day overwhelmed Ryan. That option wasn't available to her.

Keir needed an explanation to the whole situation, answers Ryan shied away from talking about. So, she offered him what she believed would appease him. "Sister stuff."

"Are you sure? The kids can stay outside for a bit if you need to talk."

"No. There's nothing to discuss."

Keir ran his hands up and down her arms. He said in a caring and gentle tone, "You know, sometimes it helps to talk things out. Maybe get a different perspective on a problem. If that's what you need, I'm here for you."

"Thanks." She handed the bowl of potato salad to Keir. "Can you put this in the refrigerator?"

"Sure." Instead of taking the bowl, he wrapped his arms around her waist and pulled her against him. Keir's erection pressed against her stomach. Her body responded, and an ache grew between her legs, slowly spreading liquid heat within her. Her body went stiff in his arms.

Slowly dropping his arms to his sides, he took a step away and did her bidding. "I need something to put the meat on. It's ready."

Relieved by the change of subject, Ryan hurried to the cabinet and removed a platter. "I'll set the table."

Leaning against the wall, he studied her, with a puzzled expression on his handsome face. He took the platter and started for the door. "I'll send Adam in to help."

"That will be good."

Fifteen minutes later, they sat down to dinner. Helen had rattled Ryan so much, she felt too anxious to respond properly to the Southhalls' queries. Adam and Emily's continual banter filled the awkward silences. She complimented the kids on preparing such a wonderful meal, although she barely ate more than a mouthful. During all of this, Keir studied her.

"Ryan," Adam began timidly.

"Hmm?" said Ryan.

"Do you"—Adam fidgeted with his fork—"do you think you'd like to come to one of my baseball games?"

The anxious expression on Adam's face tugged at her heart. Ryan refused to disappoint him, although sitting on a wooden bench in the sun didn't thrill her. Smiling reassuringly, Ryan responded, "Sure. Just let me know."

Once dinner ended, Keir rose from the table and directed, "Adam, clear the table and put the dishes in the dishwasher."

"Okay, Dad," Adam said as he picked up the water glasses and headed for the sink.

"Dad-dee, what do I do?" asked Emily.

"Pick up the silverware, and bring it to me," said Keir.

"No. No. No. I can do this," Ryan protested, reaching for the dinner plates. "You guys cooked."

Keir ignored her, pulling out a chair and patting the cushion. "You invited us to dinner and prepared most of the food. The least we can do is clean up after ourselves. Have a seat. Enjoy the show. We'll take care of the rest."

After Adam loaded the last item into the dishwasher, Keir shut it with a sharp snap. The kids flew out the kitchen door to the den. Seconds later, they were fighting over the television remote and deciding on videos.

"That's what having kids in the house will do to you. They zap all of your energy," said Keir. His remark lacked the teasing note that normally accompanied this type of remark.

"Your kids are fine. I like having them around."

"Do you? Are you sure?" Keir probed. "Because if they are a problem, I need to know."

"They're good."

Keeping a safe distance, Keir stood at the sink. His eyes searched hers for a clue to what was going on in her head. "You look worn out."

Embarrassed by his accurate observation, she brushed a hand through her hair and admitted, "Little bit. I think the week just caught up with me. Since the shutdown, it's been really busy." Boy, was that a lame excuse. But that was the only explanation she had available. She needed time to process everything, think about her husband, and get that part of her life in order.

"I'll tell you what. These two need to get home to their mother, and I've got a bit of work to finish tonight. We'll get out of your hair so that you can have an early night."

"That's probably for the best." Ryan rose from her chair and started for the door. Keir followed.

"Emily, Adam. Time to go," Keir called from the living room. The kids hurried ahead of the couple. Keir and Ryan slowly strolled up to the front door. He kept a respectable amount of distance between them.

Emily hugged Ryan and said, "Thank you for dinner."

"The dinner was delicious," was Adam's comment.

A genuine smile formed on Ryan's face. Obviously, Keir had had them rehearse their lines. "You're welcome. I'm glad you enjoyed it."

Keir stood awkwardly at the door. Slowly raising a hand to her face, he traced her jaw line with a tender finger and then kissed her gently on the mouth. "Get some rest, and I'll see you tomorrow." Hurt flashed from Keir's eyes before he quickly hid it.

Once the door slammed after him, Ryan shut her eyes and rubbed her forehead. She couldn't help it; Ryan felt such disloyalty to her husband.

Keir was rounding a corner at the studio in search of Ryan when he heard the harsh note in Glo's voice above the noise and music of workmen and the camera crew. He took a step back, out of their visual range, but close enough to see and hear.

"Ryan," Glo called, hurrying after the younger

woman. "Set five needs to be prepared ASAP. The director wants to shoot an additional scene before the end of the day."

Voice filled with exhaustion, Ryan faced her boss, with a cart filled with accent pieces. "Glo, I've only finished half of set two. Plus, I need to break down set four. Is there anyone else available to help?"

"No. We're stretched to the limit today. All I can say is get two finished ASAP, and then get your ass over to five."

Concealed behind a wall, Keir listened to the exchange. The demanding note in Glo's voice begged him to step in. Although he'd promised Ryan he'd steer clear of interfering on her behalf, Glo's tone made him instinctively want to correct the situation. Only the certainty that Ryan would never speak to him again if he interceded held him back.

A flash of annoyance crossed her face before Ryan arranged her features in a calm mask. She started down the hall, with a dismissing wave of her hand. "Okay," she called back to Glo.

Hands on his hips, Keir frowned. What in the hell was going on? Ryan had just rolled over and played dead. Since that fateful day when her sister paid a visit, all the fight had gone out of Ryan. It didn't matter what people said to her; she went along without uttering a word. Something was very wrong. Keir made a silent promise to find out the details and get to the bottom of the situation.

As he made his way down the corridor, the voices of actors, workmen, and crew faded. He gave Ryan ample time to make it to the set before following her into the room.

"Hi," he said.

She glanced in his direction and stiffened before she visibly calmed down and resumed placing the decorative vases and plants in their proper place. "Hi. How are you?"

What the hell was going on? Lately, whenever Keir got near her, Ryan stiffened like she'd just encountered a rapist. "I'm good."

The set was completely deserted except for him and Ryan. He moved closer and lifted a gold-rimmed black vase from her cart. "Where does this go?"

She pointed at a wooden curio loaded with framed smiling faces. "Second shelf between the parents' photos."

He completed this task and asked, "So how have you been? I haven't seen or talked to you in days."

"Good. Busy."

"Everything going okay?"

"Mm-hmm," she muttered, placing items around the room and then checking the sketch of the floor plan.

"How are things between you and Glo?"

"We make it work."

With his back turned to her, Keir groaned softly. For the past week, their conversations consisted of work and inquiries about his kids. She avoided any discussions about herself or what was really troubling her.

"Emily and Adam want to know when they can see you again," said Keir. "They informed me that they are now gourmet barbecue chefs, and you are just waiting for them to come over and cook for you."

That brought a petite smile to her face. "Your kids are so funny."

"Funny to you because you don't have to live with them." Keir immediately regretted that comment. What if they did decide to live together? He didn't want her to believe or feel his kids were a burden.

Silently, the couple worked together for several minutes while Keir tried to decide how to get the information he needed. There must be a way to break down the barriers separating them. If she refused to confide in him, how could he help her?

Watching her out of the corner of his eye, Keir considered ways to get her to open up. Ryan needed a safe haven. A place where she felt comfortable to discuss things with him might help. Maybe dinner away from their day-to-day life might be the answer.

Clearing his throat, Keir approached Ryan. "You know, although I enjoyed having the kids, I really missed spending time alone with you."

A spark of wariness clouded her brown eyes. She studied Keir but remained silent.

"How about a date night? Just you and me." Smiling encouragingly, Keir added, "Dinner and dancing work for me. I'd love to hold you in my arms."

Ryan took a step away from him. Her face contorted into a mask of conflicting emotions as she searched for the downside of this suggestion. "When?"

"Saturday."

She nibbled on her bottom lip and then hedged. "I'm not sure that day will work for me. Let me check my schedule. I'll get back to you. Okay?"

Disappointment gnawed at his belly. This was not the answer he wanted. Keir decided to give it another shot. "I'm not married to Saturday. If Friday or Sunday works for you, then let's go that route."

Her forehead wrinkled into a frown, while her fingers nervously flirted around the clipboard in her hand. "No. Sunday's definitely out. I've got things to do."

What things? he wondered, watching her closely. They needed to talk and soon. Keir refused to allow outside influences to destroy the relationship they'd worked so hard to establish. Putting on his most appealing expression, Keir lifted a green leafy plant from the cart. "No problem. Where do you want this?"

Ryan pointed to an end table. "Over there."

Once they completed the set, Ryan muttered a soft

thank you and went her way. Keir returned to the Eiffel Tower and moved swiftly across the carpeted floor to the desk.

Lips pursed, Keir switched on his computer and logged into the secure portions of One Leaf's database system. If Ryan refused to talk to him, he'd just have to find another way to help her. A twinge of guilt fluttered through his veins. Keir quickly banished the emotion and focused on learning the truth.

Ryan's employment application popped up, and he scrolled through the screens until he found what he needed. Nodding approvingly, he jotted down Helen Ford's name and telephone number. *Good,* he thought. After logging out of the computer, Keir leaned back in his chair and considered his next move. Should he make this call? Probably not. Unfortunately, the look of pain on Ryan's face made it impossible for him to think of anything else. She meant too much to him to allow her to continue like this.

Keir drew a thick black line under the name and then tapped the sheet of paper with the pen. Ryan's sister held the answers to all of his questions. He picked up the telephone and punched in the number, waiting impatiently for someone to answer the phone. After the fifth ring, voice mail kicked in, and he heard the voice of Ryan's older sister.

"Hello. This is Keir Southhall. We met at Ryan's last Sunday. If you get a chance, give me a call. I need to talk with you about your sister." He paused, debating whether he should add anything more. "Call me on my cell. My number is 333-1580."

Once he finished his call, Keir dropped the receiver into the cradle and shifted the chair toward the window. He hoped this intervention wouldn't blow up in his face. On more than one occasion, Ryan had instructed him to stay out of her business, let her run her life the way she saw fit. Keir couldn't do that. Ryan meant too much to him. If he had to take the hit for messing in her life, so be it. He refused to sit back and let her suffer in silence.

Chapter 24

Paper cup of coffee in his hand, Keir studied the dark rain clouds from the front window of Starbucks. A summer storm brewed, silently and deadly. If his luck held up, he hoped to be home before the heavens opened up and showered the area.

Keir checked the time. Helen still had ten minutes.

After nearly a week of playing telephone tag with Ryan's sister, he'd finally connected. Helen had responded to his call by leaving a voice message on his cell phone, suggesting they meet for coffee. He didn't care, as long as he got what he needed to help Ryan.

Ryan's older sister practically ordered him to show up at Starbucks. This meeting should be interesting because that idea didn't sit well with him. Keir seldom gave up control to another person. Unfortunately, his choices were few, and if he wanted information, this might be the only way to get it.

Keir chuckled nastily. He suspected Helen had her own agenda. She wanted to size him up. By meeting with him, Helen created an opportunity to get the skinny on him without Ryan's watchful eyes censoring her questions.

This discussion required finesse. Face-to-face provided more answers.

He finished the last of his coffee and tossed the cup in the trash, returning to the front of the cafe. Minutes later, Helen stepped into Starbucks, with an umbrella on one arm and a tote bag hooked on the other. She glanced around, found Keir, and marched across the floor toward him.

Hiding a smile, Keir watched the woman's approach. There were similarities and differences between the sisters. Gray sprinkled Helen's auburn, shoulder-length hair. Helen's sparkling brown eyes resembled Ryan's. But Ryan stood an inch or two taller.

Helen's strength of character and pride were visible and matched Ryan's. Although the years had added a few extra pounds to her small frame, Helen maintained a figure that turned heads. Ryan's older sibling made up a very nice package.

Helen stopped in front of Keir, taking a minute to do a slow examination of the man in front of her. Brown orbs probed him to his very core. When her gaze finally settled on his face, Keir felt as if he'd been stripped bare and examined like a human on an alien ship.

They made eye contact, and Keir felt the start of a new test. Every instinct inside him shouted, "Don't look away." He intended to pass this test and any others she might initiate. After a moment filled with enough tension to keep a soap opera junkie glued to the television for a week, Helen turned away, with a soft grunt.

Relieved, Keir dragged in a deep breath. She must be dynamite in the classroom. Helen knew how to hold a person captive with just the gleam in her eyes.

"Thanks for meeting with me," he offered.

"You're welcome."

Turning away, Keir took a quick sweep of the small

cafe before spotting an empty table near the back. That locale would buy them a bit of privacy. "Let's sit over there."

With a curt nod of her head, she marched across the floor after him. At the table, Keir pulled out a chair, offering it to her. Instead, Helen moved to the opposite side of the table and sat.

Okay, he thought. *This is going to be one interesting meeting.*

Helen took her sweet time settling down at the table. She placed the tote and umbrella on the chair next to her and then unbuttoned her sweater.

Keir sat patiently waiting as she completed her tasks. The woman had perfected the art of putting a man in his place while gaining the upper hand. Until he got what he needed, Keir intended to bow to her whims.

"Can I get you anything?" Keir waved a hand at the food counter. "Cup of coffee? Muffin? Cinnamon roll?"

"No. I'm fine."

Silently, the pair sat. As if she'd come to a decision, Helen cleared her throat, leaned forward in her chair, and placed her linked hands on the table. "We might as well get down to business. What do you want?"

Straight to the point. Keir liked that. "After you left Ryan's house last week, she seemed upset, and I haven't been able to get her to open up about what happened between you."

Eyes narrowing, Helen answered, "When I landed on Ryan's doorstep Sunday, my sister made it clear you were her priority. Doesn't she tell you everything?"

"Obviously not."

She hunched her shoulders and smirked. "Sorry."

Keir fought the urge to cuss. He stayed focused on his goal. "Please help me. Ryan's hurting, and I won't let it go on if I can help it."

"What does Ryan think of you getting in her business?"

"She doesn't like it."

Chuckling, Helen replied, "That's what I thought."

He demanded, "Are you going to help me?"

She leaned back in her chair and folded her arms across her chest. "No. I know my sister. If Ryan wanted you to know her business, she would have told you."

No point in lying. The truth always worked better for him, anyway. "You're right. She doesn't want me to know what's going on. Ryan's very important to me. I want and need to help."

Helen smirked.

"What?" said Keir.

"You are very different from her husband."

Keir blinked. That was the last thing he expected to hear.

"Really?"

"Mm-hmm."

"Trust me, if Galen had lived, she'd never have looked at you."

Okay, stick it to me. This isn't going the way I planned. I'll play along because I intend to get to the truth, Keir thought.

Helen didn't back down and said exactly what she meant. "For some reason, I don't see you being the type to take time to smell the roses. You're more the type to buy the flower shop and hire someone to run it for you. Mundane, everyday things don't interest you."

"That's not always true," he insisted. "I like the simple things in life."

"No, you don't. That's why my sister appeals to you. She's rare. A unique flower that you won't find anywhere else."

He liked the description. Ryan was unique. Special. "True. Let's get back to the problem at hand. Can you tell me what's bothering Ryan? She's withdrawn, and I'm worried."

Forehead crinkled into a frown and lips pursed, Helen contemplated Keir. After a long, silent moment, she came to a decision. "What has she told you?"

"Nothing."

"Do you know anything about her husband?"

"He's dead."

Dislike flashed from her eyes, and her words were sharp and cutting. "You've got that one correct. Word of advice. A little empathy won't hurt."

"This has been going on for almost a week. I don't have time for niceties. What can you tell me?"

"Galen was a med student, soft-spoken and easygoing, very caring. He wanted to save the world."

Fascinated, Keir watched Helen's face become transformed. Her expression softened as she described Ryan's husband. This was the first crack in her armor Keir had noticed since she'd entered the coffee shop. A spark of jealousy surged through him. Had Galen been that perfect?

Her eyes narrowed to minor slits. "Why should I tell you anything?" she said.

"You don't want to see her suffer any more than I do. That's why you came over Sunday, isn't it?"

Studying the pattern in the carpeting, she admitted, "No, I don't. She's my baby sister. I promised our mother I'd watch over her."

Keir took a risk. He reached across the table and captured Helen's hands between his own. "And now it's my job. Help me take care of Ryan."

"Why?"

"Because I love her," he responded. Shocked by the truth of his declaration, he leaned back in his chair and uttered softly, "I love Ryan."

Helen smiled and nodded. "Okay. Now we're getting somewhere. I would never reveal my sister's personal business to just anyone. You had to have a vested interest in her life and future for me to say anything."

"Thank you."

"Needless to say, I keep up with my sister. I visit a lot. Since you've been around, I can barely get her on the phone."

"We have things we do together," he muttered.

"Yeah, I got that. The truth is when Galen died, I didn't believe she'd recover. No surprise, Ryan loved the man dearly. But she pulled herself together and went back to work. She does well until her anniversary or Galen's birthday rolls around. She pretty much falls to pieces. I stopped by her house to check on her and found you and your family."

"Which is it?"

"His birthday is Sunday."

"What does she normally do?"

"Goes to the cemetery and cries her eyes out."

A current of protectiveness surged through Keir. Poor baby. She needed him. Keir glanced across the table at Helen and noted the expectation in her eyes. "It's my turn to reassure you."

"I'm listening."

"I love her. And I'll fight anybody that gets in the way of her happiness."

Giggling, Helen asked, "Interesting. Does my sister know about this alpha male attitude of yours?"

"She's learning," he answered. "And she doesn't always like it. But it's my job to take care of her. Protect her. Love her. And that's what I plan to do."

Chapter 25

The sun beat down on Ryan. Perspiring, she blew a strand of hair from her eyes. It had been a while since she'd visited, and it showed. An empty yellow potato chip bag, twigs, and leaves brown from age littered the grave site.

Ryan deposited the trash in a black garbage bag at her side and then leaned back on her haunches, studying the area. She nodded approvingly at her handiwork. "There. That looks better."

A family of ducks quacked as they waddled past her on their way to the man-made pond. The wind stirred, creating a gentle breeze. Ryan tilted her head, enjoying the cool air as it caressed her hot skin. "I'm sorry I haven't been here in a while. I started this new job, and I really like it. But, it's keeping me busy."

She paused. Her stomach churned, cramping. She always told Galen the truth. Clearing her throat, she amended her previous statement. "That's not completely true. I do have a lot of responsibility on this job. Other things have kept me away."

Sadness overwhelmed her as she gazed at the computerized image of her husband etched into the black marble headstone. Fresh tears threatened to fall. Galen James Mitchell had died far too young.

The impact of his death had deeply affected and permanently scarred Ryan. How had she survived without him? The answer was simple. She'd done it for her husband. Galen would have wanted her to get on with life, to enjoy everything the world offered.

"It's a different studio, with lots to learn. I'm on a weekly television series again. Set designer. You'd be happy to hear I get to do sketches. Sometimes I even use one of those computerized programs to create the sets. It's nothing like designing clothes, but I enjoy using my artistic abilities."

Hands covered in dirt, she rubbed her cheek. "Oh, Galen. It's what I've worked so hard for. It's great. The money's pretty good. I've been saving. And I plan to do some improvements on the house. I think I'm going to start with the kitchen. Have new cabinets installed. Those are good things."

For several minutes, she cleared away trash so she could add a new batch of fresh flowers. "And, of course, there's bad stuff. There's always a drawback or two. Unfortunately, the show shoots all times of the day and night, and a member of the design team has to be present."

Ryan halted, drawing her tongue across her dry lips. This part was hard to say. But, she had to. She owed him that much.

"That's not the only reason I'm here." She cleared her throat and began to speak. The words quivered on her lips. "There's something I need to tell you. I've met someone new. It's nothing like what we had," Ryan rushed to say. "This relationship is very difficult to describe." She laughed softly as an image of Keir filled her head. "He's very different from any man I thought I'd be with. Go figure."

"First of all, he's a divorced man. And he's the boss.

The big cheese. He owns the studio where I work. It's not all good." Ryan worked the soil as she continued. "And my supervisor, Glo, gives me a lot of grief about Keir. She doesn't like the fact that I'm involved with the boss. Honestly, I still have my problems with that. It's not the way I like to handle my business. You know that. I walk a fine line to keep the two parts of my life separate.

"This stuff makes me nervous. I'm a bit worried about what other producers will think and how it will affect my career. I don't want my reputation to take a hit because of my involvement with the boss." She laughed. Pride edged her words. "As if I would agree to sleep with someone to boost my career. You, above all, know how important it is for me to succeed on my own.

"That's another story. I want to talk about this new man in my life. His name is Keir. Keir Southhall. It's weird. When I first met him, I thought he was cute in an interesting sort of way. This is California, so you know what I mean." Ryan dug a spot for new flowers. "Everyone is beautiful and tanned, with perfect bodies. Something in his eyes beckoned me and made me look beyond the handsome face to see a man with ideas and morals."

Shaken by what she'd just revealed, Ryan sat silently for several minutes before continuing. "I don't like the boss thing. You know how I feel about my work. I like a clear division between work and home. Keir doesn't give a damn. He threw that particular issue right out the window the first time I mentioned it, just like he did my objections about his children. I wasn't sure if I wanted that complication in my life. The next thing I knew, I was having lunch with Keir and his kids. It didn't make a difference to him. He encourages me to enjoy the benefits of being involved with the boss. A man with a great deal of power doesn't understand making it on your own. I've worked too hard to have my accomplishments sabotaged by gossip."

Ryan sat there, enjoying the sense of peace surrounding her. It felt good to unburden herself and talk things out. "Keir's tolerant and yet . . ." She paused, searching for the proper words to describe this new and unique man in her life. Hands covered in dirt, she moved them aimlessly in circles as she conjured the perfect description. "When I wanted to keep our relationship private, he used logic to change my mind. That's not quite right. He shows me a different way of viewing things."

She pulled absently at the weeds surrounding the headstone. "I have no idea where we're headed. Certainly not marriage. But . . ." She sighed, remembering how wonderful it felt to be in Keir's arms, the sense of security he brought to her life. "I love being close to someone again. It's been a long time since I've had you with me. I miss having someone to talk to, confide in, and to rant and rave with. And believe it or not, I still miss you. He didn't take your place. That will always be yours. Keir created his own place in my life. His alone.

"What we have is for us. I didn't want to get tangled in his family and then things don't work out between us. And he's almost ten years older than I am. So there are some major differences. Ex-wife, kids, and studio. Can you imagine us as one big, happy family? That's one of the reasons I don't think marriage is an option. I just go with the flow and enjoy what the day brings.

"Well, I didn't come here to dump all my problems. I'm here to say happy birthday and tell you how much I miss you. I love you." Rising from the green pallet she'd used for her knees, Ryan gathered her gardening tools and tossed the empty flower cartons in the trash bag.

She dropped the bag in a stone receptacle at the end of the path and then started down the walkway to her car. There was no other car in sight. Next to her car stood Keir.

Shocked to find him there, she halted in the center of

the road, speechless. After a moment, she found her voice and asked, "What are you doing here?"

"I thought you might need me," Keir answered.

"Thank you." Ryan didn't care how he got there. All she knew was she was happy he'd found her.

Keir stepped away from the car, removed his shades, and shoved them into the pocket of his shirt. He opened his arms, and Ryan stepped into his embrace, allowing Keir to gather her close. She wrapped her arms around his waist and laid her head on his chest. Inhaling his scent, she snuggled closer. It felt so right to be here with him, in his arms.

Other feelings emerged, taking charge, demanding release. Pain and sorrow welled up, and tears fell. Once they started, they were impossible to control. She cried silently for all she'd suffered and lost—the death of her husband, the fight to build a life after Galen died, and the pain and loneliness of three long years.

Through all of it, Keir held her, rocking her back and forth while whispering soothing words of love into her ear. She began to heal. After a few minutes, she gained a level of composure.

"You okay?" Keir asked as he took a step back, examining Ryan's face.

Embarrassed, Ryan wiped at her dirty cheeks with her hands. She succeeded in smearing the dirt and stains.

"Here." He removed a handkerchief from his pocket and dabbed at her cheeks. Kissing the top of her head, he said, "This may not be the right moment. But I want you to know I love you."

Ryan's heart swelled with happiness. She raised her head and said, "I don't know if it's the right time, but I like hearing it. I love you, too."

"I'm glad to hear it. That makes life easier. Come on. Let's get you settled." With a hand on each of Ryan's shoulders, Keir guided her around her SUV, opened the passenger door, and helped her inside. Once he shut the car door, Keir started toward the grave site.

Puzzled, Ryan asked, "Where are you going? I thought we were headed home."

"In a minute," he called over his shoulder. "I want to talk with Galen."

"Galen?"

"Yeah," he answered.

"Why?"

"We've got a few things to clear up. Sit tight. It'll only take a sec."

Following the path that Ryan had used, Keir searched for the proper area. He found the grave and hunched down to look at the image on the headstone. It was the handsome face of a man who had died too young. Such a shame. Right now he had things to say to Galen.

"Hey, man. I'm Keir Southhall. I think Ryan told you about me."

He stooped to one knee in front of the headstone, gathering his thoughts. He'd never done anything like this before. But he believed it was the right thing. "I don't know how much of this truly works. If you can hear me. I hope so. If our roles were reversed, I would want you to come to me and tell me what's on your mind. I'm here for Ryan. So that she has a sense of peace about you and the years you spent together."

Keir glanced around. It was so quiet here. Peaceful. He refocused on his reasons for being there. "I love Ryan. Truly love her. Rest easy. I'll always cherish and take care of her. Everything I have is hers."

Swallowing loudly, he brushed the back of his hand across his forehead. This wasn't easy to do. But, he needed to do this for Ryan.

"I'll do all I can to make her happy. To make our life

good. She deserves that and so much more." *Now what?*
"I know she needs to come here and see you sometimes.
I won't interfere. I think I understand why she needs to
visit."

Keir got to his feet, looked down at the grave. "We'll
be back, I promise."

Returning his sunglasses to his face, Keir moved along
the walkway to the car. Ryan sat where he'd left her. He
got behind the wheel and held out his hand for the keys.
She dropped them into his palm.

"What was that about?" she asked.

"I wanted Galen to know that I am here for you. That
he could rest knowing I would always take care of you."

"Oh," she muttered softly.

He shifted, facing her. "Are you all right with that?
Can you let me help you when you need it? I don't want
to run your life. I love you. So I want to be available
when you need me. Okay?"

"Okay." Ryan studied the landscape around them.
"Keir, where's your car?"

"At home."

Frowning, she asked, "How did you get here?"

"Phil Berger dropped me off."

"You are amazing."

"Remember that when we get home." Keir started the
engine and put the transmission into drive, slowly
pulling away. His free hand eased over the gears and captured hers. "We've got stuff to talk about."

Smiling at him, she nodded. She felt strong, confident
that she could weather a deep discussion about the
future.

Chapter 26

After a long day at the studio and an even longer drive, Ryan pulled her car next to the curb in a middle-class subdivision of Los Angeles. She absently hummed along with Sister Sledge as they sang of family and sisters. With the engine running, she sat outside Helen's two-story town house. Lights blazed from the house's interior. Her sister's Chrysler Pacifica sat in the driveway.

I don't want to have this conversation, Ryan thought. *Maybe I shouldn't go in. All of my life Helen has cared for and protected me. How do I tell her she doesn't have to do it anymore? It's time for her to stop. I'm capable of taking care of myself.*

Sighing, Ryan mentally searched for the proper strategy to deal with her sister. She loved her older sibling and wanted to make things right between them. Unfortunately, there were times when Helen acted as bullheaded as any two-year-old toddler. Helen stood her ground and refused to budge, which helped explain her success as a middle school teacher. Students never got the best of Helen. She always ran the show, or the classroom, in this case.

Sitting in the car wouldn't solve the problem. Ryan switched off the engine, grabbed her purse, pushed open the driver's door, and got out of the car. She ran up the walkway to the tiny porch and rang the buzzer. A welcoming wreath of white and pink dried flowers hung from a hook on the door. Baskets of flowers decorated the tiny porch.

From the house's interior, she heard approaching footsteps. A tall, athletically built teenager answered the door.

Andre, Ryan's nephew, greeted her. "Hey, Aunt Ryan." The young man stepped onto the mini-porch and gathered her in a bear hug. She hugged him back and added a kiss to his cheek.

"Hi." Ryan entered the house. Although she had noticed the car in the drive, she still asked, "Is your mother home?"

"Yeah. Mom's cooking dinner. Come on in." He shut the door and then led her into the living room.

Helen loved to cook. Working full time didn't dampen her desire to prepare a home-cooked meal for her family. "You can go on in there if you want," added Andre.

Apprehensive regarding the coming confrontation, Ryan lingered in the living room with Andre. "Where's your dad and sister?"

Andre jumped over the back of the sofa and then dropped onto one of the cushions, picking up the remote and clicking on the fifty-inch television/DVD combo. "Gee's at basketball practice. Dad went to pick her up."

Good. She had a little time before they would be disturbed. Nodding, Ryan started for the door. "Check you later. I'm going to talk to your mother."

Andre waved a hand in the air and concentrated on swaying to Kanye West's latest rap video. Ryan made her way down the short hallway, passed the dining room and Helen's office, and entered the kitchen. Her sister stood at the counter, fussing over the George Foreman grill.

She lifted the lid and poked at the skinless chicken breasts with a three-prong fork before returning the lid to its previous position.

Ryan cleared her throat and said, "Hey."

Helen turned. Surprise flashed in her brown eyes, and then her body went stiff. "What are you doing here?"

Moving farther into the room, Ryan responded, "I came to see you."

"Where's your friend?"

"Which friend? I have lots of friends." Ryan decided to play dumb.

Helen scoffed at her sister's comment. "Keir."

"I don't know. Probably with his kids or at work."

Helen crossed the tile floor. She stopped at the range, stuck her hand inside an oven mitt, and lifted the lid of a steamer. Steam rose from the lid, warming the room. The aroma of broccoli and carrots mingled with chicken and garlic, permeating the room. "Are you here for dinner?"

"That depends on you."

Brows knitted into a frown, Helen asked, "What does that mean?"

Agitated, Ryan blew out a hot puff of air and moved closer to her sister. "The last time we were together, you gave me the impression that you didn't want to see me again."

"Nooooo." Helen shook her head. "I think you've forgotten or just plain left out a few facts. Ry, you were the one with the new family. Not me. Boyfriend, kids, cozy dinner at home. I was the intruder."

"That's part of what I want to discuss."

Laughing, Helen crossed the room and opened the refrigerator. She rummaged through the crisper and removed a bag of lettuce, tomatoes, and cucumbers. At the sink she turned on the faucet and washed the vegetables.

"Interesting. A week ago you were too wrapped up in your friend and his kids to talk to me. Now you have time." Glancing at Ryan over her shoulder, she asked, "What happened?"

"Nothing. Me, Keir, and the kids are fine." Ryan strolled across the room and placed her purse on the blue, yellow, and white ceramic tile table and then turned to her sister. "But, you and I aren't. That's why I'm here."

Unmoved, Helen continued the preparations for dinner. She chopped and dropped bite-size portions of tomatoes and cucumbers into a bowl. "What do you want me to say?"

"Please listen. You are my only sister, and I don't want you to be upset over Keir."

Helen snorted. "You're a little late on that one."

"Okay. This is going to be difficult no matter what. So I'm just going to say my piece. You're my sister. And I love you. I know you feel that you need to protect me."

Ryan paused, waiting for some form of response from Helen. None came. She drew in a deep breath and let it out slowly, giving herself a few seconds to decide how to proceed. "I need you to be my sister, my friend. Not my keeper or protector."

Helen whipped around to face Ryan, with a knife in her hand. "I've never done that. Whenever you needed me, I've tried to help. I promised Mom I'd watch over you, and that's exactly what I've done."

Stunned into silence, Ryan stared at her sister. She'd never suspected. Looking back at their lives, Helen's need to watch over her suddenly made perfect sense. "Ma told you to keep an eye on me?"

"Yeah. Before she died. Mommy wanted to make sure that you'd be okay."

The sense of responsibility Helen felt needed to be put to bed. They deserved a new and better relationship.

"I know our mother is resting better because you've kept your promise," said Ryan. "I thank you for being so caring. What I need now is different."

"What do you mean?"

"Don't be my mother. Be my friend and my sister. And be happy for me and Keir. I need someone to share things with. We're too old to hide from one another. Stop being my substitute mother, and be my confidante. Listen to me, and offer advice that a sister would give. I'm not Gee. Can you do that? Is there too wide an age gap for us to bridge?"

"I only wanted to protect you. Help you after Galen died."

Ryan hurried to her sister and took her hand, squeezing it reassuringly. "I know and thank you for that. I was a mess back then. There were times when I didn't think I'd recover. You helped me over that dark period. I'll always be grateful. Like with most things, time dulls the pain, and I've gotten on with my life. Whatever happens, Keir is my future. Galen is now part of my past. Can you understand that?"

"Yes, I can. When I walked into your house, I felt as if you didn't need me anymore. You had your life, and I wasn't a part of it anymore. I guess you could say it was the empty-nest syndrome." Her voice quivered. "It felt as if I was losing part of myself."

"No. No, you weren't. You'll never lose me. Things change. That's all."

"I don't want to lose my sister. And I'm worried that Keir may hurt you."

Smiling, Ryan replied, "That might happen. Galen hurt me. He didn't mean to, but he did when he died and left me alone. Keir taught me that you have to risk your heart to get the happiness you want. Sometimes there's pain. We hope for love. I'm risking my heart again. It's both exciting and frightening. Helen, be happy for me, please? I didn't believe I'd find someone to love."

Helen wrapped her arms around Ryan and held her close and leaned her forehead against Ryan's. "I am, sweetheart. I am. You deserve to be happy. And I want that for you."

"I'll always need you in my life. You help anchor me and provide the support I need when life gets too hard. Ma would be proud of you."

"I can do that. But I have to tell you one thing. Sometimes the people who love you can see things clearer than you can. That's my job. One more thing. I'm never going to stop caring about you."

Grinning, Ryan said, "I wouldn't have it any other way."

"Sometimes when people get into new relationships, they forget their family. Their thoughts are on the new person in their life. Please don't let Keir separate us."

"I won't."

"How can you be so sure?"

"We're going to get him involved with our family."

Waving a hand in the air, Helen said, "Honey, be real. He's a big-time Hollywood director and producer. Do you really expect him to have time for our little family?"

Ryan held her sister's gaze. "Yes."

"Are you sure?"

"Well, there's only one way to find out. Invite us to dinner next Sunday. If he doesn't show up and doesn't have a good excuse, then you'll know. And so will I."

"True."

"Are we good?" Ryan asked.

"Yeah. I think we are." Helen returned to the counter and unplugged the grill. "Are you staying for dinner?"

"Everything smells really good. Do you have enough?"

"Sure. I always make more than enough."

"I don't know." Ryan grinned. "Who was that man who

opened the door? If that's Andre, you need to stop feeding him. What are you putting in his food? That boy has grown a foot in the last month. Are you sure you have enough to feed us both?"

Laughing, Helen answered, "Tell me about it. You should see our grocery bill. Don't worry about it. There's always room for you."

"Then, yeah, feed me."

"Set the table."

Ryan burst out laughing. This friendly banter reminded her of so many times when she was a child and Ma would have them set the table while she finished preparing dinner. For the first time in a long time, she felt as if she had made Helen see her as an adult. Ryan went to the cupboard and removed plates and cutlery.

As they worked, a huge shadow fell over the women.

"Hi, sweetie."

Helen and Ryan turned in time to see Larry, Helen's husband, enter the kitchen. He strolled purposefully over to his wife and took her in his arms and then kissed her passionately. Coming up for air, he waved. "Hello, Ryan."

"Hi, Larry," said Ryan.

"Are you here for dinner?" asked Larry.

"Looks like it," Ryan replied.

"Good," Larry said as he set his wife on her feet and hurried to the refrigerator. "It's been a while since you've been over. I want to hear all the details about this new man in your life."

Ryan rolled her eyes. She should have known. Helen always confided in her bear of a husband. Larry was like a second father.

"Where's Gee?" Helen asked, switching off the stove.

"Upstairs. She needed a shower," replied Larry.

"That I don't doubt," said Helen. "Ryan, let's get this

meal on the table." Helen took a platter from the cupboard and placed grilled chicken breasts on it and then returned to the range for the vegetables. She stepped to the doorway and yelled, "Okay, folks. Dinner's ready. Wash your hands, and get to the table."

Chapter 27

Normally, Keir and Ryan shared their days off together. They relaxed and enjoyed each other's company in the privacy of the home of their choice. After a late morning brunch, Ryan stretched out on the sofa in Keir's entertainment room, watching a program on annual and perennial flowers presented by the Discovery Home Channel.

Humming softly to a Prince tune, Keir entered the room, plucked the remote from her hands, and switched off the flat-panel television.

"Hey! I was watching that," Ryan said as she stood, reaching for the remote.

Avoiding her eager hands, Keir placed the remote on the coffee table. "Not anymore." He wiggled his fingers and smiled encouragingly. "Come on."

Trustingly placing her hand in his, she allowed Keir to tug her along behind him. "Where are we going?"

"You'll see," Keir said suspiciously, wrapping an arm around her shoulders as he steered her through the house to the garage.

What the hell? Ryan thought philosophically. As she settled into the passenger seat of the Jaguar, she realized it didn't matter where they were headed as long as they were together.

Keir pulled into a parking space outside a store in Santa Ana. After he parked the Jag, Ryan glanced at Keir and asked, "What are we doing here?"

"It's time for me to put some furniture in the great room. You and the kids keep making cracks about my empty great room. Today is the day I'm going to finish off the house."

Stunned, Ryan stared. "You're kidding, right?"

"Does this look like a joke?" He pointed a finger at his face and the solemn expression he wore.

Pensively, she studied his expression. It was true she teased him about the furnitureless room. Normally Keir ignored her. It had never bothered him before. Why now? What was going on in his head?

"No. But why today? I mean it's been what?" She tossed her hand in the air. "You've been in that house three years, and today you need furniture. It doesn't make sense. It's odd."

Shrugging, he glanced out the car window before answering. "I've got plans for a big event later this year, and I want the place to look great before I invite people in. Is that a good enough answer for you, Mrs. Mitchell?"

Grinning, Ryan replied, "Absolutely, Mr. Southhall."

Hand in hand, the couple entered Jo Del Creations Inc. Designer Showroom. They halted inside the entrance, taking a moment to adjust to the soft lighting after the harshness of the bright afternoon sun.

A gentleman dressed in an elegant navy double-breasted suit, pale blue shirt with a white collar, and a multicolored tie with geometric designs approached them, stepping into their path. "Hello. How are you folks?"

"Fine," Ryan answered.

Scowling, Keir remained silent at her side.

Flashing a smooth smile of confidence, the man asked, "Is there anything I can help you with? Are you looking for anything in particular?"

"Actually," Ryan began, looking at Keir for confirmation, "we want to look around. If you don't mind?"

"Help yourself," replied the salesman.

"We'll call you if we need anything," Ryan added.

"Certainly," said the salesman as he gave them a tiny bow. "My name is Blair. Ask for me when you're ready for some help."

Keir dragged Ryan past the salesman to a living room display. "Come on," said Keir.

Ryan sighed dramatically. "If we must."

Confused, Keir turned to Ryan and touched her arm, asking, "What's wrong? A minute ago, you were gung ho."

"Nothing."

He tilted her head up to face him. "Something."

"I haven't done any furniture shopping since Galen died," she admitted.

"Maybe it's time to make new memories. I promise it will be painless. In an hour, we'll be on our way."

Perching on the arm of a sofa, Ryan laced her fingers with Keir's and let their linked hands swing between them. "I'll hold you to that promise, Mr. Southhall." Standing, she glanced around the display and asked, "Have you thought about what you want in the room?"

Grunting, he shook his head.

"I think you should stick with contemporary furniture. The room is large and airy. A sofa, couple of chairs, and some accent pieces would do the trick."

"Sounds nice."

Ryan ran a caressing finger along his arm. "Let's look at the upside of this situation." She moved closer, brushing her breast against his side. "We need to check the furniture thoroughly. Make sure it's comfortable and safe for everyone. That will take time together in close quarters, testing to be certain it's right for you."

His eyes lit up as he wrapped an arm around her waist, lightly dusting her lips with his kiss. "I can do that."

"I thought so."

For the next hour, they tested furniture, laughed, snuggled, and kissed on the different couches. What started as a chore turned into an afternoon filled with fun and love.

With his arms wrapped around her, Keir held her against him while kissing the side of her neck.

"Is this the Keir Southhall I know?" said a voice out of the blue.

Keir stiffened against Ryan. Turning, Ryan studied his face. An intense expression of dislike glared from his green eyes. Keir's arms dropped away from her and hung loosely at his sides as he faced the intruder. "Lakeisha," he said.

The woman sauntered up to them, with an outstretched hand. Keir ignored her hand, and eventually, it dropped to her side. Lakeisha gave Ryan approximately three seconds of her time before dismissing her, focusing on Keir.

Ryan got her first good look at the intruder. Tall, with the build of a model, the woman stood in front of them, with a hand on her hip. Hair the color of midnight, she tilted her head to the right, allowing the long tresses to fall over one bare shoulder.

"I haven't seen you since I moved. How's your family?" Keir asked politely.

"Good. Malcolm is twelve. He's in Little League with Adam. And my daughter just turned seventeen. Passion wants to be an actress." Lakeisha moved close to Keir, softly rubbing against his side.

Ryan's blood pressure shot up a notch. Who did this

woman think she was? Ryan inserted herself between the two.

Ignoring Ryan, Lakeisha added, "If you need an extra on one of your shows, give us a call."

Lakeisha's blatant plug for a job for her daughter made Keir clench his jaw. He stepped closer to Ryan and placed an arm around her shoulders. "What about your husband? What's Derek doing these days?" he asked.

"Still at the post office. I swear that man has been there for a million years. He's the district manager for the Orange County area."

"I never see you when I pick up the kids. Do you and Shannon still hang out?" asked Keir.

"Some," Lakeisha answered, studying Ryan.

"I'm sorry," Keir said and turned to Ryan. "When I lived in Malibu, Lakeisha and Derek were our neighbors. Lakeisha Foster, Ryan Mitchell."

Lakeisha nodded at Ryan and then refocused on her true prey. "Where are you living now?"

"I bought a house close to the studio," he answered evasively.

"How's that little Emily? She was always such a character," Lakeisha said as she flipped a lock of hair over her shoulder.

"Still is. Are you and Derek still in the same house?" said Keir.

"Yeah," replied Lakeisha.

Keir nodded and then cupped Ryan's elbow. "Well, we have our day planned, so we'll be moving on. Tell Derek I said hello. Take care."

"You, too," said Lakeisha. She took Keir's hand as they passed her and kissed his cheek, following that gesture with a seductive stroke of her hand on his arm. "See you soon."

"Not if I see you first," he muttered.

"That was interesting," Ryan stated, watching the

retreating figure. "Care to add in the backstory? Bring me up to date."

"Next-door neighbors when Shannon and I moved into the house. The woman wouldn't take no for an answer. Royal pain in the ass most of the time." His voice had a bitter edge.

"I gathered that."

"I'd come home from work, and she'd be sitting in the kitchen with Shannon. We didn't have a moment's peace. Lakeisha always flirted with me." His face scrunched up as he spoke of this awful time in his life. "Came to the house in revealing clothes and hung around when Shannon wasn't there. When I mentioned it, Shannon didn't see it. She thought I wanted to isolate her, to keep her from having any friends."

"My poor baby."

"Hopefully, we won't see her at Adam's games. I'm not in the mood for a game of dodge her busy hands."

Taking pity on him, she asked, "How would you feel about my hands spending some quality time in new and interesting places on your body?"

"Anytime. Anyplace."

"Well, not anyplace. Certainly, not here. But, I can think of a few locations that'll work for me."

Keir pulled her into a loose embrace and hugged her. "I love you. You know that, don't you?"

"You've mentioned it a couple of times. But, it's always good to hear it again."

Slipping his arm around her shoulders, he guided her back to the living room displays. "Come on. Let's finish shopping and go home."

"Sounds good to me."

Chapter 28

The hot July sun beat down on the trio as they made their way along the fringes of the baseball diamond. Leading the way, Ryan climbed the stairs to the top row of bleachers and walked along the narrow edge of concrete until they found the perfect spot to watch the baseball game. Emily held Ryan's hand tightly, trailing the woman as her father brought up the rear.

Ryan chuckled, marveling at the changes her life had undergone since meeting Keir. Her eyes lovingly stroked his features. He represented more than a boyfriend. A new blended family had emerged from the rubble of Keir's divorce and the death of her husband.

If anyone had told her she would be looking forward to attending games for her boyfriend's son, she'd have laughed in their face and then called that person a liar. But here she stood, eager to spend the next two hours on a hard wooden bench, cheering on Adam's team, the Raptors.

Keir slipped into the space next to Ryan, placing a picnic hamper loaded with plastic containers of Sunny Delight, Subway sandwiches, fruit, and bags of potato chips on the bench next to them.

Commandeering the middle section of the top row of wooden benches, Ryan and Emily settled on the wooden bench and gazed toward the baseball diamond, searching for Adam's blue and white no. 12 Raptors uniform.

"Have you spotted him yet?" Keir asked.

"No," Ryan answered.

He studied his watch for a second. "We've got about fifteen minutes before the game starts. We can relax."

Several rows below them stood Lakeisha Foster. The woman looked exotic and enticing. Lakeisha stood in the stands, dressed in a fuchsia halter top and tight black racing shorts. Dark hair flowed freely across her bare back. "Keir! Keir!" she shouted.

In contrast, Ryan felt like a frump in a loose-fitting cinnabar-colored top and chocolate shorts.

Emily pointed a finger at the woman and said, "Look Dad-dee. That's Miss Foster."

Instantly, Keir stiffened beside Ryan. She placed a hand on his thigh and whispered, "Don't let her get to you. Remember, when we saw her at Jo Del's, she told us her son played ball with Adam."

Nodding, he tried to relax, and some of the tension oozed from his body. "You're right. It doesn't look as if we're going to be able to get away from her. We might as well get used to seeing her."

"Or ignore her," Ryan added, with a grin.

Laughing, Keir nodded. "Hold on. I think the game is about to start."

The teams ran out on the playing field, and everyone stood to sing the national anthem. Once the last note faded into the air, the team managers ambled purposefully to the mound. The umpire produced and tossed a coin in the air. The Falcons won, giving them the first turn at bat. The Raptors took their places on the field as the first Falcon player stepped up to the plate.

Two hits, one run, and three outs later, the bottom half of the first inning started. One strikeout followed, and then it was Adam's turn at bat. He walked up to home plate, with his blue helmet in place and the bat slung over his right shoulder. As he prepared for the first pitch, words were exchanged between Adam and the catcher.

Adam grabbed the handle of the bat tighter. Between swings, several verbal exchanges occurred. Keir and Ryan were too far away to hear what was said. From both boys' body language, it wasn't good.

Leaning forward, Ryan strained to see what was going on. Frowning, she turned to Keir. "Something's not right."

Stretching forward, Keir said, "Yeah. I know. I don't know what."

The umpire flashed one finger in the air. "Strike one."

Nodding, Adam stepped away from the plate and tapped the dirt from his shoes. He repositioned himself at the plate, ready for the next pitch. Ryan bit her bottom lip, waiting for the next throw. "Come on, Adam," she muttered softly. Suddenly, Adam's head turned toward the catcher as the ball zipped by.

"Strike two," came the umpire's call. The umpire flashed two fingers.

"The catcher is messing with Adam," Ryan said to Keir. "Do you know the catcher?"

"No. Hopefully, Adam can settle down and ignore the idiot."

Three balls later, Ryan and Keir were on edge waiting for the final pitch. Nervous, Ryan nibbled on her nail. Keir's hand found hers, and he held her hand. "Come on, Adam. Come on," he said under his breath.

The pitcher wound up and threw the payoff pitch. Adam swung and hit a line drive between the shortstop and second base. He dropped his bat and raced to first base.

Emily, Keir, and Ryan hopped up like tops, yelling

encouraging words to Adam as he rounded first base and sped toward second. By this time the shortstop had recovered the ball and tossed it toward second. Adam slid into the plate, missing the second baseman by inches.

Thrilled, Ryan tossed her arms around Keir and jumped up and down. Excited beyond words, they clung together for several long moments. "He did it! He did it!" she chanted.

"That's my boy," Keir said, with pride.

People stared at them. "I guess we should sit down," Ryan suggested, following the idea with action.

As the day and game wore on, the score flip-flopped several times before the Raptors came out victorious. After the game, Ryan, Emily, and Keir went down to the playing field, searching for Adam. As they descended the stairs, Lakeisha Foster appeared. "Hey, Keir," she said.

"Lakeisha," Keir said matter-of-factly.

A large boy strolled toward the small group. When he reached Lakeisha's side, they saw that he carried the catcher's headgear for the Falcons. This was the child who had possibly upset Adam. Lakeisha placed a hand on the boy's shoulder and asked, "You remember Mr. Southhall, don't you?"

Malcolm nodded.

"His son played on the other team today," Lakeisha added.

Keir held out a hand to the boy. They shook hands. "Well, see you. I've got to find my son," said Keir. With a slight nod of his head, he moved away.

Adam appeared from the dugout and started for his family. Ryan reached him first, wrapping her arms around him. "Congratulations! We were so proud of you," she told him.

Grinning broadly, Adam hugged her back. "Thanks."

Keir hugged his son close. "You did a wonderful job. Great game! I told you anything worth having has to be worked for. You worked hard, and I'm proud of you, son."

Adam's gaze slipped past them to where Lakeisha and her son stood. His eyes narrowed to slits, and there seemed to be a menacing glare in the boy's eyes. Malcolm's gaze landed on Adam, and they exchanged a meaningful look.

Curious, Ryan followed the direction of Adam's gaze and found his eyes on Lakeisha's son. Her gaze shifted from one boy to the other and then back again. Okay, what was going on here?

Malcolm had been the catcher while Adam was up to bat. What had the child said to Adam? Was this more than simple competition? Ryan wasn't sure. The situation didn't feel right.

She wasn't the only one who noticed the silent exchange. Keir studied the boys for a moment. He grabbed the hamper and said, "Let's get out of here."

Emily slipped her hand in Ryan's. Ryan laid a hand around Adam's shoulder, and they trekked after Keir to the parking lot. Once the picnic hamper had been stored in the trunk of the Hummer and everyone was buckled up, they pulled out of the lot and onto the street, heading to the expressway.

It didn't take long for Emily to fall asleep. She laid her head against the door frame and promptly shut her eyes. Minutes later, they heard the soft hum of her snoring. For several minutes everyone was silent. Once Keir got the car on the highway, he asked, "Son?"

"Yeah," said Adam.

"Did something happen while you were up to bat in the first inning?"

Adam hesitated. He fidgeted with the shoulder strap of his seat belt, plucking at the harness cutting across his chest. "Why?"

"Well, you didn't seem as focused. It looked as if something was going on, and Ryan and I were concerned," replied Keir.

The boy sighed. "It was okay."

"Was Lakeisha's son bothering you? Saying stuff that upset you?" asked Keir.

"Yeah, Dad." Adam's lips were pursed as he considered his answer. "He was being a jerk, trying to mix me up."

"What happened?" asked Keir.

The boy shot a quick glance at Ryan before saying, "Mal kept saying stuff."

"What kind of stuff?" Keir's forehead was crinkled into a frown. There was a cautious quality to his questions.

"About us. Momma and you," said Adam.

"Really. Mm," replied Keir. His calm tone belied the way his hands gripped the steering wheel. "Whatever Mal said doesn't mean anything. He doesn't know anything about our family."

"It just made me mad," said Adam.

"I know you don't want to hear this. But you're going to have to learn to control your feelings," said Keir. "Tune out the bad stuff so that you can concentrate on the game."

Head lowered, Adam muttered, "I know."

"Son, don't get me wrong. I'm not criticizing you. Talking bad to you is how people make you lose your cool so that you can't do your job. They talk a lot of junk, and before you realize it, you've screwed up. Don't let that kid destroy all the hard work you've done this summer. Understand me?"

"Yeah," Adam whispered.

"Good. Let's get back to the good stuff. Your team won, and we're proud of you," said Keir.

Ryan remained silent throughout the discussion. Something in Adam's face and tone bothered her. The way he glanced at her when Keir mentioned the stuff Mal had said. She had to get to the bottom of things. Whatever Mal had said, it had greatly upset Adam.

Chapter 29

"Strike three. You're out," the umpire yelled.

The young boy's shoulders slumped, and dejectedly he dragged the bat through the dirt as he slowly headed back to the Raptors' dugout.

Ryan's heart went out to the child. She wished she knew of a way to make him feel better and to remove that forlorn expression from his face.

Keir turned to Ryan. Frustration was etched deeply into his features, and he warned half seriously, "If this game doesn't pick up for the Raptors, it won't last much longer."

"I hear you. But, we can't give up," said Ryan. Ever the optimist, Ryan patted Keir's thigh reassuringly. "There's still another hour to play. The Raptors can rally and win the game."

Slowly shaking his head from side to side, Keir grimaced. "I hope you're right. With a score of four to zero, their hopes are fading."

"We've got to keep a positive attitude, Keir. It's not over until it's over."

"I know."

She glanced down at the sleeping child. Emily's head rested in Ryan's lap, and her little body stretched along the opposite side of the wooden bench. Fifteen minutes into the game, she'd dropped her head onto Ryan's thigh and had promptly gone to sleep. Ryan stroked the little girl's cheek. Baseball moved at too slow a pace to hold Emily's attention.

Frowning, Ryan focused on the game, doing a mental check of the number of batters who went down in order. So far, five of the nine batters had had some sort of verbal interaction with the Falcons' catcher.

Ryan rested against the warm lines of Keir's body, watching the teams switch positions. "Each time the Raptors come up to bat, the catcher stirs them up. Could he be messing with their concentration? You know, like before. Like he did with Adam?" she asked.

Keir's dark eyebrows were slanted in a frown. He leaned over the bench to get a better look at the catcher and player. "Could be. I know they're kids. But they're supposed to be trained to ignore stuff like that."

"You just said it yourself. They're kids. It's not that easy," Ryan said dubiously. "There are adults who can't ignore stuff like that."

"True."

The Falcons went down without scoring a run. The Raptors ran to their dugout as the Falcons trotted onto the playing field. When Adam jogged to home plate for his turn at bat, Keir rose and cupped his hands around his mouth. "Adam, stay focused."

The boy waved at his dad and then readjusted his helmet, preparing for the first pitch. Without warning, Adam stiffened as the bat fell from his shoulder. He turned to the catcher. His lips moved rapidly. They were too far away to hear the details of the scene unfolding in front of them. Ryan leaned forward, intent on Keir's son. *Come on, Adam. Don't let Malcolm get to you,* she said to herself.

Regaining his composure, Adam took several practice swings and then took his position at the plate, waiting for the pitch. The first ball left the pitcher's hand and flew past Adam.

"Strike one," cried the umpire, flashing one finger.

Beside Ryan, Keir winced, while the line of his mouth tightened a fraction.

Ryan's fingers crept between Keir's as they sat together. Tension floated through the air as they waited for the next pitch. One strike and two balls followed. Adam stood at the plate, waiting for the next pitch.

Screaming furiously, Adam threw down the bat and helmet and charged at the catcher. He flew across the small space. The full force of Adam's body sent Malcolm smashing against the ground. Seconds later, they were rolling in the dirt, tossing punches.

Surprise siphoned all the blood from Ryan's face, and she cried, "Ohmigod!"

"Holy shit!" In a lightning-fast move, Keir sprang up and bounced down the long flight of stairs.

A huge crowd of players from both teams spilled onto the baseball diamond, surrounding the fighters. The umpire and managers fought their way through the hordes, aiming for the boys in the center of the dispute. Finally, the umpire got to the center of the group and pulled the two boys apart.

Malcolm kicked at Adam, missing him by inches. Adam broke away from the umpire and landed a punch on the catcher's jaw. The kid staggered backward, toppling over.

When Keir reached the bottom of the cement stairs, all hell had broken loose. A Falcons player had bumped against a member of the Raptors team, and a shoving match had commenced between them. Within seconds players from both teams were fighting, tossing punches, and shouting threats.

The brawl on the baseball field rivaled any professional hockey game scuffle. Chaos reigned.

Worried Adam might be hurt, Ryan gently shifted Emily's head off her thigh and placed the child's head on the bench and stood, trying to see the playing field above the heads of other curious onlookers. The crowd gathered around Adam and Malcolm made it impossible for her to get a glimpse of Adam or see what Keir was doing. *Please don't let him get hurt,* Ryan silently prayed.

A bullhorn blew from somewhere in the stands. The sound jolted everyone on the baseball diamond. This ruse gave the umpire and managers time to separate the players. The umpire held on to Adam with one hand and Malcolm with the other. The catcher continued to take swings at Adam. One of his punches landed on the umpire's chest.

"You're out of here," the umpire yelled at Malcolm, pointing a finger at the dugout. "Get your gear and go."

Adam grinned. A devilish bearing of his teeth revealed how much he was enjoying Malcolm's dilemma.

The umpire shifted his attention to Adam. Ryan felt her heart slam against her chest as she gnawed on her bottom lip. Things weren't over. Adam needed to pay for his part in this brawl.

"What are you laughing at?" The umpire gave Adam a hard, quick shake. He pointed at the clubhouse and added, "You do the same thing. Neither one of you guys will be playing for a while. The next time you feel the urge to toss a punch, you'll think twice and have more respect for the game. Go!"

Finally, Keir appeared on the baseball diamond, on the fringes of the crowd. He squeezed between the outer circle of players and spectators. Keir pushed his way to the center of the group, taking charge with quiet authority. "Do you know what caused this?" he asked the umpire.

"It doesn't matter. I won't have this type of behavior at my games," replied the umpire. "Both boys displayed poor sportsmanship by inciting this free-for-all. I can't allow that to go unpunished."

The Raptors' top man nodded, pointed a finger at each boy and then shoved his thumb towards the clubhouse. "Game over. Dugout."

In contrast, the Falcons' manager began to talk fast and furious. Pointing at Adam, he said, "My player didn't start it. Why should he be kicked off the team for something that kid started? That's where the poor sportsmanship comes in."

"Don't blame all of this on my son," warned Keir as he pointed a finger at the manager. "There were two people involved in this."

The umpire concurred. "They both participated, and they'll both receive the same punishment."

"Son, come on. Get your stuff," Keir said as he placed a hand on Adam's shoulder and steered him away from the group.

Ryan picked up the still sleeping child and hurried down the steps. She met Keir at the bottom of the stairs, and they left the ball field together.

Tension stretched the silence to the breaking point. Everyone climbed into the Hummer and sat, still and quiet. Keir maneuvered out of the parking lot and made his way to the highway. Once he merged into highway traffic, Keir asked quietly, "Son, what happened?"

An expression of pain and then regret flashed in Adam's eyes, surprising Ryan. What had Malcolm said to upset Adam so much?

"Well?" Keir said.

"He made me mad," replied Adam. He poked out

his bottom lip and stared out the window at the moving traffic.

"How?" asked Keir.

Adam pulled at the leather strings of his baseball mitt and then rubbed a hand against his forehead. "Mal kept talking junk."

"Junk? Like the last time?" replied Keir.

"Sort of," the boy answered evasively.

"Mm." Keir mulled that comment over before asking, "If it was the same crap, why didn't you ignore him?"

Agitated, Adam admitted in a tone rough with anxiety, "Because he kept saying bad things, and I couldn't let him get away with it."

"What kind of bad things? About you?" Keir asked. He took his eyes off the road to glance in the rearview mirror at his son huddled against the back door.

Up to this point Ryan had stayed out of the conversation. The pain in Adam's eyes unnerved her. A shadow of alarm touched her heart. There was much more to this story. Ryan felt it.

She glanced at Keir. His closed, guarded features increased her misgivings.

She touched Keir's arm, drawing his attention away from the child. "Why don't you let it go for now?" she asked.

Keir shook his head. "Can't. I need to get to the bottom of this. That's the only way I'm going to get it sorted out. If Lakeisha is behind Malcolm's remarks, then I've got to get my facts right so I can talk to her and Shannon."

Ryan tried another approach, lowering her voice so only Keir could hear her. "Adam's really upset. A lot has happened today. Give him a little bit of time to recover. You don't have to talk to Lakeisha today."

"No," Keir vetoed. "I need to sort this out now."

There wasn't much she could do. Ryan turned to Adam and mouthed the words, "I'm sorry."

"Adam, what kind of junk did Malcolm say?" asked Keir.

The boy squirmed in his seat. Finally, he said, "He said stuff about us!"

"Us? Like what?" asked Keir.

Shaking his head, Adam scrunched up his little face, and his eyes darted in Ryan's direction. A wave of apprehension swept through her, turning her stomach into knots.

"Stop pussyfooting around and tell me," Keir demanded. His eyes darkened with anger. "I'm not going to punish you. You didn't do anything wrong. I want to put the blame exactly where it belongs. I believe it belongs on Lakeisha and her son. Nothing can be done until you tell me everything."

This story was far from complete. In the months Ryan had known both of the Southhall children, they had never raised a hand at each other or at anyone else. The pair teased, but a malicious word never left their lips. Whatever happened between Malcolm and Adam had pushed the boy to the breaking point. He was not the kind of child to instigate a fight for the fun of causing a ruckus or being the center of attention.

From the expression on Keir's face, ferreting out the information wasn't improving his mood. He wanted answers, and Adam's responses were not dampening Keir's frustration, they were adding to it.

"Adam?" Keir prompted. The stern note in his voice sent a chill coursing through Ryan.

Grimacing, Adam quickly turned away. He tied and untied his baseball mitt's loose strings into knots. Finally, he answered. "Mal kept saying bad things about Ryan."

"Ryan?" Keir repeated.

Ryan gasped. What could Malcolm possibly know about her? And the more important question, why would he talk about her?

"What did he say?" she asked.

Adam's head hung, and his cheeks turned red. "I don't want to say."

"It's okay," Keir assured him. "Tell us."

"Malcolm called Ryan a b-b-bitch," said Adam. He hesitated over the next part. "Like a prostitute."

Embarrassment flushed Ryan's face beet red. Appalled, she turned toward the window so that they couldn't see her. *Ohmigod.* Why would a kid talk like that about someone he didn't know?

Keir reached across the transmission gear and touched Ryan's arm. "You okay?"

Nodding, she continued to stare out the window. She didn't want him or the kids to see the tears swimming in her eyes.

Whispering softly so that the kids didn't hear him, Keir assured her, "This is not your fault. Don't think it is."

Now that Adam had made his confession, the words practically spilled from his lips. "Malcolm said Ryan broke up you and Mom."

Keir's hands were clenched tight around the steering wheel, but he spoke calmly. "Adam, you know that's not true. Your mother and I were divorced before I met Ryan."

"I know. He made me mad," replied Adam. "Malcolm called Ryan a home wrecker. And that's why you and Mom can't get back together. Ryan keeps you apart."

Awakening from her nap, Emily added, "He don't know anything about our family."

"Honey, you're right. Sometimes people make up cruel things to hurt you," Keir explained to the little girl. "That's what Malcolm did to Adam. He wanted to make him feel bad so that he'd mess up when it was his turn at bat."

"Malcolm's stupid," the girl stated. "He never

comes to our house. How does he know anything about us?"

Grinning, Keir responded, "Exactly. Think Adam. He knows nothing about us."

But Lakeisha does. Either she said those things to her son or to someone else, and he heard her. Home wrecker? Ryan thought. Keir and Shannon had made several attempts to make their marriage work before divorcing last year.

"Is that why you went after him?" asked Keir.

"Yeah," Adam answered softly.

"Malcolm doesn't know jack about our family. It's obvious that he was making things up. Don't let him or the things he said get to you. Besides, they're only words, and you shouldn't let anyone bring out your anger that way," said Keir. "But I understand how you felt. I don't want anyone saying cruel things about Ryan, you, or your sister. Especially, if they're untrue."

They were silent for a moment, and then Keir said, "Thank you for defending her."

"Your welcome," murmured Adam.

"From now on, when someone makes cruel remarks like that, talk to the umpire, team manager, or come to me. Don't let things boil over or take them into your own hands. When you do, the situation could end like it happened today. Think, Adam. You may not be allowed back on the team," said Keir.

"But, Dad—"

"No. Son, listen to me." Keir waved away Adam's objections. "Defending Ryan was a good thing. But, it cost you three games and possibly your part in the championship. Let an adult handle it. Do you understand me?"

"Yeah," muttered Adam.

"Good," said Keir.

Throughout the exchange, Ryan sat quietly, staring out the window. Name-calling and lies didn't bother

her. Using Adam to hurt her and Keir did. He was just a little boy trying to have some fun. He didn't deserve that.

Keir glanced Ryan's way as he stroked her cheek. "Ry?"

"Hmm?" Ryan whispered.

"Are you all right?"

She nodded.

Keir's hand found hers and linked them together. "Want to tell me what you're thinking?"

What exactly was she thinking? She wasn't sure. This should not have happened. He was a child trying to enjoy a game. Instead, Malcolm had subjected Adam to the taunts and lies of another. Lies specifically designed to hurt him. No child deserved to be treated that way.

Keir's gentle voice penetrated the fog of pain she felt. "Don't let this upset you," he said. "It's the cruel gossip of someone who doesn't know us. Please don't let it stress you out. We'll get everything figured out together."

Nodding, she sat silently, replaying Malcolm's vicious words in her head. She came to one conclusion. Something had to be done, and she was the person who had to do it.

Chapter 30

Keir turned off the lamp and switched on the night-light. He brushed the hair away from Emily's sleeping face. Grinning, he leaned close and kissed her cheek. "Good night, baby."

Satisfied his little princess was out for the night, Keir tiptoed out of the room and gently shut the bedroom door before moving across the hall to Adam's room. After peeking at his son, Keir felt secure in the knowledge that both children were fast asleep after devouring two large pepperoni pizzas and a liter of orange soda.

Drawing in a large gulp of air, Keir headed for the stairs. Now the real work began.

Ryan needed his full attention. Although she tried to hide it, he knew today's events had shaken her to her core. Keir didn't want Ryan obsessing over the incident. His tenderhearted woman took everything so personally.

He entered the kitchen and found her stuffing the empty pizza boxes into the trash. "Hey," he muttered, with a smile. "You didn't have to do that."

"No problem."

"Thanks."

"Are the kids asleep?" Ryan folded the dish towel in half and returned it to the counter to dry.

"Dead to the world." He moved close and wrapped his arms around her shoulders and swayed back and forth, gazing into her troubled brown eyes. "How about you? Are you all right?"

"I'm okay. Just a little tired." She held him close, with a hand around his waist.

Brushing a gentle finger across her bangs, he kissed her forehead. "Let's chill out awhile before you head home."

"Okay."

Keir led her to the entertainment room. She sat gingerly on the edge of the sofa and waited for him to take his place next to her. "Want a glass of wine?" he asked.

"Nah. I've got to drive home. I'm fine."

Nodding, he sank into the spot beside her and rested his arm loosely around her shoulders. Her body felt like a board against him. Tension radiated from her. A quick and disturbing thought entered his mind. Ryan was psyching herself up to tell him something major. Keir glanced at the closed, uncompromising expression on her face and clenched his hand into a fist along the back of the sofa. Whatever she planned to say, Keir felt certain he wasn't going to like it.

Never one to back down from a fight, Keir decided to meet this crisis head on. With a little finesse, he might be able to defuse the situation. "What's on your mind?"

Surprised, Ryan's lips parted. "Am I that obvious?"

Amused, he planted a quick kiss on her lips, admitting, "Only to people who know you. Come on. Care to tell me what's going on in your head?"

"My mom," she stated softly.

Thrown to the left by her comment, Keir shook his head. "What?"

"While I was putting away the pizza, I thought of my mother and the way she raised my brother, sister, and me. How she believed every child deserved a good start in life."

Okay, now he was nervous. Ryan's topic of the conversation confused him. A flutter of uneasiness surged through him. Although she'd opened up more about her past, Ryan didn't make trips down memory lane without a reason. When he'd sat down next to her, Keir had fully expected Ryan to talk about Adam and the fight between the boys. No way had he been expecting a discussion about her childhood and her mother.

"No matter what happened around us, my mother always made sure we were untouched, protected from the bad things going on in the world," she said. Her faint smile held a hint of sadness. Ryan's words were softly uttered, but an ominous quality surrounded them. "I believe whatever happens in your childhood colors the rest of your life. Mom believed strongly, almost obsessively, that every child deserved a good start."

Lost regarding what Ryan wanted him to understand, he remained quiet. As long as she talked, it gave him an opportunity to glean her thoughts. Hopefully, that would help him plot out a course of action that would counter Ryan's plans.

"When I was about three, a new family moved on our block. The couple had two kids, a boy about eight and a daughter of about four or five." A tiny smile came and went on her lips. "It's been so long, I don't remember their names." Forehead wrinkled into a frown, she dismissed the thought with a wave of her hand. "That's not important. Domestic violence surfaced between the parents soon after they settled in. And then signs emerged that the boy might take after his father. He kept bullying his younger sister. Jealousy fueled his anger. I remember a couple of times, my mom mentioned her concerns to the wife. The woman refused to listen and accept responsibility for it."

Ryan paused, fidgeting with her fingers.

Keir waited, wondering what he could do to turn this around. Ryan's ramblings didn't offer any insights into what road she planned to take them down.

"Anywho, when nothing changed," Ryan continued, "my mother refused to let me play with them because she felt they were a bad influence for a three-year-old. Mom believed in removing us from any unpleasant environment. She didn't want that negative attitude around her children."

"Ry," Keir prompted, touching her hand.

She shook it off before continuing. "There were a few situations like that while I was growing up. But my mom always took charge and immediately pulled me from the bad stuff." Her voice broke miserably. "My life is filled with good memories. She made sure of that."

Listening, with growing dismay, Keir sought a way to comfort Ryan.

Swallowing loudly, she stated thickly, "Emily and Adam have been through a lot."

Okay. This conversation kept going all over the board. He couldn't keep up. What new torture was Ryan planning to inflict on him?

"What do you mean?" he asked.

"They've suffered through the breakup of your marriage. A divorce. And they're shuffled between your and your ex-wife's homes. That's a lot for kids to handle."

"Don't worry about them. They're doing well. All their needs are taken care of and most of their wants."

She patted his thigh reassuringly. "I know. I'm not criticizing."

"What are you saying?"

Ryan turned on the sofa, facing him. "Keir, don't be upset. This is not about you and me. It's about your children. Adam and Emily need your protection. And to do that, it's up to me to step out of the picture."

The uneasiness that had plagued him since entering the kitchen surged into panic. "No. Stop. Listen to me. They don't need to be protected from you. Emily and Adam love you."

Tears glittered in her eyes, and her voice quivered. "Yes, they do."

"Doesn't it count for anything?"

"More than you know. And that's why we have to end this."

Keir threw his hand in the air. "No. We're not going down that road a second time. I refuse to accept that."

"You can't deny it. This is a far cry from what I want from you. Keir, I love you and don't want to leave you."

"Then don't. And I love you," he added.

"It doesn't matter how we feel. Your kids have to come first. They deserve a good start in life. Emily and Adam need the stability and security that you can't offer them with me in the picture. It's time for me to leave."

It's time to take charge of this situation. Make Ryan realize that she's not responsible for what happened today. None of this is her fault, he thought. "What we encountered today could have happened any day. Don't take on a situation you didn't instigate. Lakeisha fed her son a bunch of crap, and he bought it. It's not your fault."

"I know. My being around doesn't help the situation. Your kids need your attention full time. Your loyalties are divided with me being around. Concentrate on them."

Desperate to make her understand, he held her hands between both of his and tugged until she looked at him. "No. No. No. You're wrong. You're a big part of their lives. How do you think they'll react when they find out that you don't want to be around them anymore?"

"It'll hurt at first. But after a while the kids will be fine. If you do your job, it'll all work out."

Sighing heavily, Ryan rose from the sofa and dug in her pants pocket for her keys. She left the room and started down the marble hallway to the front entrance. A sense of helplessness and terror raced through Keir as he followed Ryan out the door and down the front walkway. Panicking, he reached for her, saying the first thing that came to him. "You can't do this. We've gone through so much to get to this point. Think about that."

Ryan allowed him to pull her into his arms, holding him as if she'd never planned to let him go. "I love you," she whispered and then backed away and climbed into her car. Seconds later, she pulled out of the driveway and drove the car out of the gated community.

Keir tossed and turned most of the night. Around four he gave up and climbed out of the bed. Although it would be hours before the kids stirred, he needed to do something. He ambled into the kitchen and made a strong pot of coffee and took a cup into the great room.

Keir stood in the center of the room, looking at the furniture Ryan and he had chosen. That Sunday afternoon seemed so far away. They'd laughed and teased each other, enjoying their time together. After everything had been said and done, they had made the selection for this room as a couple, like a family.

He chuckled softly, remembering how Ryan insisted they try out each piece of furniture. It had been one hell of a ride. She was an essential part of his life. Keir didn't know what he would do without her.

Shutting his eyes, Keir relived the last moment Ryan

had been in his home. With a heavy heart, he shook his head, turned out the lights, and returned to the kitchen. Ryan's presence lived in every room of this house. How had that little woman stamped herself so completely in every nook? After all, they'd only been together a few months.

I'll get her back, he vowed. All he needed to do was give her a little space and time to think the situation through. Ryan loved him, and she'd come back. There were other issues to deal with. What should he tell his kids?

The truth always worked best. Kids smelled a lie quicker than a prosecuting attorney.

Keir checked out the contents of his refrigerator and cabinets. Sausage and French toast might keep them occupied so they wouldn't ask too many questions. Keir chuckled. He could hope.

Emily would be the one to question her father. She loved Ryan and would expect to see her.

Although Ryan refused to stay overnight when the kids were visiting, she always returned for breakfast, or they packed in the car and went to her house. She never missed a meal because she loved his cooking.

A couple of minutes after nine, the children stirred. Emily tended to be the early bird of the pair. Keir heard the bathroom door slam, and a few minutes later, the toilet flushed. Soon afterward, the action was repeated. They were both up and would expect their breakfast.

He removed a skillet from the overhead rack and placed it on the range, adjusting the flame underneath it. As he placed sausage patties in the skillet and stood at the counter, mixing eggs and milk, Emily entered the kitchen. Keir hid a smile. His baby girl was quite the princess. His princess looked adorable with her Dora the Explorer pajamas buttoned up wrong. Emily's hair stood all over her head. One side was flat from the position she'd slept in.

"Hi, Dad-dee," she greeted, slipping into a chair at the island.

"Good morning, baby."

Puzzled, the little girl looked around the room and asked, "Where's Ryan?"

Before Keir formed an answer, Adam shuffled slowly into the room. "Mornin'," said the boy. He took the chair next to his sister. "What you fixin' for breakfast?"

"French toast and sausage," replied Keir.

"Sweet!" said Adam. He was quiet for a moment. "Hey. Where's Ryan? Are we going to Ryan's house?"

No point in putting it off. Keir drew in a deep breath and let it out. "No."

"Why not?" asked Adam, his brows knitted together in surprise.

"Ryan won't be here today," said Keir.

"Why?" his daughter asked.

Keir took another deep breath, giving himself a minute to think. "Ryan decided she needs a little alone time."

"Not from us," Emily responded confidently. "She loves us."

Keir couldn't deny that. "Yes, she does. But, things are a bit more complicated."

"How?" Adam quizzed. A suspicious line marred the corners of his mouth. "Dad, she's not mad at me, is she? 'Cause I can call and say I'm sorry."

"No. Ryan's not mad at you," Keir said. He felt as if he were walking on shifting sand. That much was true. Her pain was directed at herself.

"This is my fault," Adam decided in a dull and troubled tone.

"No, it's not. Son, you didn't cause this."

"Is she coming back?" Emily asked. Hysteria touched her words.

"I think so," said Keir. "She just needs a little alone time. We have to give her that."

"Dad-dee, I want to talk to her. Can we call her?" said Emily.

Fighting the pounding in his head, Keir thought, *Jesus!* This was harder to do than he'd expected. The kids had gotten really attached to Ryan, and he wasn't answering their questions effectively. *Hell!* He didn't know how to respond.

"Not yet. Soon," said Keir. "I want you guys to understand, Ryan isn't mad at you. There's a lot going on, and she needs a break." Keir turned to the range and flipped the sausage. "Ryan will be back. I'm sure of it."

At least I hope I'm right, Keir thought, grabbing a loaf of bread and removing several slices. *If I'm wrong, I'll have to find some way of convincing her to return to us.*

Chapter 31

Adam had a plan. At night, in the quiet of his bedroom, he mapped out the details.

Since the baseball game, they hadn't seen Ryan. He felt really bad about what happened that day and how it changed his father and Ryan's relationship.

Dad was a wreck. Although he tried to pretend everything was fine, Adam knew different.

And he missed Ryan. She was so cool. When he first asked her to come to his baseball games, he thought she'd make up some excuse, but she hadn't. She always showed up to cheer him and the team on.

She was family, his family, and he wanted her back in his life. Even Emily kept questioning Dad about Ryan and asking him to take them to visit Ryan. Dad talked and talked, but he never gave them a straight answer. Dad needed Adam's help. It was his job to help his father make up with Ryan and put things back on track.

His father looked so sad all the time. He tried to hide it. But, Adam saw how Dad gazed at Ryan's picture. And he kept it on the nightstand next to his bed.

Adam blamed himself for the breakup. His father kept telling Adam that he hadn't done anything wrong and repeating that Ryan would return to them after she had time to consider things. But Adam knew better. If he'd stayed cool at the baseball game and hadn't fought with Malcolm, things would be different. Dad wouldn't feel so alone.

The next morning, Adam felt the time had come to put his plan into action. In exchange for baseball, Mom and Dad made him attend a summer school enrichment program. He didn't mind because summer school lasted only a few weeks. Although what he really wanted to do was sleep late, stay home, and watch TV.

Monday morning, Mom pulled the car up to the front of the school. Adam hopped out of the car and waved good-bye. His mother waited at the curb while he strolled up the long concrete stairs, opened the red double doors, and entered the private school building. The central hallway was cool, dark, and practically empty.

Adam started down the hall to the community room. Each morning the students and faculty met there before classes began. The teachers took attendance, described the day's program, and then sent the students on their way to the appropriate classrooms.

The principal dismissed the students, and they dispersed to their classrooms. Adam shot down the hall to the lavatory. He listened at the lavatory door for the halls to clear. Once the halls emptied, he planned to sneak out of the building through the side door. He leaned against the door, listening. It took forever for the laughing and screaming to fade and eventually die away. Adam pushed the door open a crack. The halls were deserted. *Cool!*

Easing out the lavatory door, Adam raced down the hall, slowing as he neared the school's main office. Ducking away from the door, he tiptoed past the office and out the side door. He let out a sigh of relief when the alarm didn't go off.

Once he made it to the street, Adam pulled out his cell phone and called a taxi from the list he'd made yesterday. Ten minutes later a yellow sedan pulled up to the curb. He climbed into the backseat and said, "One Leaf Studio."

The driver studied him from the rearview mirror. One eyebrow rose skeptically. "Kid, how do you plan to pay for this trip?"

Adam considered showing the driver the money he'd siphoned out of his piggy bank. But, the driver didn't need to see it. For now all the cabbie needed to know was if Adam could pay the fare. And he could. Using his fiercest voice, Adam responded, "Don't worry about me. My dad is meeting me at the studio. He'll pay the bill when we get there."

The driver scratched his head, examining the boy in the mirror. "Okay, kid. Just so you know, if you don't pay up, I'll call the cops."

Adam leaned back in the seat and placed his book bag on his lap. "It's not going to be a problem."

Nodding, the driver pulled into traffic, and they made the drive to the studio in silence. Adam didn't care. The less said, the better. Besides, he wanted to rehearse his speech in his head before doing it aloud.

Thirty minutes later, the cabbie braked outside the main gate of One Leaf. The man behind the wheel turned to face Adam, saying, "What's your father's name?"

"Doesn't matter." Adam shoved the money into the slot and left a twenty-dollar bill for a tip. He scooted out of the backseat and stood on the curb for a moment before tossing the book bag strap over his shoulder and approaching the guard's shack.

"Hi, Clay," Adam called.

The uniformed man smiled down at the boy. "Hey, Adam. What's going on?"

"Nothing. I'm here to see my dad."

Nodding, the guard pulled out a computer printout and scanned the pages. "You're not on the list, but that's okay. That sometimes happens. Do you want me to get you a cart and driver? Or call your dad to come and pick you up?"

Shaking his head, Adam shifted the book bag from one shoulder to the other. "Nah. I'll walk. I know how to get to the Eiffel Tower. Besides, I don't want to disturb him."

The guard studied the distance between buildings. He clipped a badge to Adam's polo shirt. "I don't know. I'll watch you, okay? That way I'll know you made it safe."

The guard stepped out of the shack and locked the door. "Be careful. Watch for cars. I don't want your dad on my back if something happens to you. And I'll see you on the way out."

"Thanks, Clay. Bye." Waving, Adam hurried up the driveway toward the studio. Before he entered the building, he glanced back at the gate and saw the guard waiting, with his hands on his hips. Adam waved and darted inside the door.

He strolled through the studio like he owned the place. No one questioned his right to be there. Kids were a common sight on the sets. Plus, most adults were too busy doing their own thing to worry about one lone child.

Dodging construction workers and camera people, he finally reached Ryan's office. He stood outside the room, mentally rehearsing his speech. Pacing, Adam crossed his fingers, hoping Ryan would be alone. The possibility of having to talk personal stuff around Glo bothered him. Besides, the old lady might take it into her head to call his dad, and the whole trip would be messed up.

Biting his bottom lip, Adam softly knocked on the door and then turned the doorknob, peeking inside the office. Ryan sat at her desk, with a sketch pad in her hands, facing the window.

"Come on in." She swiveled the chair toward the entrance. She gasped, and her eyes grew large. "Adam!" Standing, Ryan dropped the pad on the chair and hurried across the room to the door. "What are you doing here?"

"I came to see you," Adam answered simply.

Ryan's look of surprise quickly shifted to suspicion. "Does your father know you're here?"

He shook his head.

"Where are you supposed to be?" asked Ryan.

Adam looked away as heat warmed his cheeks. She'd put him on the spot, and he was embarrassed. "Summer school."

"Then why aren't you there?"

He hunched his shoulders but remained silent.

Ryan took his hands and drew him to a chair against the side of her desk and patted the cushion. "Sit down," she said as she sank into her spot and then reached for the phone.

Obeying, Adam dropped the book bag on the floor and sat. "Don't," he said a moment later. "Please."

She replaced the receiver without dialing. "Okay, Adam. Come on, honey. What's going on?"

"I came to talk to you."

"With me? About what? Why didn't you use the phone?"

"I wanted to tell you in person that I'm sorry."

Ryan's forehead became crinkled. Leaning back in her chair, she said, "I'm confused. Sorry? About what?"

"Fighting with Malcolm and letting him say those bad things about you. I didn't mean to cause trouble between you and my dad."

"I know you didn't. Don't worry about that. It's all forgotten."

"But you don't talk to Dad or Emily and me. So I thought you were mad at me, and I needed to tell you, I was sorry."

She took Adam's hand. "Honey, listen to me. You didn't do anything wrong."

"If I didn't do anything wrong, then why did you leave us?"

"I didn't leave you," Ryan denied quickly. "Keir and I decided to cool things down a bit."

All the words rushed out of his mouth at once. "You don't come over to Dad's anymore. We miss you. And Dad's so sad. I'm sorry. I didn't mean to cause trouble. Please come back."

Grimacing, Ryan shook her head. "No. Not now. Everyone will be fine. Just give the situation a chance."

"Emily and me, we miss you. Dad needs you."

Tears appeared in Ryan's eyes. She cleared her throat and turned away, brushing at her cheeks. "Your dad and I decided to spend a little time apart. This will give your dad more time with you and your sister."

Ryan's version made Adam mad. She had never treated him this way. He jumped to his feet, sending the chair flying against the wall. The cushion went in one direction, and the steel frame teetered back and forth on its back legs before righting itself. "Don't talk to me like I'm a baby. I know how things are going between you and my dad. Emily and me saw the same thing happen with my mom and dad."

This time Ryan's cheeks flashed red. "No, honey. You're wrong. It's not the same."

"Then what is it?" he demanded.

"I'm sorry. You're right. I shouldn't treat you like a baby. You're not. So I'll be honest with you."

Nodding, Adam returned to his chair, waiting.

She brushed her bangs from her eyes. "After the stuff at the game, I got really upset. I didn't want you and Emily to be hurt that way. It wasn't fair. I talked with your dad and explained to him that I felt you and Emily needed more time alone with him. We agreed to stop seeing each other for a while."

"How long is a while?"

"I don't know."

"That's not right," Adam declared.

"What do you mean?" she asked.

"Nobody asked us. Everybody's making decisions about us without talking to me or Emily. How would you feel if somebody did that to you?"

Ryan swallowed loudly before admitting, "Not real good."

"Maybe I didn't want you to stop coming around. Maybe I had something real important to tell you. You should have talked with Emily and me before running away."

For a moment, Ryan sat, fidgeting with the sketch pad. She turned to him and said, "You're right. I shouldn't have left without explaining the situation to you and your sister. I left the explanation in Keir's hands. I believed your father could do a better job than me."

"Ryan, do you love my father?"

"What?"

"You heard me? Do you love my dad?"

Ryan looked away. When she spoke, her voice trembled. "Yes."

"Then why can't you be together?"

"Things are complicated. There's more involved than

your dad and me. I don't want you guys to be hurt by things people say about me. You were defending me when you should have been having fun."

"You're my family. My dad taught me to take care of the people I love. And I love you."

"Oh, honey." She pulled him to her and hugged him close. "I love you, too."

Adam wrapped his arms around Ryan. He'd missed the hugs and kisses she always gave him. "Please come back," he requested softly. "We miss you."

"I miss you, too."

Adam took a step away, holding Ryan's gaze with his own. "Then why won't you be with us? Having fun, going to the park or movies?"

"I just can't right now."

"When?" he pressed.

"I don't know."

"You don't like us anymore, do you? Because I did a really bad thing."

"No. It's not you. It's me. I can't talk about this anymore." She rose and held out her hand. "Come on. Your dad needs to know where you are."

He took her hand. "Ryan, will you at least call sometime so I can talk to you? I have a cell phone."

"We'll see."

"Which means no," he mumbled bitterly.

"No. It means we'll see."

Following her out of the office, Adam fought the urge to cry. He'd failed. He hadn't been able to convince her to give them a second chance, and he didn't know what to do.

Adam pulled his emotions together and made another promise. There had to be another way. He'd find it and bring his dad and Ryan back together.

Chapter 32

Phil Berger paced the Eiffel Tower, with a clipboard in one hand, a pen in the other, while an unlit cigar hung from the corner of his mouth. "Those last two episodes went way over budget, my man. We're going to have to scale back for a few weeks to stay within the quarterly projections."

Keir sat with his legs propped on top of his desk, watching Phil work his way through a list of issues. "Yeah. I caught that."

"I'm shifting some of the shooting schedules so that we won't accrue as much overtime."

"That'll work." Keir dropped his feet to the floor and jotted a few notes on a yellow pad. "I'm going to have my assistant schedule a meeting with the department heads to make certain they are aware of the tight budget and limit their spending."

"Good move." Phil checked an item from his list.

"I've already shifted some funds to handle the deficit. We're going to have to hold down the costs until we balance this out."

"I hear you, boss."

"Are the sets completed for the next few shows?" Keir rose and then strolled across the floor to the window.

He hoped to get a glimpse of Ryan on the set. Since their breakup, he'd rarely seen her. Ryan kept to herself, did her job, and went home without making any fuss.

Waiting until he regained Keir's attention, Phil chewed on the end of his cigar. When Keir glanced his way, Phil answered, "Sure are. We can save some dollars there. The shooting schedule for the next couple of weeks will use previous sets. They're ready to go."

Keir nodded. "Good. That's what I want to hear. Anything else?"

"No. That's the end of my list." Phil slipped his pen inside the slot at the top of the clipboard. "We're all set."

"Good."

While Keir leaned against the floor-to-ceiling window, he felt a shift in the room. Tension filled the room. Phil shifted uncomfortably from one foot to the other. It reminded Keir of one of those climactic moments in the movies when all of the secrets are revealed. With a raised eyebrow, he waited, focusing on Phil.

Phil cleared his throat. "I have a question or two regarding another issue."

"Go for it."

"It's a delicate matter."

"Personal stuff?" Keir asked.

Berger grinned.

Sighing, Keir shook his head. "My personal stuff."

"Pretty much, my man."

The studio gossipmongers were buzzing with questions about him and Ryan. No one but Phil Berger had the balls to bring it up with Keir. Lifting a dismissing hand at his production manager, Keir faced the window, searching for Ryan. "Not today."

Phil raised a hand. "Hey, my man. It's not my business, and I won't push. But, if you need someone to talk to"—

Phil shook his free hand as if there was a phone in it—
"give me a call."

"Thanks, man. I'm okay." *No, I'm not*, Keir thought.
But I'm a man. We don't discuss our personal feelings that way.
"I appreciate the offer."

Phil shoved the cigar into the breast pocket of his
shirt, strolled across the office floor, and opened the
door. "Anytime, my man. Anytime. I'll catch you later. I
need to have a word with the director's assistant."

"Later."

Keir scanned the sets, searching for Ryan. He felt so
alone without her. What was he going to do? After three
weeks, Ryan remained aloof and as stubborn as she had
been the night she left his house. The only reason he
allowed her to leave without a fight was that he truly expected her to come back after a few days of thinking the
situation over.

Boy, had he been wrong. Ryan barely acknowledged
his presence when she found herself in close quarters
with him.

Somewhere in the back of his mind, he expected to
make her see reason or corner her and force her to talk
about their problems, work out a solution, and find a
way back to each other. A sour smile spread across Keir's
face. Seeing Ryan at the studio was a rare occurrence.

Dwelling on his problems didn't seem to help, so Keir
decided to return to his desk and get some work done.
He reached for an envelope loaded with bills requiring
his signature. Work always provided the best therapy
until he figured out his next move. As he worked his way
through a stack of invoices and checks, his cell phone
rang.

He brought the phone to his ear and said, "Southhall."

"Keir?"

"Who else would it be, Shannon? It's my phone."

"I don't have time for this. Play those games with your girlfriend."

He leaned back in his chair, twirling the silver Cross pen in his hand. "Love you, too. What do you need?"

"Is Adam there with you?" she asked urgently.

Keir's brows furrowed over his green eyes. What was Shannon up to? "No. Shouldn't he be in school?"

Hope dashed. Shannon's voice picked up a note of panic. "He's missing."

Shocked, Keir sat up straight in his chair. Fear caused his heart to slam against his chest. He squeezed the pen in his hand so hard that it left an imprint in his palm. "Missing? How?"

"I-I-I," Shannon stammered.

He didn't give her time to answer. Instead, he bombarded her with more questions. "What do you mean? Nobody snatched him, did they? You took him to school this morning, right?"

"Of course, I did," she answered defensively. "Just like every morning. I waited at the curb until he went through the front doors, and then I took off. I had things to do."

Frowning, Keir asked, "Where's Emily?"

"Right here next to me."

He sighed, happy one of his children was safe, and then asked, "Has Adam said anything to you? Maybe he wanted to get your attention?"

"No. Although, he has been a little quiet since he got back from your place. Preoccupied, rather than unhappy, would be the way I'd describe his mood. Otherwise, he's been fine. Did anything happen at your place that might have upset him?"

Immediately, Keir's thoughts shifted to the fight at the game and the subsequent fallout with Ryan. He didn't plan on exposing his private life to his ex-wife. Instead, he gave Shannon the trailer instead of the whole movie. "The incident with Lakeisha's son, Malcolm, really upset Adam. He's not the kind of kid to get in trouble. I'm sure it's probably still preying on his mind."

"Could be."

"What about his friends?" Thinking fast, Keir tried to consider every option. "Anyone he might go to if he felt he was in trouble? Or needed a break?"

"No one I can think of. But the school called a few minutes ago. Father Perrin said Adam disappeared right after they took attendance this morning. He never showed up for his first class."

Keir glanced at the clock on his desk. Shaking his head, he said, "It's damn near eleven o'clock. Why are they just calling me?"

"From what the Father explained to me, the office never calls parents right away. The kids hide everywhere, including in the lavatories or in other classrooms. So they do a thorough sweep of the building before alarming anyone."

"I'm on my way." Grunting, Keir rose from the desk, fished the keys from his desk drawer, and shoved his wallet in his back pocket. "I should be at your place in twenty minutes."

Shannon asked hesitantly, "Should we call the police?"

"Not yet. Hopefully, he just skipped class and is hanging out with his buddies."

"Is there anything I need to do?"

Standing in the center of his office, he debated for a moment. "Shannon, why don't you call the parents of the neighborhood kids while you're waiting? If they know anything, maybe we'll get lucky, and they'll tell us. And don't forget to ask Emily. She always knows what's going on."

"I hope you're right."

"Me, too," Keir admitted, taking note of the fact that his hands were shaking. "Sit tight. I'm on my way."

"Please hurry," she said softly.

"I will. My cell's on. If you hear anything, call."

"I will."

"And Shannon?"

"Yeah?" she answered in a worried tone.

"We'll find him."

Keys in hand, Keir headed for the door, intent on leaving the building. Since the incident at the Little League game, Adam had been acting differently. For the past few weeks, his son had been quiet and withdrawn. No matter what outing Keir suggested, the kid didn't show any interest. He suspected this disappearance was related in some way to the incident with Malcolm. Whatever the reason, he planned to find his son and bring him home.

Storming out of his office, Keir barely missed running into Ryan. "Sorry," he muttered, reaching out a hand to steady her. Before he could wrap his head around the fact that she was at his door, Keir noticed his son at her side. His eyes went over the boy, searching for any signs of injury. Ryan wrapped a protective arm around Adam's shoulders and pulled him against her side.

"Adam!" Keir exclaimed, hugging his son. "Where have you been? Your mother just called. She's frantic!"

Embarrassed, Adam hunched his shoulders and refused to look at his father. The boy shuffled from one foot to the other as a dull streak of red crept up his neck and settled into his cheeks.

Shrugging, Ryan explained, "Adam's fine. He came by the studio to talk with me."

Shifting into father mode, Keir faced his child. "Son?"

Ryan cleared her throat, gaining the attention of Keir and Adam, and said, "I can see that you two have things to discuss. I'll leave you to it." She kissed Adam on the cheek and turned away. "Keir, it was good seeing you."

"Thanks for bringing Adam back to me." Keir said as he pulled out his cell phone and hit the prepro-grammed number for Shannon. "I just got off the phone with his mother and was on my way to search for him."

Smiling gently, Ryan touched Keir's hand. He squeezed her hand and held it a moment longer than necessary. "No problem. Go easy on him. Adam's heart was in the right place."

"I'm calling your mother, and then we're going to talk," Keir said as he tipped his head toward his door. Head bowed, Adam shuffled into the room.

"Shannon. I got him," Keir said into his phone.

"Thank God! How is he?"

"He's fine. I'll tell you the details when I bring him home. We're going to have a little talk first."

"How long before you get here?" she asked.

"Give us an hour. See you." Keir disconnected the call and shoved the phone into his pocket before reentering his office and shutting the door after himself. He marched across the room and sat on the edge of the desk, folding his arms across his chest. "Want to tell me what's going on?"

Silent, Adam stared at the carpeting.

Voice edged with steel, Keir asked, "Care to tell me how you got here?"

"Taxi."

Jesus! Keir felt his blood pressure soar as his face scrunched up. Using superhuman control, he quickly re-arranged his features into a calm mask. Anything could have happened. Kidnap, rape, even death might have been the outcome if the driver had any nefarious ideas or an inkling as to the identity of the boy he was chauf-feuring around town. "You realize you might not have made it here? The cabbie could have done anything to you."

"I was careful."

Hands clenched into tight fists, Keir bit the soft inte-rior of his jaw, fighting to hold on to his temper. "Where did you get the money?"

"My bank."

Shaking his head, Keir moved behind his desk. Adam slid into the chair in front of his father.

"Why?" said Keir.

Silence filled the room. Adam refused to look at his dad. He rubbed his nose and played with the strap on his book bag while chewing on his bottom lip.

"Adam?"

"I wanted to talk with Ryan. Me and Emily miss her."

Holding Adam's gaze with his own, Keir asked, "Did your sister help you do this?"

"No."

Putting on his sternest father's voice, Keir said, "You realize you scared your mother and me to death."

Fidgeting with his hands, Adam mumbled, "Sorry."

"Sorry is not what I'm looking for." Keir jumped out of the chair and rounded the desk, standing over the boy. "You're my son, and I love you. I want you to be safe. Anything might have happened, and that's part of the reason we were so worried."

"I know."

"Don't do this to us again," Keir demanded.

"Dad, do you love Ryan?"

Adam's question caught Keir with his mouth open. The last thing he expected to hear from his son was a question about Ryan.

"What's that got to do with anything?" Keir asked.

"Well, do you?" Adam's eyes compelled his father to answer.

At once it felt as if their roles had been reversed. Keir was the child, and Adam, the adult. Through the years, Keir always told his children the truth, and today wouldn't be any different. "Yes, I do."

"She loves you, too, Dad. Did you know that?"

Those words swelled in Keir's heart. Keir wanted nothing more than to go to Ryan and demand she end this self-imposed exile and come back to him. But the reality of the situation was love wasn't enough.

Adam approached his father and placed a hand on his shoulder. "If you love each other, why can't you be together?"

"It's more complicated than that, son."

"How? Tell me."

Keir tiptoed through this situation. "It's not just about Ryan and me. She's concerned for you and Emily."

"You always told me that anything important in your life was worth fighting for. Don't you want to fight for Ryan, Dad? Isn't she important enough?"

"Adam—"

"Ryan's great! She loves you and us. If you love her back, you should fight for her."

Keir ran a tired hand over his face. Lord, so much truth all at once was making his head hurt.

The boy continued to hammer at his father. "Dad, we miss her. Things feel as bad as they did when you left home. Please don't let things go the same way. Emily and me want to go to Ryan's house and do things with her like we used to. You know, like go to the park, the zoo, and dinner."

His son had a major point. Wasn't Ryan worth fighting for? Like a person emerging from the depths of a drug-induced sleep, Keir cleared his head, and he realized his son was correct. Why had he rolled over and played dead for the past few weeks? Ryan was truly worth any effort, and it was time for him to fight and win her back.

He patted his son on the shoulder. "Thanks, son."

With a puzzled expression on his face, Adam mumbled, "Huh?"

"Thanks for waking me up, making me see the light."

Keir missed Ryan and the time they spent together. The nights they enjoyed together, holding each other and just talking. Evenings dining out, followed by hours of making love.

Laughing, Keir hugged his son. "You're right. Ryan is worth fighting for."

Adam drew one hand into a fist, jerked it down, and yelped, "Yes!"

"Adam, don't get your hopes up," Keir cautioned. "I can't guarantee anything."

"You're going to try? Right, Dad?"

"Absolutely." He placed an arm around his son's shoulder. "Come on. Let's get you home to your mother."

"Okay." Adam grabbed his book bag and trailed after his father.

Keir stopped in the doorway. He shut and locked his door after Adam. The pair started down the hall to the front of the building. "You're in trouble with your mother. You know that, don't you? That is not a good thing."

Head bowed, Adam nodded. "Sorry."

Keir steered his son through the studio maze. At the exit, he turned to Adam. "When we get you home, you better do some Oscar-worthy apologizing to her, or you will probably be grounded until you're fifty."

"Can you help me out, Dad?"

Pursing his lips, Keir shook his head. "Sorry, Charlie.

Not this time. You made this bed. Now you have to sleep in it."

Sorrowfully, Adam sighed.

When they reached the Jaguar, Keir watched Adam climb into the car and buckle his seat belt. Chuckling softly, Keir shook his head and thought, *My twelve-year-old son has more sense than I do.*

Chapter 33

With a heavy heart, Ryan slowly returned to her office. Even though she and Keir had only been together for a few moments, seeing him had stirred all her emotions into a fiery ball of frustration and pain.

Ryan halted outside her office, praying her pigheaded boss was on the set and not in the little cubbyhole they shared. Pacing back and forth, Ryan grimaced, fighting the cramps created by the stress of this situation. Seeing no point in delaying, she turned the knob, opened the door, and stepped inside.

Good! An empty office.

With a sigh of relief, Ryan hurried across the floor to her desk and sank into the chair. She swiveled toward the window, finger combing the hair at her nape.

Lord, she couldn't keep this up. All of this drama had her on edge, affected her sleep, and hindered her ability to eat. Adam's visit to the studio had sent Ryan into a tizzy. Since the night she left Keir's house, she'd cut off all contact with the man and his children, hoping this would make separation easier. Unfortunately, Adam's insights into her relationship with his father had been right on target. But, Ryan refused to relent. Above all else, Adam and Emily's happiness remained paramount. Her own well-being came in a poor second.

With the scent of Elizabeth Arden's Red Door perfume, Glo burst into the office. Arms loaded with scripts and sketch pads, she stopped and looked around the small space before heading to her desk. The mass of paper slipped from her arms and landed on her desk, sliding across the surface. "Where's your company?" Glo asked.

Surprised, Ryan stared at Glo. How did she know about the child? "You saw Adam?"

Glo shook her head. "No. My hand was on the door-knob when I heard his voice. I kept going so you two would have a bit of privacy."

Not sure how to respond to this act of kindness, Ryan mumbled, "Oh. Thank you."

Glo sank into her chair and began to clear her desk. She gathered the scripts and sketch pads, stacking them into neat piles. Next came the loose pencils and pens. Glo bunched them together and dropped them into the middle desk drawer. "So tell me. When did you split with Keir?"

Ryan's eyes grew large, and her cheeks burned scarlet. Her feelings were too raw to discuss, so she needed a topic change. Besides, why would she talk with Glo? The woman had made it clear how much she loathed their pairing.

Stalling, Ryan ran her tongue across her dry lips before deciding to ask a question of her own. "How do you know about that?"

The older woman scoffed, leaning forward in her chair like she was talking with an old buddy. "Please. It's all over the studio."

Great! Her coworkers were spreading rumors about her and Keir. Ryan turned toward Glo. "I hate this kind of gossip. It was one of the reasons I didn't want to get involved with Keir."

"That's something you need to get over," Glo advised, tucking her feet under her body.

"What?"

"Honey, people are going to gossip whether you like it or not. It's human nature to be curious. And let's be honest. Keir is too interesting a topic to ignore. The gossipmongers want all the gory details when the story involves someone big at the studio."

"I've never wanted my private life to be on display."

Shrugging, Glo said matter-of-factly, "Get over it. It was. It is."

Ryan moaned sorrowfully.

"Oh, come on. It's not going to change how you do business. Ryan, you've always worried about your reputation and how being linked with Keir would affect your career. It never mattered. You already have a spotless reputation. Everyone knows you get the job done. Your skills speak for themselves. So stop moaning and pissing over what other people think. They don't pay any bills in your house. It really doesn't matter."

Doubtful, Ryan replied, "I guess you're right. Everyone already knows that Keir and I split up."

Glo remained quiet for a moment. "Emily and Adam got to you that much?"

Confused, Ryan stared at her boss. "What? How do you know that? Did Keir tell you that?"

"Well, there's no point in me lying. I heard you talking to Adam."

Embarrassed, Ryan swiveled the chair away from Glo and faced the wall. Generally, people who eavesdropped pretended they didn't know the details of the conversation they overheard. Peeved, Ryan glared at Glo, saying, "Who told you about us?"

"Nobody. I listened at the door." Without a speck of remorse, Glo added, "What happened?"

Ryan waved away the question and said, "Nothing." For a beat she sat silently, and then she said, "Something." She wondered what was inciting her to confess all of this to Glo, a woman who had treated her cruelly. Maybe she needed to tell someone, and Glo was in the right place at the right time. Whatever the reason, Ryan started to talk. "There was a big upset at a baseball game, and Adam got into trouble. I found out later that it was over something the other kids said about me. Adam and Emily are great kids. I don't want to see them caught in the middle of a lot of adult crap."

"What about Keir?"

"What about him?"

"Oh, come on, Ryan. He's done everything within his power to make you happy. I can't believe he'd let you walk away that easily."

An overwhelming sense of sadness and loss washed over Ryan. She wanted to cry her heart out for all that she'd never have again. But she refused to shed a tear in front of her boss.

Ryan loved Keir so much. This was the second time she'd lost someone she truly loved. It didn't get any easier. Actually, she felt as if she'd left her heart at Keir's house. *God!* She rolled her eyes. That line sounded like dialogue from a soap opera.

"Your concern for Keir's children is commendable," said Glo. She stood and approached Ryan's desk, perching on the edge.

"I'm not doing this for brownie points." Ryan's voice trembled. "This is damn hard."

Glo ran her manicured fingers through her hair, fluffing the blond locks. "I'm sure it is."

An uneasy silence followed. Wallowing in her own misery, Ryan ignored the older woman.

"Honestly, I'm seeing you in a different way," Glo stated.

"How so?" Ryan inquired. Maybe focusing on something besides her own problems would make her feel better.

"Over the last couple of months, I've accused you of a lot of things. For lack of a better term, I thought you were a gold digger. Within months of getting this job, you started dating the head of the studio. In my gut, I believed you were using Keir to further your career. And then Keir began to make changes on the set to accommodate you. That burned my ass." Glo hissed between clenched teeth.

Yeah, Ryan remembered all of that and more. Plus, how difficult it had been to work with Glo.

"But that was only one of my issues," Glo admitted softly. "Your presence threatened me. You did excellent work, and people liked you. I got really worried about my position."

Shaking her head, Ryan said, spacing the words evenly, "I don't want your job. I like what I do. It's satisfies my creative nature, and I can leave the rest of the studio crap to you."

"Thanks. I think." Glo's hand dropped to her side. Her tongue ran across her red painted lips. "I'm beginning to believe I might have misjudged you."

Ryan snorted. "What brought you to that decision?"

"Your eyes are full of pain. And nobody in this business puts anyone ahead of their own needs."

Embarrassed, Ryan turned away. She didn't want Glo's sympathy. What happened between her and Keir was their business, and she could handle the fallout.

"You love Keir. Don't you?" asked Glo.

Instead of a question, Glo had stated a fact. The lightbulb had finally switched on.

"Yes."

"I would suggest you take a minute and think long and hard about your decision to split with him."

"I can't let his kids take the hits for what we've done. Adam was protecting me. He shouldn't be doing that. Emily and Adam deserve to be happy, to have a safe and comfortable childhood. Every child deserves that."

"You're right. They do."

"They've already been through enough. Their parents are divorced, and now they're shuttled from house to house. I won't add more problems to their young lives."

"What about you?" Glo's voice had an infinitely compassionate tone.

Frowning, Ryan answered, "I don't understand."

"You've suffered, too. Your husband died in a tragic and totally unnecessary accident." Glo stood, with her hands on her hips. "What do you deserve? Haven't you earned a shot at happiness?"

"I can't put myself before Keir's children. That wouldn't be right."

"Where did you get that idea?"

"My mother. And she backed up those words with action."

Glo folded her arms across her chest. "Maybe your mother did. But, this is your life. You don't have any kids."

"Keir does."

"You don't have to sacrifice your life. I assume your mother was talking about your family."

"Of course," Ryan responded cautiously, uncertain where Glo was headed with this train of thought.

"You don't owe Keir's children anything."

"Yes, I do."

"I don't believe that. Think back. Did your mother save your family or every child in the neighborhood?"

"My family."

"Exactly. Here's my take on the situation. In theory, your mother's right. Children should always come first.

But, we're talking about your future with a man you love. I don't think your mother would have approved of the way you've handle this thing with Keir. Above all else, I'm sure she wanted you to be happy." Stopping in front of the younger woman, Glo continued, "Here's the big question. What do you really want, Ryan?"

"Keir," Ryan said confidently.

"Then go for it."

"How can I? I don't want to hurt anyone."

"What you're doing now is hurting everyone. You, Keir, and his kids. It's time to put an end to it."

Shaking her head, Ryan admitted, "I don't know."

"Well, I do," Glo stated. "Have you considered how being with Keir enhances the kids' and your lives? All of your experiences with your mother are things you can pass on to Adam and Emily. Leaving them is not the only way you can make them happy. Matter of fact, Adam sounded pretty upset."

Ryan studied her boss, dissecting her comments. Glo was making sense.

"Keir has always been one of my favorite people to work for," Glo continued. "And because I've been with him so long, I worry about him. Even though he's this tough businessman, he's a good guy at heart." Glo moved around the small space, pacing their cubbyhole. "I felt as if you were coming between us. I also suspected, eventually you'd hurt him."

"I just wanted to do my job. Meeting Keir was not on my agenda. But I did. And I'm glad I did. Keir refused to let me ignore him."

"I can see that now," Glo admitted.

Ryan studied the older woman, with sadness in her heart. "It's done now. Let it go."

"No. I don't think I will. I need to say this. Because I care so much for Keir, I was very protective of him. The breakup of his marriage devastated him. He'd been through so much. I didn't want to see him hurt a second time. After that one chick lost her mind, I felt compelled to protect him from predators. You were new here, and Keir tried to hide the gleam of admiration in his eyes but failed miserably. I can see that he loves you. What are you going to do about it?"

"I'm going to figure out a way to get him back."

"Now you're talking." Glo gave Ryan's shoulder a quick pat of approval.

Chapter 34

With her feet tucked under her body, Ryan lounged on the sofa, with the remote in one hand, waiting for *American Idol* to come on. After a dinner consisting of a Wendy's chicken salad and a small Frosty, she needed a little time to wind down and relax.

The day's events had been brutal. Adam's visit and Glo's about face had amazed and shocked Ryan. Glo's questions remained in the forefront of her thoughts, swirling around as she searched for the right answers.

What if she'd made her decision too hastily? Had she thrown away the best thing to happen to her since Galen died?

Groaning, Ryan dismissed all thoughts of Keir and his children. Instead, she channel surfed, looking for something to occupy her troubled mind and give her brain five minutes of peace.

She switched to the Fox network. *American Idol* flashed on the screen, and she sat up straighter, giving all of her attention to her favorite program.

Twenty minutes later, she hit the mute button and tossed the remote on the coffee table. Tonight, neither the show nor its contestants held her attention. Simon's comments had seemed snippy rather then humorous.

Ryan stretched out on the sofa and shut her eyes, debating whether she wanted to call it a night and go to bed. The doorbell rang throughout the house.

Frowning, she opened her eyes. Her feet hit the floor, and she stood. Who in the heck would drop by without calling first on a work night? Ryan strolled to the front door and called, "Who is it?"

"Keir."

Her whole body started to shake, and her knees refused to support her. She leaned against the wall. *Ohmigod!* Keir was the last person she expected to drop by tonight or any other night. What did he want? "Just a moment."

Ryan glanced down at her ratty sweats and shrugged. At this point there wasn't much she could do about her wardrobe choice. But Ryan took a second to smooth her hair into place with her hands.

As she unlocked the door, she chanted silently, *stay calm; be pleasant.* Keir probably wanted to thank her for bringing Adam to his office. The little voice in her head warned her against expecting anything more. *Yeah. That's why he'd taken the time to stop by, to talk about Adam.*

She flung open the door and hungrily ate him up with her eyes. He looked handsome, dressed in a khaki sweatshirt and denims. White sneakers peeked from under his jeans. At that moment she realized how much she missed him. Although Ryan had told Glo she would find a way to get him back, she hadn't formulated a plan yet.

After a moment Ryan shook herself, realizing Keir still stood on her doorstep, waiting for an invitation. Feeling foolish, she played with the neck of her top. "Hi," she said.

"Hey," Keir muttered back. "I know it's a little late, but can I come in? I need to talk with you."

"Sure." She stepped away from the door and ushered him inside the house.

"Thanks." Keir followed her through the hallway and into the living room. He sank into the chair next to the sofa. Ryan returned to her position on the sofa, patting her hands on her thighs as she waited for Keir to say something.

Keir studied the muted television screen for a moment. "*American Idol?*"

Ryan nodded. "It's not holding my attention tonight."

"I understand. I have days like that."

The silence that followed quickly got on Ryan's nerves, and she found she couldn't keep still. "Is Adam okay?"

He nodded. "Properly chastised by me and his mother."

"Good." She chuckled nervously as she straightened her top. "Finding him in my office shocked me."

"I can understand that. Finding you and him outside my door threw me for a loop," he replied. "Thanks for bringing Adam back to me. I appreciate that."

"Of course, I brought him to you. That's where he belonged. How did the princess take the incident?"

Smiling, he answered, "Well, you know Emily. She trailed after him, giving Adam plenty of grief. The only thing that saved him was the no entry without permission rule Shannon imposed on each kid's bedroom."

Ryan laughed. "Adam should go ahead and let Emily have her say. She'll save it up for later, and he'll still have to listen."

"That's for sure."

They laughed together. The sound filled the room with warmth but quickly died to a second awkward silence.

Ryan reached for the remote and pumped up the volume on the television. For the next ten minutes, they sat watching *American Idol.* Although the contestants were talented, her mind refused to stay focused on the show. She found herself enjoying the tantalizing fragrance of Keir's cologne and the way his sweatshirt hinted at his broad shoulders and tight muscles.

Finally, at the commercial break, Keir came to a decision. He rose from the chair and moved around the coffee table, dropping into the empty place next to her, and took the remote from her hand.

Nervously clearing his throat, Keir said, "Adam and I talked for a while after you left. My son is very perceptive, and he gave me some interesting information." Keir chuckled a bit and then continued. "The boy took me down a peg or two or three or four."

Ryan shifted on the sofa, tucking her feet under her and facing Keir. "What did he say?"

"He reminded me of something I've been preaching to him." He reached over and took her hand. Ryan let out a soft gasp as her heart rate instantly accelerated. "Before the school year ended, we made a pact. If Adam agreed to go to the summer school enrichment program, I'd work with him on his baseball game so that he could try out for the team. We practiced a couple days a week, and he did his best in summer school. Adam worked really hard in school and on the baseball field, and his hard work paid off with a position on the team and improvement in his math scores."

Nodding, Ryan waited for the meat of the story. She didn't know where Keir planned to go with this, but she let him continue without interruption.

"Today, after our talk about his unauthorized escape from summer school, he asked me some direct questions that made me take a closer look at myself."

"Like what?" she asked softly.

Eyes focused on her, Keir whispered, "Did I love you? Why had I let you go without a fight?"

Ryan's mouth went dry, and her heart raced like an overheating engine. Her eyes remained glued on Keir's face. "Why did you?"

"I told him that I didn't have a choice." Keir lowered his lids over his eyes. "You wanted to leave me. That wasn't completely true. In my arrogance, I believed all you needed was a little time, and then you'd come back to me."

Voice quivering, Ryan asked, "And now?"

"I'm the one coming back to you. I need you in my life. I'm here to persuade you to come back to me, to us. Be part of the family that we've created."

Keir had offered her an opportunity to correct her previous mistake. This second chance wouldn't slip through her fingers.

"Adam asked me why I didn't go after you," Keir continued. He focused on their linked hands. "Try to talk to you and make you understand. Then he reminded me of something I've been saying to him all summer."

"What was that?"

Keir lifted his head. Ryan saw the pain their separation had caused. Her heart went out to him. She fought the urge to draw him into her arms.

Keir lingered over her hand, kissing the palm. "Anything worth having is worth fighting for."

"Am I?"

"Absolutely."

Ryan stretched out a hand and cupped the side of his face. She'd missed him so much. Hunger flared intense and all-consuming. An answering need started in the pit of her belly and surged through her blood.

"We've got to talk about my kids," said Keir.

She nodded.

"Mrs. Mitchell, you are dead wrong if you believe leaving them was the right thing to do. We're a family.

Adam's and Emily's lives are intertwined with yours. They miss you and need your reassuring presence and love as much as they need mine and their mother's. We all need you. You make us whole."

Ryan shut her eyes, seeing Adam's troubled face. She heard his voice quiver as he apologized for something that wasn't his fault.

"You can't control what other people think or do," Keir continued. "Our job is to provide a secure, loving environment where our kids will feel safe. I want us to have a place where they feel comfortable enough to tell us anything. As long as we communicate, we can work out any problem."

Amazed, Ryan studied the man sitting next to her. Glo was right. Ryan didn't have to give up everything to care for the kids.

"There will always be Malcolms and Lakeishas," Keir added. "They always have something to say. But, that type of scum only gains power when we let their comments take on meaning. If we stick together, keep them out of our lives, we'll be fine. Actually, we'll be more than fine."

Keir cleared his throat, then continued. "Here's the deal. I love you, and I want you in my life. I'm willing to do whatever it takes to get you back. Tell me what you want."

"You."

A deep growl of satisfaction rose from Keir's throat. "That's what I wanted to hear."

Carpe Diem. Seize the day. She didn't plan to mess up again.

"I love you, Ryan."

"Keir, I love you."

Grinning broadly, Keir admitted, "That's what I needed to hear. I want us to be together. Not just today or tomorrow. For the rest of our lives. We can make things work between us. Are you willing to take the leap of faith with me?"

"I think so."

"No." He shook his head. "No thinking. I want you to be sure, be positive. We're not going back down this road again."

"Yes. I'm willing to take the risk."

"All right. Now we're getting somewhere." Keir slipped off the sofa and got down on one knee and reached inside his pant pocket and removed a velvet ring box. He opened the box. "Ryan Angelique Mitchell, will you marry me?"

Gasping softly, she touched the white-gold band with a single pear-shaped diamond. With tears falling down her cheeks, Ryan threw her arms around Keir, holding him close, kissing him with all the love in her heart.

"Absolutely!"

Breaking the kiss, Ryan muttered the word again against his lips, "Absolutely."

Keir held her away from him by her shoulders. "Is that a yes?" he asked.

"Yes." Ryan gave him a quick kiss on the cheek. "Yes." She moved to the corner of his mouth. "Yes."

Keir deepened the kiss, slipping his tongue between her lips and tasting her.

He muttered, "I love you, Ryan."

Chapter 35

Ryan and Keir chose September 1 for their wedding. Since they both had had previous marriages, they decided to keep the ceremony small and intimate. The attendees consisted of their immediate families and close friends.

Emily and Adam had ushered Ryan into Keir's bedroom to dress. Ryan sat on the end of the bed, rolling the second cream stocking over her knee and securing it around her thigh.

Panic set in as she considered her fate. In less than an hour, this would be her bedroom, her home, and Keir would be transformed from boyfriend to husband. Was she truly ready for this transition? As she reached for a cream-colored shoe, a soft tap on the door broke into her troubled thoughts.

Helen poked her head inside the door. "Need any help?"

With a wave of her hand, Ryan beckoned her sister into the room. "Come talk to me."

Her older sister entered the room and shut the door, moving across the floor to where Ryan sat. She tossed her purse on the bed and examined Ryan's face for a second. "What's up?"

"I'm not ready," Ryan answered in a worried tone.

"Sure you are." Helen sank into the soft mattress next to Ryan and massaged her shoulders. "Calm down. This is what you want."

"I guess. Maybe." Ryan shrugged. "I don't know."

Laughing, Helen wrapped an arm around Ryan and hugged her. "You two are way too happy together. Stop worrying and get married."

Giggling nervously, Ryan gazed at her sister. "You're right. This must be a case of the pre-wedding jitters."

"Mm-hmm. You're entitled. This is a whole new life for you."

Ryan watched her sister move around the room, taking the garment bag from the closet and removing the dress inside, gently placing it on the bed.

"Helen, are you okay with the way I arranged the ceremony?"

"Honey, this is your wedding. Everything should be the way you want it. It was the right choice. Don't worry about me. Besides, the last time you got married, I was the maid of honor. I like the idea of being a spectator."

"As long as you're all right with it."

"I am." She gave Ryan a gentle nudge and helped her to her feet. "Let's get you dressed so that we can start your wedding."

Helen picked up the cream tea-length dress. The beaded bodice fitted tightly around Ryan's small frame and flared from the waist into a full hoopskirt. Ryan stepped into the dress, and Helen zipped up the back.

The sisters stood before the mirror, admiring Ryan's wedding dress.

"You look beautiful," Helen said.

"Thank you."

Helen wrapped a hand around Ryan and advised, "Love each other, and the rest will follow."

"Did it work for you?"

Grinning, Helen replied, "Absolutely."

The organist began to play.

"He's playing your song," Helen said. She picked up her purse and headed for the door. "It's time for us to go."

Nodding, Ryan grabbed her bouquet of white roses and trailed her sister out the door and down the stairs. Emily greeted them when they reached the main hallway.

Earlier, after making Ryan promise to shut her eyes and not peek, Emily and Adam had led Ryan upstairs from the back of the house. Now she got her first look at the downstairs and the great room.

She gasped, stunned by the transformation. The great room looked magnificent.

Flowers of every size, shape, and color dominated the room, creating a bouquet of scents. An arch had been set up near the patio door. The white arch was decorated with multiple colored flowers.

Ryan's brother, Tony; his wife, Michelle, and their two kids stood near the entrance. Helen, Larry, Andre, and Gee waited alongside Tony. Keir's parents, Mr. and Mrs. Southhall; Phil Berger; his wife; and Glo were all present for the event.

Emily ran up to Ryan. She was perfectly attired in a tea-length, beaded Empire-style dress in ocean blue. White patent-leather shoes covered her feet, and baby's breath, secured by a ribbon, held her hair in place. A bouquet of multicolored roses filled the girl's hands.

In the great room, Keir stood tall and handsome in a dark gray tuxedo. At his side, Adam wore an identical suit as they waited in the patio archway with Reverend Aisha Wagner.

The wedding march began.

"Come on, maid of honor," Ryan encouraged. "Do your stuff."

Emily started down the three stairs into the sunken room, just the way they'd rehearsed last night. With all the elegance and grace of a seasoned runway model, the girl strolled to her father. Ryan followed at a slower pace, pausing after each step. As she drew near Keir, the small band of guests moved closer, surrounding the couple.

Ryan's thousand-watt smile refused to go away. Helen had been right. She did want to marry Keir and spend her life with him. When she stole a quick peek in his direction, the same jubilant expression beamed back at her. Keir took her hand, and they stood side by side. Leaning close to her ear, he whispered, "I love you."

Reverend Wagner stepped before the couple as the music softened and slowly died away. "Welcome, family and friends. We're here today to witness one of God's greatest gifts, the holiest of occasions. The sacred union of Ryan Mitchell and Keir Southhall. Two souls that now come together to create a holy bond."

Emily slipped her hand in Ryan's and squeezed. Ryan looked down at the girl and winked. The child grinned back.

"As in many cases, the road to love and happiness is not a straight path; there are twists and turns," said Reverend Wagner. "You stand before God and each other to enter into the hallow institution of marriage. You can proceed with your vows."

Keir turned to her. "Ryan, from the moment I spied you running around One Leaf Studio, I knew you were going to change my life. It didn't take long for that to happen. It's true, the important things in life are never easy. But loving you was one of the easiest things I've ever done. Convincing you to take a chance on us was the most difficult. Now that you've learned to trust me,

I promise you this. You and our life together will always be my first priority. I will protect you with everything in me. And I will love you, now until forever."

"Ryan," said the minister as she waved a hand in Ryan's direction. "It's your turn."

"Keir, I have learned so much in the time we've been together. You taught me how to open my heart and to never be afraid to receive and give love. I promise I'll be the best wife that I can. I'll be at your side and will support you through whatever endeavor you choose. I will love Emily and Adam and any children we create. I promise to love and cherish you, now until forever."

"What God has joined together, let no man put asunder. I now pronounce you husband and wife," said Reverend Wagner.

Keir reached for Ryan, and she went into his arms, kissing him with all the love in her heart. The soft murmurs of the audience penetrated the happy fog surrounding them. Embarrassed, they stepped away from one another.

With a child on each side of them, Ryan and Keir turned to the audience.

Reverend Wagner closed her Bible and said, "Ladies and gentlemen, I present to you the Southhall family. Keir, Ryan, Adam, and Emily."

Dear Readers;

Welcome to *Now Until Forever*. I hope you like the story as much as I enjoyed writing it.

I've carrried Keir and Ryan's story in my head for several years. It felt wonderful to finally have a chance to explore the characters' personalities and work through their problems.

Writing can be a frustrating and lonely job. It warms my heart to hear from readers who have interesting comments about the stories and the characters that I create. Don't be a stranger. Feel free to e-mail me at *romwriterkwo@yahoo.com* or drop a note at P.O. Box 40366, Redford, MI 48240. I love hearing from you.

Happy reading!

Sincerely,

Karen White-Owens

Grab These Other
Dafina Novels
(mass market editions)

Check Out These Other
Dafina Novels

Look For These Other
Dafina Novels